THE GOLD OF SAN XAVIER

THE GOLD OF SAN XAVIER

By Bruce Itule

Thunder Mountain Publishing Co.

First Edition

Text © 2003 by Bruce Itule
Photographs © 2003 by Theodore J. Sokol

Published by
Thunder Mountain Publishing Co.
8946 E. Palm Lane
Mesa, AZ 85207
www.thundermp.com or www.thundermountainpress.com

Designed and produced by Dawn DeVries Sokol
Printed and bound in Canada

ISBN 0-9725510-0-X

For my father, Joseph John Itule Sr. He has been gone for decades, but I am so thankful that while he was on Earth, he taught me to love Tucson and Southern Arizona.

Prologue

In the desert of New Spain, July 1781

Padre Hernando Díaz marveled at the stars studded against the black sky. The desert night was moonless, the air hot and stagnant, with a rising humidity that signaled a summer storm brewing in the mountains to the west.

Although past his bedtime, Díaz pushed himself to finish the day's entry in the journal he kept of his travels in New Spain. His eyes darted as he thought carefully about his experiences so far and how to put them in words, phrases, and sentences. When he wrote, his tired hand moved slowly, jittering across the paper.

> *July 17, in the year of Our Lord, 1781*
> *I long for the cooler summer days of Europe.*
> *I will be back in Spain some time in 1782 and*
> *hope I will miss another summer in this terrible*
> *desert. I think that when we get to the spot*
> *called Yuma Crossing tomorrow I can bathe*
> *in the great and cool Colorado River. I have*
> *been told it is an oasis in this place of*
> *scorpions and sand. I pray for an end to the*
> *incessant heat. Even at night, my body is*

soaked in sweat. We might have rain soon.
Mendoza says perhaps in a day or two.

Díaz, a slight man with a long nose and pocked face, took frequent breaks as he wrote. He knew that no one else would see his writing, yet he agonized over every sentence. He frowned constantly and used his silk scarf to wipe sweat from his face.

The padre wrote in his journal every night during the 240-mile journey from San Xavier del Bac Mission near the presidio of Tucson to La Purisima de la Concepción, the mission at Yuma Crossing. On this torrid night, the flickering light of a campfire illuminated him dimly and sent eerie shadows dancing atop the barren ground and then off into the darkness.

If I am so hot, the soldiers in their thick
uniforms must be worse. Our long robes
cannot be as bad as the soldiers' uniforms and
tall boots. It will be good to get to Concepción
and unload the gold ingots and coins we carry.
I wonder if the other half of the gold will remain
at Bac. We lived comfortably with the other
Franciscans and the mission Indians. There are many
bars of gold. They are heavy and make the horses sweat
even more on our harsh journey, but the gold will
finance our work on the frontiers of New Spain in
what is known as California. Our treasure is a
blessing from God, though I fear some of the soldiers
may look upon our heavy load as a curse. I am sure
Padre Garcés and the Indians will be happy to see
us at Concepción. Besides the gold, we bring with
us beads and Christian writings for the Indians.

"You're always writing, Padre." The grumpy soldier's words jarred Díaz from his concentration.

"I'm sorry," he said as though he needed to apologize to the conquistador he knew only as Mendosa. He looked at the large man whose pointed metal helmet made him two heads taller than anyone in camp. "What time will we be at Yuma Crossing tomorrow?" Díaz asked.

"If we leave before daybreak when it's cool, we can make it before the hot sun is overhead. We'll camp on this side of the river during the heat of the day, and then in the evening the Quechans will help us cross to Concepción. Once we have you safely at the mission, my men and I will join the other soldiers at the crossing."

Before Mendosa finished speaking, Díaz took his journal and carefully wrapped it in a piece of deerskin as he did each evening when he finished writing. He then put it in the small studded oak box in which he also carried his rosary.

Fifty years had been kind to Díaz, not a young man for his time. Only a few wrinkles notched his face, and hardly any gray streaked his black, thick hair. Thinness and the gentle life of a missionary had distanced him from the ruin of age.

"Do you know much about the Quechans?" Díaz asked, once again wiping the salty sweat from his brow before it could run into the tiny canyons around his eyes.

"They're heathens," Mendosa shouted, his dark brown eyes narrowing. "We've done everything we can to civilize them, but they remain barbarians. You padres have established the missions to bring them religion and culture. We all have given them food to make their stomachs bulge. In the beginning they liked us, but no more. I've heard talk they will rebel some day. Then we'll kill them. At least when Concepción was built a year ago, it was built on a hill, from where we can keep our eyes on the uncivilized children of the devil."

"I pray there is no rebellion and the Quechan learn to live with us side by side," Díaz said. "They were never asked if they wanted Spanish religion, culture, and language, yet we loved them and gave them everything. Since Padre Kino came to this area we've tried to uplift these people by Christianizing them. I've only been to the missions at Tumacacori and Bac, and our efforts worked there. I'm anxious to get to California and help Padre Garcés, even if it's only a short while before I return to our homeland. Maybe we've pushed the Quechans too much."

The big soldier did not reply quickly. Both men peered at the fire's golden dancers until Mendoza finally threw a mesquite log into the flames and said, "Yuma Crossing opens the trail into California, and it's nearly impossible to cross the river without the cooperation of the savage Quechans."

"Yes, I know that. Padre Kino's map of 1710 designated Yuma as a crossing on the Colorado to California. It's an important area for us. That's why I am sorry to hear that we have angered the Quechans."

Mendosa shook his head, saying nothing, but as he stared at the padre traveling to Quechan land for the first time, he thought to himself that he was seeing a fool. Too bad he'd been ordered to escort more fools to Yuma Crossing. He knew better than the padres how to handle the Quechan.

The soldier cared nothing for the Indians. The Quechan men were farmers, not soldiers, and their women ran in fear. More than once he had publicly whipped Quechans who protested when settling Spaniards took possession of the best farmland. To him, the Spanish were the rulers of Yuma Crossing, their reign guaranteed by their swords, muskets, helmets, and shields. The conquistadors let their horses, mules, and cattle destroy Quechan crops and eat the mesquite beans that were so important to the Indian diet.

Díaz tucked his oak box into one of the four rickety wagons that had been snaking slowly across the desert for nearly two weeks. The padre pulled a wool blanket from the wagon and spread his bed for the night in the dirt.

He concentrated on sleeping, but nothing worked on this restless night. Sweat dribbled down his head for hours. A recurring dream in which he was screaming and running away from a faceless intruder jarred him into consciousness for hours. The rain never came.

⌒

By midmorning on July 18, the three padres and their escort of ten conquistadors could see black smoke rising from Yuma Crossing. The dark fume in the distance jumped like a smoke signal and lured them closer.

As they neared the crossing, they heard musket shots. Then from the distance a priest stumbled toward them. Blood streamed down the side of his face.

"Who are you?" hollered Mendosa as the man tripped and fell twenty feet in front of them. The red-faced and animated conquistador waved his left arm as he shouted again angrily, "Who are you?"

"Please, my friend, help me. I'm Father Felipe. I carry great sadness."

Díaz and the others surrounded him.

"The Quechan attack began yesterday on the other side of the river," the terrified priest told the travelers. Like Díaz, he was a Franciscan priest who wore a hooded brown wool robe and a wooden crucifix around his neck. "They're clubbing everyone to death. They crossed the river and attacked this morning. They're lead by their chief, Salvador Palma. The massacre of children, women, soldiers, and my fellow priests is senseless. I saw a young girl of ten or eleven plead desperately for her life just before a stone club crashed into her skull."

Terror filled Felipe's bloodshot blue eyes. He began to weep. He wiped blood from his face, but it kept dripping, some of it splashing on his feet and strap sandals. He weakened. The priest focused on no one in the group of listeners, but each one of them watched him in deathlike silence.

"When Captain Rivera and his troops arrived from California earlier this year, the whippings of Quechans increased," Felipe said. "Some of the conquistadors stole food. Padre Garcés lost contact with the important chiefs, including Palma, and he feared that the Indians were planning a revolt. He warned Rivera of a possible attack, but Rivera didn't believe him."

Díaz shook his head in disbelief as the priest continued.

"Rivera camped on this side of the river, and he underestimated the strength of the Quechans. They rebelled yesterday. They attacked Concepción and San Pedro y San Pablo de Bicuner upstream. I was one of the few who escaped from Concepción. God sent me a cottonwood log that I clung to until I reached the bank on this side of the river. The Quechans set fire to the churches and homes. Rivera watched helplessly from his side of the river. He was unable to cross. Too many Quechans for the few dozen Spaniards. The Spanish muskets and swords could not stop the clubbing."

Díaz held Felipe in his arms for several minutes after the priest quit breathing. He lay the man's head gently on the sand and walked to the wagons to retrieve a shovel.

"No time to dig a grave," Mendosa ordered. "My men and I must ride to Rivera's camp to see if we can help."

The blaring sunlight reflected brightly off the polished silver on the conquistadors' helmets and shields. Their somber mood revealed an impatience to get moving.

Díaz and the other priests had no choice but to follow; they knew they would die in the desert if they tried to return to Bac without adequate supplies or soldiers to kill game along the way.

⌒

By late afternoon, they were dead, clubbed to death brutally like the other Spaniards. Blood from their slaughtered bodies stained the dirt of Yuma Crossing and mixed with the blood of the fallen Quechans.

Díaz died proudly in his God's arms. He had found shelter in an adobe home near La Purisima de la Concepción and was drinking a cup of hot milk when a group of Quechan surrounded the dwelling and yelled in broken and guttural Spanish for him to come out. He walked out, unarmed.

He stayed on his feet until a club smashed into his left thigh and commanded him to his knees. For several seconds he stared into the flaring eyes of a Quechan smaller than he. The Indian's black eyes never left those of his victim.

Díaz refused to plead for his life. He begged only for forgiveness from his God.

A half dozen more Indians surrounded the priest. Their clubs came crashing down on his head, breaking through it as though it were a soft melon. Díaz died near the mighty river in which he never had a chance to bathe, the fiery sun turning his blood black before it could soak into the dirt.

The Indians were exhausted after two days of fighting, yet they continued their vicious advance against the dwindling ranks of Spaniards. At least a half dozen of their bodies littered the ground around each of the slain conquistadors.

After the third day of the battle, the Quechans had killed the one hundred or so Spaniards at Yuma Crossing. The victors were not interested in the Spaniards' weapons, clothing, or animals. Nor did they care about the gold the travelers brought from San Xavier or the studded oak box that held a rosary and daily journal. They thought only of ridding their land of the ruthless conquistadors and the priests who tried to force them to follow an unknown God.

The Colorado carried away most of the smashed and mutilated bodies, as well as their belongings. It would be more than a century before any of the Spanish relics showed up in European museums or libraries.

Chapter 1

Long Island, New York, February, 1993

Nick Genoa left his reporting job at *The New York Times* two years ago, but he remained addicted to newspapers and couldn't pass a news rack without stopping.

The front page of *USA Today* on a vacated table inside the Amityville Cafe caught Nick's eye. In his maiden State of the Union speech to Congress, President Bill Clinton had called for one of the biggest tax increases in history. Serb tanks had attacked a key suburb of Sarajevo in Bosnia-Herzegovina. *Another year has started typically,* Nick thought. *The good cheer of the holidays fades after a few days and barbarian madness returns to a world rioting over race and religion.*

Today's gray and frigid winter morning in New York didn't bother Nick in the least. He had signed a contract a day earlier with *Smithsonian* magazine and would be leaving for warm Arizona in a few days to research and write an article on the art conservation project at San Xavier del Bac Mission, a two-century-old Spanish church south of Tucson. He planned to be gone a month or two and miss the worst of the snow and sleet.

Since his divorce, he had converted the upstairs of his Seaford, Long Island, home into an apartment, and, as always, his tenants agreed to look after the place during his absence and feed his fat and spoiled cat, Typo.

"Must be tough as hell to trade this for the sunny and wide-open

Southwest," Phil Mitchell said when his friend Nick joined him at a small table near the cafe's front window. Whenever they had the time, the two men sipped coffee and ate breakfast early in the morning.

Nick took a bite of a strawberry jelly-filled pastry and smiled without responding. He pinched his lower lip with his left index finger and thumb as if deep in thought, but he really only wanted to flick away the powdered sugar left from his first bite. The coarse hairs of his black mustache always swept up various foods as he ate them.

Nick and Philip S. Mitchell, as his byline proclaimed but who was known to his colleagues as "Mitch," had been good friends for years, since they met on the federal courts beat. Mitch, a burly, balding redhead, had come to New York from Atlanta for a job with the *Daily News*. Nick, a svelte, five-foot-ten Italian-American with black wavy hair and a caterpillar mustache, arrived at *The Times* after a stint at the *Star* in Kansas City.

The two men were in their early thirties when they moved to the big city for their careers. Despite the competition between their newspapers, Mitch and "Nicky" became friends because they spent so much time together in the cramped press room of the federal courthouse on Centre Street downtown. They debated every issue, from the beauty of a woman, to the Yankees and Mets, to U.S. policy in China.

Unlike Nick, Mitch remarried, happily, after the break-up of his first marriage. He looked married. Men like him were easy to spot: wrinkled, inflating tires around their guts, secure.

Mitch envied his friend for having the courage to quit daily journalism, but he never admitted it.

"Who'd you sell this one to?" Mitch asked, smoking, as usual. He often held his cigarettes between his lips until ashes tumbled onto his tie.

Nick stroked the end of his mustache with his left thumb and looked out the window at a college-age blonde rushing into the next-door laundry. There were no other people on the street. Too blustery.

"*Smithsonian*," he said. "I'm leaving Monday morning on an all-expenses-paid trip for a story about conservation at San Xavier Mission south of Tucson."

"Santa what? Christ, I can't even pronounce the place."

"It's sahn hahv-YAIR. It was founded in 1692 by Father Eusebio Francisco Kino, a Jesuit missionary born in Italy. He named the place for St. Francis Xavier, his patron saint. It's still an active Catholic church. Always has been. It serves the Tohono O'odham Nation."

"Toe-ho? Sounds foreign to me, or some kind of health food."

Nick smiled. "Toe-ho-no o-OD-ham. They used to be known as Papagos, but they go by their traditional name now because Papago means something disparaging. Bean eater, I think."

Nick loved to talk passionately about stories, particularly those he was planning. An introvert, he needed time to warm up even among friends, but once he did, he was relaxed and open. He was best one-on-one, worst in a crowd.

They had been in the cafe for about an hour when Mitch moved his chair back from the table and announced, "I need to make some room for more coffee. Back in a minute." While he was gone, Nick stared out the frosty window. His mind flashed from his assignment in Tucson to the changes in his life over the last two years. It still appeared odd to him that he could simply pick up and leave his home for a season. He should have been happily married by this time in his life, with children and a booming career. He grew up in that kind of family. He thought he would work in a job where he would have a regular paycheck and full benefits. He would have a home in a safe, middle-class neighborhood. A Beemer, vacation home, and boat. Perhaps a . . .

"Earth to Nick, come in, Nick," Mitch said when he sat again, heavily.

"I was thinking about my story," Nick said.

"No problemo. Tell me about the women you'll be working with. Anyone loose and lonely?"

"We always turn to women, don't we, Mitchy?"

"Forget women. Let's talk sex, or the possibility that you might get a little."

Nick wasn't comfortable talking about his exploits as an unmarried man, but the topic always somehow popped up around Mitch. Usually Nick didn't have much to tell. His writing schedule kept him busy, at least busy enough so that he could avoid dwelling on the loneliness that a man without a woman feels. Never much of a barroom drinker, he seldom took the train into the city to visit popular nightspots and meet women. Women and quick relationships emerged here and there, but he had not found anyone yet with whom he could share his heart and soul. He wondered if he ever would. The last woman he'd been with lamented her marriage but then only desired a "soulfriend," her term, not his.

His married friends admired the single lifestyle, sometimes longed for it, and enjoyed living it vicariously through Nick Genoa. Too bad he usually disappointed them.

"There are four conservators, two from Italy, one from Turkey, and one from England," Nick said. "I don't know all their genders and probably wouldn't tell you if I did, but the team is led by an Italian woman. Her name is Rosa Zizzo. She and the others are supposed to be the best in the world, and even helped restore the art in the Sistine Chapel. They've hired three Tohono O'odhams to work with them and are going to teach them conservation so the Indians can become caretakers of the church."

"You haven't lost it, Nicky. You're one hell of a reporter. You've got a lot of the story already."

Nick smiled again, this time more broadly, revealing the lines of aging that already had started to spread like tributaries from his eyes to his closely cropped curly sideburns. He kept his hair short, which made it straighter and easier to comb. The longer it got, the wavier it got. He never much liked dealing with the waves, nor his two cowlicks. A few strands of gray salted the sides of his pepper-black head.

Nick looked away from his friend, remembering a payment to the vet for Typo's shots, one more little thing he needed to do before he left New York. He would drop it off later today.

He hesitated for several seconds, took a sip of his coffee, and resumed talking. "People in Tucson are trying to make the interior artwork look as it did when San Xavier was completed in 1797. They hired the chief conservator at the Guggenheim here in New York as a consultant because he's recognized as one of the world's best for murals. He recommended that the Tucson group hire the woman from Rome. She's the best conservator he's ever worked with."

"So what makes San Xavier so special?" Mitch asked.

"The Guggenheim guy says the mission is the only one of its kind in the United States. He says it has the most beautiful Spanish colonial wall paintings in the nation, and they are incredibly high quality and well preserved."

"So why does it take Europeans to restore the art? Why not a few Yanks from here in New York, or maybe Philly? There are great churches around here."

"The Europeans are the best conservators. It's the only Spanish baroque church in the country. There aren't any American art conservators like these people. They aren't restoring the artwork. They're just cleaning it and bringing what's left of it back to how it looked in the 1790s."

"Just Indians go there?"

"Hell no. It's packed every Sunday with people from the reservation, Tucson, and tourists from all over the world. The conservation project is a multi-year thing. The Europeans are only doing small sections of the church at a time, so that they don't disturb the faithful. They're working on one of the side chapels this year. The church is shaped inside like a big cross with two side chapels and then the main altar area, which is supposed to be pretty spectacular."

"Sounds fascinating," Mitch said between bites of eggs and bacon. Nick wasn't much of a breakfast person. A sweet roll and coffee were all he could take. Mitch enjoyed the full blast of cholesterol and fat. He'd given the health thing a shot during the eighties when it was the in thing. He even tried running awhile, but that craze didn't last long.

"I really can't wait to get there," Nick said confidently. "I talked to Father John, the Franciscan who is now the San Xavier pastor and guardian. He told me the place is a shrine church, for pilgrims. He said that between 200,000 and 300,000 churchgoers and tourists visit each year."

"Nicky, my boy, I hope you do more in Tucson than get a story and maybe some religion. Like find a woman."

"I'm not looking for a woman, at least a permanent one. You know that."

"You never know. Those Europeans might like an Italian-American like you. You've got the Omar Sharif look, and maybe that's just what they're looking for."

"Omar Sharif is Egyptian. Don't you mean Italian Stallion?"

The two men laughed and asked for refills on their coffee.

"I've never been to Italy, but I remember my grandmother talking fondly about it," Nick recalled as he watched the waitress clear the breakfast dishes from their table and walk away. She had a walk that he liked. He observed it and her for months when he came into the cafe. Although he smiled at her, he never bothered to ask her name, give his, or attempt a conversation. He much preferred just looking at her walk without the hassle of trying to get involved, or much worse, risking rejection.

"Tell me something," Mitch said as he and Nick walked out of the cafe and paused on the sidewalk. Nick was blowing his hot breath into his cupped hands, smelling the four cups of coffee he'd downed. "What's the payoff on these feature stories you do? You're not doing any heavy investigations. You're not going to reveal wrongdoing by anyone or be a watchdog on government. Is the only reward the money you're paid?"

Embarrassed, Nick stared into the street. He disliked having to respond to such questions from his peers. He considered himself a journalist, *dammit*, and a fine writer. "You never know what might turn up," he said. "This story might not win me a Pulitzer, but it'll be more satisfying than dealing with the scumbags you have to talk to every day. Think about that when you're freezing your ass off here in the city without me."

Chapter 2

Tucson, Arizona

Maria Gomez, the cleaning lady, found Father John Duvall's body at nine in the morning in his living quarters behind San Xavier Mission. Her shrill scream reported the murder.

Two Mexican plasterers working near the priest's quarters jumped in fear when they heard the scream. "*Llama la policia*," one worker shouted. He sprinted toward Father John's front door while the other man rushed for the nearby church office to telephone the police. Other people already had spilled out of the office and church and were running toward the commotion.

The hysterical housekeeper inside the apartment crossed herself wildly, the thumb and first two fingers of her right hand pinched together so tightly that they were ghostly white. Over and over again, she moved her hand in the sign of the cross, from her forehead to her chest to the top of each breast to her lips. She wailed, "*El padre esta muerto, el padre esta muerto!*"

Maria shut her eyes tightly, but she still saw the brilliant image of death, and it made her nauseous and weak. She stuck out her arm as though she needed to motion for someone and cried "*mi corazón*." The worker who'd run into the priest's quarters helped her sit on the recliner in the living room. He feared the worst: a heart attack.

"Take it easy, *mi amiga*," he told her. "You don't want to have a heart attack."

She kept screaming, "*El padre esta muerto. El padre esta muerto*" and refused to open her eyes.

Police arrived within five minutes and pushed away the three dozen workers and tourists who had crowded around the door to glimpse at death. News of the priest's slaying spread through the church and surrounding grounds as quickly as a desert wildfire sparked by lightning. The pastor and guardian of the Franciscan community at San Xavier Mission had been stabbed to death. It had been an easy death. No bombs. No bullets. No innocent bystanders killed or injured. No fuss. No mess. Simple. Direct. The weapon had been pushed in the right place. A life had been erased.

The officers covered the body with a white sheet. It lay in the middle of the kitchen floor, where it would remain for more than an hour while they began their preliminary investigation. With his soul now in the hands of his Lord, Father John's lifeless body had become police property ready for the routine of a robotic murder investigation. His eyes were stuck open in death, as though he stared in terror at the early end of his life.

A female police officer slid a kitchen chair next to the recliner and sat with Maria, holding her hand and whispering, "*Está bueno, está bueno. Calmese.*"

A man not wearing a police uniform walked to the recliner and bent in front of the cleaning lady.

"Mrs. Gomez, I'm Detective Anderson of the Pima County Sheriff's Department. Please, can you open your eyes? I'd like you to look at me and talk to me."

She did as instructed. She made low whining sounds, like a child nearing the end of a tantrum. Her eyes weren't focused.

Slowly, she looked at the handsome, unsmiling red-haired cop. In his blue blazer, white Oxford button-down shirt, and silk tie with blue and red stripes he looked too fancy for a policeman. Maria dabbed her eyes with the tissue given her by the female officer, who introduced herself as Deputy Portillo.

The deputy put her hand on Maria's shoulder, hoping the personal touch would help quiet her. The sheriff's department always sent a female officer to a crime scene if a woman was involved.

"I know the pain you are feeling," Anderson said. She looked in his eyes that showed no emotion. How could he know her pain? He kept clicking his ball point pen open and shut, which annoyed Maria. She noticed his manicured fingernails.

"Why don't you tell us what you saw when you walked in here this morning?"

She shrugged, hesitated, took a deep breath before speaking. "I knocked on the front door to the living quarters like I do every day. I can just walk in, but I always knock first because sometimes if Father John is here, he opens the door for me. We know each other well. He's my priest, and I have been his cleaning lady for ten years."

Anderson helped Maria move from the recliner to the frayed brown velour couch in the living room, where he could sit with her and she could not see the sheet-covered body in the kitchen. She sat forcefully, her thin body sinking into the soft, worn-out cushion.

"He didn't answer the door today, and you used your key?" the detective asked.

"No, the door wasn't locked. He usually was in the church office next door, where he took care of church business. He wasn't here most mornings. He trusted everyone, and he saw no need to lock his door."

"You thought he wasn't here?"

"Yes. Still, I called out, 'Father John, it's Maria. Housecleaning.' I always did that because I got in the habit when I worked at a resort in the foothills."

Anderson let her drag through the conversation. He wouldn't rush her, and he didn't want to deal with more hysteria. She wore no makeup, only red lipstick, some of which had stained the back of her hand when she rubbed her lips. "So you just began cleaning like you do regularly?"

"I smelled something in here. It was faint, something unusual. I'd smelled it in other places, but never here, but I didn't know what it was. I told myself to quit being silly and go to work."

Anderson made a note about the strange smell. Maria kept talking.

"I cleaned the living room first. This room," said the tiny woman whose hair had grayed gracefully over the years. She covered it with a hair net when she worked. "It is a simple job each day, just dusting the bookcases, picking up the newspaper, and pulling down the recliner. Father John had a habit of getting out of his recliner without pushing down the foot rest."

She looked at the brown leather chair across from the couch and forced a smile. She'd sat in it for the first time minutes ago. When she got up, she'd pushed down the foot rest.

Anderson looked at the recliner, too. It, the couch, and a cheap veneer coffee table were the only pieces of furniture in the sparse front room about the size of the tiniest bedroom in a tract home. A small framed photo of a priest and a man in a business suit hung on the white plaster wall, the room's only ornament. The detective stood and walked to it.

"Was this Father John?"

"That's him and his brother. He was proud of that picture. His brother lives in Tennessee, I think Nashville. He's something in the music business. Not a star or anything, but he has a good job." Maria shook her head. "Who'll tell his brother?" she asked no one in particular.

Deputy Portillo spoke first. "We'll make the necessary calls, Mrs. Gomez. You don't have to worry about a thing. Just relax and try to answer the detective's questions."

Maria smiled slightly. She liked the young woman who couldn't be twenty-five or twenty-six. She reminded her of a niece who lived along the Mexican border near Nogales.

Anderson looked at the photo. Father John, a thin, balding man, had a smile that revealed straight, white teeth. In his hooded habit and strap sandals, he looked medieval.

"Did you hear anything?" Anderson asked, turning back to Maria.

"Como?" She didn't catch the question and asked him to repeat it.

Anderson had worked in Tucson for a decade and knew Spanish, although he understood more than he spoke. "Did you hear anything?"

"No. I hum while I work."

"What do you hum?"

"A simple tune that my mother taught me. A song of childhood, of love, and happiness."

"Where did you go after the living room?" Anderson knew it had to be the bathroom, kitchen, or bedroom. They were the only other rooms in the adobe house. The rectangular structure was a simple expression of plain living, the home of a man who lived a modest life. Adobe brick outside, plaster and Saltillo tile inside, the home offered nothing to suggest the riches of the Roman Catholic Church.

"The kitchen was next," Maria said. "I have to clean the gas stove and the table and four chairs. Last year, Father John splurged and bought a microwave oven so that he could warm his meals or make popcorn at night. He liked microwave popcorn because all he had to do was put the bag in and push a button. The stove wasn't dirty much. He liked the low-fat popcorn without the butter flavor. . . . empty bags in the garbage all the time."

The detective could see the microwave from the living room. It was on an oak cabinet in the corner, next to the small refrigerator-freezer.

"Cleaning the kitchen is simple," Maria said. "Father John was good about washing his own dishes, putting the garbage in the can underneath the sink. All I have to do is tidy up, sweep the tile floor, and put away anything he might have left on the stove or counter. On Fridays I also take some fish or meat and vegetables out of the refrigerator and put them in the crock pot so that Father John would have meals for the next few days."

Maria started crying again. She closed her eyes and crossed herself.

"Mrs. Gomez, please tell me what you saw." Anderson put his hand on her shoulder. Deputy Portillo sat next to her on the couch. Maria stared at Anderson, wondering how many murders he'd investigated. This one was just like any other, probably. It meant nothing to him.

"When I first saw him on the kitchen floor, I didn't even think anything. My first thought was, how odd, Father John is sleeping on the kitchen floor. He looked so peaceful. His left arm was next to his body. The right one was stretched out to the side, like many of the statues of saints inside San Xavier. I didn't see any blood."

Anderson glanced at one of the Polaroids that had been taken of the body. The sharpened screwdriver used to kill the priest had been jammed efficiently through his right eye and into his brain. He had dropped face down, and his head covered most of the blood that had seeped out. Anderson, a hard-boiled cop who'd seen plenty of gruesome killings, had never seen anything like this one. He thought without speaking: *What kind of bastard would shove a screwdriver into the head of a beloved priest?*

"When did you realize what had happened?" he asked Maria.

She shook her head and sobbed deeply. Anderson handed her more tissues. "When I saw the small amount of blood that had come out from under his head and dried on the kitchen floor," she said.

Anderson knew to ease off. He had done this many times before and knew that people who discovered murder for the first time could not be pressured. He'd talk to her again tomorrow, after she had time to share her agony with her family. "Mrs. Gomez, your son is here to take you home. We'll have a car follow you to make certain you are comfortable. Why don't you take it easy, and I'll talk to you again in a day or two."

She nodded.

"Let me see the screwdriver," Anderson said to a uniformed officer after Maria left the living room with help. "Where'd you say you found it?"

"A few feet from the body, nearly underneath the microwave stand."

Anderson looked at the six-inch-long screwdriver that had been placed in a plastic bag. Its tip had been ground down to an extremely sharp end. Its smoothed shank and wooden handle had blood on them.

The officers needed to be careful, to gather as much trace evidence as possible. Hair. Pieces of clothing. Dirt under fingernails. Blood sample under the victim's head. Saliva from his mouth. Anything that looked out of the ordinary. Everything they found went into bags.

The commotion outside startled Anderson. A woman yelled at the police officer trying to protect the front door from the onslaught of people.

"I'm Rosa Zizzo," she shouted without hysteria. "I need to get inside. Let me in. I worked with Father John and I can help." She was yelling. Her accent and loudness caught Anderson's attention.

The officer at the door would not budge, but Rosa appeared ready to push the much larger man out of the way. He looked at Anderson and then moved out of her way as soon as the detective's head nodded up and down.

In the dimly lit room, Rosa looked younger than her thirty-four years. She wore her "work clothes": tight-fitting, button-fly Levi's and a white V-neck T-shirt with a lacy white bra underneath.

"Can I help you, Miss. I'm Detective Anderson." He walked toward the door, casually looking at the Italian with her deep whiskey-colored eyes, narrow and straight nose, and pouty lips. Her olive skin looked healthy. She did not need makeup to be attractive.

Rosa walked inside the quarters quickly. "I think I might know why he was killed," she said. "Look in his bedroom and see if there is a large black suitcase in the closet."

The detective motioned his head again and a uniformed officer walked into the small bedroom down the hall from the kitchen. He returned several seconds later, shaking his head no.

Rosa dropped her head and ran her hands through her long black hair. "The gold is gone. They got the gold."

Chapter 3

"I understand a New York journalist is coming today to do a story on us. He'll interfere with our work." Turkish conservator Ali Bahadir spoke in broken but understandable English. Rosa Zizzo heard Ali but didn't respond or look at him. She didn't like the Turk, or his usual condescending tone. The flash of heat rolling down the back of her neck could have easily fired up her sharp tongue, but she didn't feel like battling with him this early in the day or anytime today. Her head pounded after an exhausting weekend of little sleep and extreme stress over Father John's murder.

Rosa and Ali had been on the job for only two weeks, and already had argued several times about the project. It didn't take much to set them off. She had been chosen as the chief conservator on this project, and he had trouble reporting to a woman. The self-absorbed Turk quickly and proudly told people that, as the best art conservator in the world, he didn't need direction. He saw no value in other people, particularly women, unless of course they could do something for him. Rosa acknowledged him as a master conservator and picked him for her team, but she also viewed him as arrogant, self-centered, and disrespectful.

She shrugged off his comment. She put her delicate hand on the black iron handle forged in the shape of a slithering rattlesnake and opened the narrow mesquite plank door into San Xavier Mission.

On this Monday morning shortly before 8 A.M., the sun had risen but hadn't yet erased the desert chill. A few clouds lingered; there wasn't enough breeze to carry them away.

As she stepped inside, Rosa recalled Sunday's beautiful funeral Mass for Father John. She felt connected to the graceful old building. The warmth from the ever-burning candles on the walls near the main altar and in the two side transept chapels comforted her. The candles emitted an inviting aroma that reminded Rosa of her mother's kitchen.

"The New Yorker must be doing a major project," Ali said, unrelenting until she finally had to answer his questions.

"Yes, it's for *Smithsonian* magazine," she said, hoping Ali would go right to work and leave her alone. "They're interested in our project because San Xavier is so important to their art history."

"What art history? America has none. This church should be part of Spain's history."

Rosa didn't respond. She agreed with most of what Ali said, but she'd be damned before she let him draw her into an argument. She and the others were used to journalists trailing them up and down the thirty-foot-tall scaffolding erected in one of the mission's chapels, asking the same inane questions. Why are you working on this mission when there are more famous ones in California? Is the art really that special? Can you save it? Why aren't you repainting it? Where do you stay while you're in Tucson? How much is this costing and who is paying? What do you think of Arizona? The desert?

Most of the writers and photographers who'd come to the mission so far had stayed a day or two. A television crew stayed five days, and a team from *National Geographic* for four. But the journalist from New York planned to remain for more than a month. He'd rented a one-bedroom apartment at the same complex in Tucson where the conservators were staying.

"How good is he?" Ali asked.

"I've heard he is one of the best," Rosa said, dropping her defenses only slightly. She realized Ali wasn't being combative, but she couldn't bring herself to relax in front of him. Be on guard; be careful, she reminded herself. Never know when he'll strike. "He's in his late thirties and worked for *The New York Times*," she added. "He's written about the Indians in the Southwest."

Rosa showed little emotion as she spoke. Her responses were matter-of-fact. Like Ali, she knew that the journalist would be just one more distraction she and the others would have to deal with during their time in America.

Her mind wandered from Ali to Father John to the work she had to begin on "Our Lady of the Rosary," a mural spanning an entire wall. It depicted the Virgin Mary holding a rosary in one hand and the Christ child in the other. She didn't want to work today but knew that, somehow, she had to. She'd told the conservators after yesterday's Mass for Father John that they should get back to the project right away. Ali had griped about her decision, saying they needed some time away from San Xavier.

She knew better. The foreigners needed to stick together and find solace in their jobs. American police had to deal with the murder, the missing gold, and the hunt for a suspect. That's what she told her comrades. Rosa implored them not to discuss with anyone their discovery of the gold treasure or Father John's murder. Detective Anderson had told her the police were close to arresting a suspect.

She wanted to change the subject, to move Ali from the journalist to the task at hand. She wanted to stay focused on the beautiful art of San Xavier.

"Don't worry about the American journalist," Rosa said. "He's coming here to do a job just like us. You don't have to talk to him if you don't want to. Worry about your work here. Everything is so overpainted. We have much to do."

Ali grunted. Her transparent attempt failed to move him, and he wanted to know more about the New Yorker. He would change the subject only when he decided to go on to something else.

"Is he coming alone?" he blurted out, ignoring what Rosa had said. His walnut-colored eyes were intense.

"Yes, alone," she said gruffly, her English thick but easier to understand than the Turk's. She'd earned a degree in foreign language and literature at Universitá Cattolica in Milan before she went to art conservation school. Besides Italian, she could speak English, Spanish, and French. "The magazine also hired a photographer from Phoenix who's supposed to be an expert on the Southwest. He'll be in and out quite a bit while the writer is here."

Rosa stood five-foot-five in heels and was tiny next to the spindly six-foot-three Turk. Even though he could overpower her easily, she considered him harmless, yet at this moment she wanted to move away from him. She walked quickly down the center aisle of the church. If she started working, so would Ali. No one else had come into the building yet. They could hear a gasoline blower running outside as a Tohono O'odham worker cleaned the walkways and prepared for the tourists and pilgrims who would filter through the plank door before sunset and gaze at the church's beauty and the conservators overhead. Officials of the church had decided that, despite the slaying of Father John, it would be best to keep the church open, as it had been, every day, for so many generations.

There would be more tourists than usual today. Some would enter the church only to seek a connection to their Lord. Most would come to somehow connect to the remnants of murder. A killing had that impact. It always seemed to lure people to its grisly scene. They would stand for hours near where it happened and try to replay the events as though they were eyewitnesses, even though their only accounts had come from the media.

The other two Europeans and their three Indian trainees entered the church and began taking their places at various locations on the massive metal and wood scaffolding spread like a spider web in the east chapel. There was little talk. They headed for their routines, as though routines were some type of protection from the last few days. Absent were the easygoing grins. They'd become robots set on forward, chess pieces headed for their squares.

Rosa shared their emptiness, yet she greeted them with a stoic "Good morning." Her large eyes were as warm as she could muster.

"*Ciao, Francesca. Come va?*" she asked Francesca Vitucci, greeting her with good morning in their native tongue.

Francesca smiled weakly and said, "*Abbastanza bene, grazie.*"

Rosa used English to greet the three Tohono O'odhams and Elizabeth Smythe, the conservator from London. Her voice was soft and maternal, and even though she could be stern when it came to the preciseness their work required, people always felt comfortable around her. She acted like a mentor, not a dictator.

She paid particular attention to the three Indians because their culture fascinated her. They were quiet men, all in their twenties. To them, San Xavier represented their heritage, and they took heartfelt pride in their work. They were always on time and were excellent students. They showed little emotion. In their culture a man who showed his feelings to a woman was weak.

Jimmy Longfellow did most of the talking for the trio. Born off the reservation in Tucson, he had spent most of his twenty-three years among his people. He usually arrived at the church right after Rosa and often left after everyone else.

"We'll be working on the red wall in the east chapel today, right?" Jimmy asked Rosa after nodding only slightly to her daily greeting. As usual he wore a heavy red-and-black plaid wool shirt over a black T-shirt. By noon, he would shed the wool shirt. He never took off his Los Angeles Raiders cap, which he wore backward. His ebony hair flowed without a wrinkle to the middle of his back.

"You'll need to move some of the lights down there so you can see," Rosa responded. She gathered her hair and put it through a rubber band so it wouldn't bother her face while she worked. Her hair also cascaded to the center of her back.

Before today Jimmy always had a quick smile. Rosa felt an urge to say something to him, although she didn't know what. "We're all so sorry about Father John, but it's probably best for us to continue with our work," she said reassuringly, trying to convince even herself.

"You know, they didn't have electric lights when they painted this church," Jimmy said without acknowledging Rosa's statement. He wanted to work. He wouldn't talk about his parish priest, particularly to a white person. Whites weren't easy to trust. Most disliked Indians and refused to believe that they were anything but worthless drunks on welfare. Jimmy didn't view Rosa that way, but he couldn't nudge the feeling from his heart. The beauty of art on the walls around him seemed much easier to handle.

Rosa spoke with her busy hands, pointing her unpolished fingers. The Indians joked among themselves about her hands, saying, "*I ñeid g e-mamwuligk am d'aga.*" She was forever plucking, poking, touching, and pointing. They laughed whenever one of them called the constant movement of her fingers "an Italian thing."

"They really were craftsmen, weren't they?" Rosa said to Jimmy. "It's hard to believe that such wonderful art was produced by candlelight or sunlight streaming through the small windows in the domes."

"I know," Jimmy said. His eyes, which were glued to the ceiling, had become as soft as the light inside the church. "The colors are what get me. Incredible. And there's fifty-four statues in the church. The carving's beautiful. You know how we say incredible and the carving is beautiful?"

"Tell me."

"*Pi ta-wohokam. Sa'i si s-keg e-hiwckwau.*"

"Wonderful. I agree, even though I can't say it," Rosa responded, arcing her head upward and admiring the magnificent display on the walls and ceilings. "The artwork here resembles that in the beautiful churches of Europe. The pigments in the wall paintings were very expensive. I'm sure they were imported from Europe. None of them would have been found locally. The colors were meant to be bright."

"That red wall I'm working on sure turns bright as I clean it," Jimmy said. "Before I started, the red receded into the wall. Now it jumps off."

Jimmy silently walked up the first flight of steps on the scaffolding to retrieve two clip-on metal lights. Within minutes, he had the lights set up on the floor and lay on his back, underneath the first level of scaffolding. Above him, Francesca Vitucci cleaned the three-dimensional blue, red, and yellow checkerboard design painted on the lower portions of San Xavier's walls.

It was an hour before Jimmy spoke again. "Should I wash this part of the wall twice?" he asked Francesca as he stood up and pointed to the wall where he'd been working. He whispered and she strained to hear him.

Francesca couldn't respond quickly. Her difficulty to communicate in English made her come across as reserved and aloof, although she was neither. In her embarrassment, she spoke only when she had to and in short bursts. She couldn't form literate sentences in English, which made America a prison for her. She only served her time, hoping her inability to communicate wouldn't get her into trouble. She wanted to return home as soon as possible. She knew that this place wasn't where she could make friends.

She looked at Jimmy's pointing finger and said, "Yes, twice. Then you see difference better."

On the level above Francesca, Ali used a foot-long orange brush to clean a statue of the Virgin Mary. It was one of three statues of Mary in San Xavier. In this one, she portrayed the sorrowing mother in a radiant crown, veil, and dress, her hands clasped in prayer. The long slit on the left side of her torso indicated that a dagger had been removed from her body.

In his white coveralls, Ali resembled a house painter, but his hands moved with a jeweler's precision. He gently dabbed the 200-year-old paint with alcohol to soften it. Next, he squirted glue from a syringe, one drop at a time, behind the paint to reattach it to the wooden statue.

Suddenly, he grumbled in disgust and yelled, "Goddamned birds."

Several early morning tourists sitting in the pews nearest the scaffolding lifted their heads and stared at him.

"The birds shit everywhere, and the acid in their shit has ruined much of this art," he said loud enough to be heard clearly by the tourists below. "They weren't even smart enough to keep the goddamned birds out of here."

With stealth quickness, Rosa moved up the scaffolding toward Ali.

"Ali, stop it," she ordered in a whisper, knowing the people below were watching them and listening. "There are people in the church. Why do you keep forgetting that we're all under a microscope?"

He looked at her crossly. "Tough shit what we're under." He spoke lower now so that only Rosa could hear him. "The bird shit has done so much damage. This paint is like potato chips. I touch it and it crumbles. There's so goddamned much work to do to clean it."

"I know there is," Rosa said, trying to control herself. *You bastard. We're all grieving over a murder, trying desperately to act healthy enough to work, and you're griping.* "Get back to work and keep your thoughts to yourself. And quit using the Lord's name in vain in a church where people can hear you. You need to act here like you did when we did the church for the Vatican in Rome."

She had been the boss there, too, and their relationship had been just as fiery. At best, they tolerated each other. He put up with her because he needed to as a professional being paid a hell of a lot of money. She tolerated him because she wanted to work with the world's best art conservators. They were co-workers, nothing more.

Chapter 4

Nick's window seat provided a delightful preview of the desert mountains and valleys. Five hours ago, he'd been in an icebox. Now his plane had landed and he stepped into a squint-your-eyes brilliant Tucson day that had warmed into the 70s. He needed the sunglasses and tube of sunscreen he'd bought inside the airport terminal.

He walked outside the terminal a little after noon. Like every other first-timer to Tucson, Nick gazed immediately at the imposing Catalina Mountains. The faded purple mountains north of the city were across the desert valley from the airport, but they appeared to be at the end of the runway, watching over Tucson as its guardian. The Catalinas were Tucson's Empire State Building. Its Grand Canyon. Its Big Ben.

Nick kept his eyes on the mountains as he walked to the van that would deliver him to his rental car. He could understand how the Indians of the Southwest worshipped the mountains. The Catalinas were a temple, a religious icon. They protected the desert from storms and brought it water from melting snows. They gave Tucson its identity, its beauty. They were its heart and soul, the home of its gods.

"Can you tell me how to get to San Xavier Mission?" Nick asked the pert clerk in the car rental office. He thought he'd look at the church and then take his bags to the apartment he'd rented. He had scheduled his first meeting for 3:30 at the church with Carlos Corona, a Tucson car dealer who was president of Patronato San Xavier, the community group raising funds for the conservation project.

"It's just west of here," the pretty blonde said as she swept her hair from her violet eyes. "Just a few minutes away. It's like one of our landmarks." *In her early twenties,* Nick thought as he watched her warm smile reveal two long, white front teeth that resembled Chiclets stuck in the middle of a set of bleached dentures. She wore a tight red miniskirt made of a light fabric that failed to hide the thin thighs beneath it.

Nice, but I don't like the peroxide hair look. He did like her flirt, but he knew this moment would pass quickly and go down as another enjoyable flash in his life that would work best as a memory. Still, he hoped more women in Tucson would be this friendly.

"I know the mission is one of your landmarks," Nick said as he looked at his Timex and tried to ignore her eyes. "Do I have time to go there, then to an apartment on Broadway, and get back to the mission by 3:30?"

"Oh, absolutely. Here's a map we have for our customers. You get on Valencia over here," she said, pointing out the window behind her with one hand and holding a pencil to the map with the other. She talked and pointed like a television weather person. "Take Valencia to I-19 toward Nogales. Then take the San Xavier Road exit, number 92, to the mission. You'll see it from the highway. We call it the White Dove of the Desert."

Nick nodded. "I read a book that described the mission as the White Dove," he said. "Why's it called that?"

The clerk giggled. "You'll know when you see it. The mission totally stands out and you'll see it from miles and miles away. It's bright white, and like all peaceful and everything."

Nick winked at her, snapped his fingers, and pointed his right index finger all in one quick motion. "Must be why it's the White Dove of the Desert," he said.

"Isn't it sad about what happened there Friday?" the clerk said, her face suddenly turning serious, ending the flirt.

The look puzzled him. *What the hell are you talking about?* "What happened there?" he asked.

"Oh, sorry. I thought you were like some type of investigator or lawyer or something here to work on the priest's killing. It was terrible. And the TV said some gold was stolen from his room. A treasure in gold."

"Did you get the priest's name?"

"John, I think."

Nick felt numb. The initial fun in Tucson had vanished. He stood with his mouth open, unable to ask another question, feeling closely attached to San Xavier and a priest he'd never met.

He stared past the clerk, but she no longer looked at him. Her wide smile framed by fluorescent red lips already welcomed another business traveler to Tucson.

Anxiety raced through Nick. He wanted to get to San Xavier quickly. He'd spoken to Father John less than a week ago. Now the priest was dead.

As instructed, he aimed his rented Nissan Altima west on Valencia Road and then south on Interstate 19. It didn't take long before the desert encircled him. Green bushes and cactuses dotted the brown tableau. People who'd never been to the Desert Southwest thought of it as sand and rattlesnakes; they couldn't envision an oasis with tributaries of dry washes flanked by mesquite, palo verde, greasewood, and the regal saguaro cactus.

"Wow," he said aloud as he looked through the right side of his windshield. "Could that be San Xavier?"

In the distance he saw a white domed building, but he didn't yet recognize it as a church. It appeared tall, but except for a taller hill to the east, flatness surrounded it. He squinted at the structure, and then reminded himself that he had to keep his eyes on the road and look for the right exit off the freeway.

He had indeed been looking at the mission, Nick realized once he exited at San Xavier Road. The closer he got, the more spectacular it looked. It wasn't one of the grand churches he'd seen in New York or other cities, but its out-of-place, simple beauty stunned him.

Its snowy whiteness popped up from a brown field. Like the undeveloped desert around it, San Xavier stood incomplete. Only one of its two towers had a dome topped with a cross.

Nick parked his car in a dirt lot across from the church entrance. He examined the brown facade set up against the white towers. Every inch had something at which to marvel. Statues were even built into the exterior.

He glanced at his watch. He had an hour to drive into Tucson, leave his bags in his new home, and get back to the mission.

Nick wanted to go inside, but figured he'd wait until he met Carlos Corona, the car dealer and expert on the history of San Xavier and its interior art. He assumed Corona would tell him what happened to Father John.

Chapter 5

"Nick Genoa?" The words floated in the air as he stepped from his rental car and walked toward San Xavier. They'd been spoken loudly, but they passed though the speaker's mouth slowly, drawn out, as though they were filtered to remove impurities.

He turned and saw a tall man walking toward him.

"Yes, I'm Nick Genoa. Carlos Corona?"

"Glad to meet you, *amigo*," Corona said, sticking his big right hand out several feet from Nick. His arms were long, like his legs and speech. He had the body of a college track star.

"But call me Carl, *por favor*. My friends call me Carl. And everyone's my friend. Only my mother calls me Carlos, or speaks to me only in Spanish." He laughed dramatically, drawing it out like his speech.

They shook hands, and Carl's tight, enthusiastic grip impressed Nick. A strong handshake revealed something about a person, but Nick didn't know for sure what. Whenever he met a man or woman, he noted the firmness of the handshake. Maybe it had something to do with a person's passion.

The car dealer pumped Nick's arm up and down and wouldn't let go. The writer didn't see car dealer when he looked at Corona, but the Tucsonan certainly shook hands like one. Nick had envisioned a car salesman wearing a wool suit, silk tie, and sporting a prize-winning smile. Carl, with skin the color of copper, wore a long-sleeve blue denim shirt, a bolo tie of silver and turquoise, white jeans, a tooled leather brown belt, and plain brown cowboy boots. His thin body covered at least six-feet-four from boots to head. The slow talk, almost a drawl, came through thick lips, and his wire-rimmed glasses and balding brown hair pegged him as an anthropologist or historian, certainly not a person who owned Pontiac and Toyota dealerships in Tucson.

"Welcome to our church," Carl said in a booming, deep voice, finally releasing Nick's hand. His broad smile revealed white, straight teeth, obviously the result of a middle-aged man's ability to afford excellent dental care.

"Thank you. This church is really something," Nick said, looking up into the taller man's creamy-coffee eyes. "I understand you've had quite a weekend here."

Carl lost his smile. "Yes, it has been terrible. I didn't know if you'd heard, and I was hesitant to tell you right away. I wasn't quite sure how I'd bring it up. We're still in shock."

"I heard about it, but not until I arrived in Tucson."

"Father John was a wonderful man, loved by all of us," Carl said, his speech quickening. "I don't understand why they didn't just take the gold and leave him alone. And the way he was killed was so vicious and horrible. People aren't safe anywhere anymore, even in a church."

Carl talked faster now, and the quicker he spoke the more he twirled his *r*'s, revealing the remnants of the Spanish he'd spoken as a child.

"Father John was such a young man," Nick said, his voice solemn. The news of another senseless killing saddened Nick, but the reporter within him smelled a hell of a story. He somehow felt close to this victim, even though their only contact had been a quick telephone interview from New York.

"It's hard to believe," he added. "I read a story in this afternoon's paper that mentioned the gold bars, coins, and a cross. Said they'd been found in a secret compartment inside the church."

Nick handed Carl the *Tucson Citizen*. "Have you seen today's afternoon paper? The story is in the second section."

Carl read the story with interest. He'd not seen it yet.

> Police officials from Pima County and the
> Tohono O'odham reservation continued searching
> today for suspects in the robbery and brutal
> killing of Father John Duvall, pastor of San
> Xavier del Bac Mission.
>
> The Franciscan priest was found stabbed
> to death Friday morning in his living quarters
> behind the church. An undetermined number
> of 200-year-old valuable gold ingots and coins,
> as well as a priceless emerald and gold cross,
> also were missing from his bedroom. The gold
> had been discovered a day earlier in a hidden
> compartment inside the church.
>
> "We're close, but we aren't ready to
> arrest anyone yet," said homicide detective
> Ashton Anderson, who is leading the team of
> Pima County and Native American investigators
> who have been called into the case.
>
> Father Duvall was 52 years old. He had
> been at San Xavier for five years and helped
> bring a group of international conservators
> to the mission to restore the interior artwork
> in the two-century-old church. They are
> continuing their work in the church, which will
> remain open for daily masses and sightseeing.

Carl returned the newspaper to Nick slowly and searched for the next
thing to say. "The art conservators discovered the treasure based on information

left on a sheet of paper they found in one of the statues," he said. "They called me in to help locate it. Once they found the gold, they turned it over to Father John immediately. It was their obligation."

Carl paused and stared into the dirt below him, gently kicking it with his boot. He'd become somber. "And now he's dead. Yesterday's funeral Mass was beautiful, and today we're trying to return to normal. It'll take time, but we need to continue with the restoration of the church. He'd have wanted that. None of us who knew Father John will rest until the murderer is brought to justice."

Carl now spoke without looking directly at Nick. His statements sounded rehearsed, as though he'd already talked to the police and reporters.

"Why don't we talk about the mission?" Nick said to change the subject.

"Yes, let's do." A slight smile returned to Carl's face, and his eyes brightened. "Let me give you a quick tour out here and fill you in on some of the history. Then we'll go in and meet the conservators before they quit for the day. They usually work until five, but I think they're planning to leave early today. It's their first day on the job since Father John's death, and there's a lot of stress in there."

Nick pulled a reporter's notebook from the back pocket and a pen from the front pocket of his khaki Dockers. He felt overdressed in his long-sleeve, button-down blue dress shirt and a silk tie splashed with bright flowers. He'd lose the tie and long sleeves after today.

Carl took several steps to the right and began talking. "That dry riverbed you crossed between the freeway and here is the Santa Cruz. I should say it was once the raging Santa Cruz, which made this a fertile valley and the headland of the Sonoran Desert. It ran until the 1890s, but long before that, it made this a perfect location for Indians to settle and then a perfect spot to build a church."

Nick wrote a few words in his notebook. He didn't interrupt Carl, but he hoped the car dealer would quit lecturing and they would move into the church. He would be in Tucson for awhile and could read about the history of San Xavier later.

"The river helped in the construction of San Xavier," Carl said, suddenly waving his left hand wildly next to his face to shoo a stubborn fly. "Water was brought here by irrigation ditches. Damn flies. I hate flies. The burned bricks were made from nearby clays, grasses, and sand. There were limestone deposits near here, too, which gave the builders material for mortar and plaster."

Nick glanced oddly at Carl, who dressed and spoke initially like a Westerner but talked now as fast as a New Yorker. What a change. At first the language came from a slowpoke, but after several minutes Carl could've been a street vendor in Manhattan giving directions to a tourist.

"There are even statues in the alcoves on the exterior of the church," Nick said, hoping to move Carl onto something else.

"Yes, there are." The more Carl talked the louder he got. "Let's start up there," he said, pointing up to the top of San Xavier's brown facade. "The statue on the top, with its head, shoulders, and arms missing is Francis of Assisi. Notice the corded Franciscan habit."

"And these two?" Nick asked, pointing to the two statues on the west side of the facade.

"The one on top is Barbara, we think. She supposedly was a Roman girl locked in a tower and tortured by her pagan father to prevent her Christian worship. Below her is Catherine of Siena, the twenty-third child of a painter. She resisted her parents when they arranged her marriage and instead became a penitent of the Dominicans. Died in 1380, I think, and was canonized in 1460 or '61."

"How do you know so much about these statues?"

"I grew up in Tucson, *amigo*. My father owned the Pontiac dealership before me, and he was always a patron of the arts. I fell in love with San Xavier when I was a school kid and we came on field trips here. I've always been interested in it. My degree from the University of Arizona is in history.

I wanted to go for the doctorate, but I realized that I really was part of my family business and would some day take it over. A Ph.D. running an auto dealership is a bit of overkill, don't you think? Maybe I should be selling antique cars."

Carl laughed like an actor on stage. Nick smiled and nodded. "So you head the Patronato to restore the church?"

"I do a lot more than that. The Patronato is raising money now to conserve the interior artwork, but I've been involved in many projects here, which require a lot of my time and money. For instance, we had to raise money to fix the exterior of the church. We needed to repair and replaster the domes so that the roof would quit leaking and damaging the artwork inside. Decades ago, the roof was patched with concrete, which of course expanded and cracked and let in even more water. We finally figured out how to do things right. Today, I can say proudly that we've gone through three generations of the same family of plasterers in restoring the exterior. They even use cactus juice in their plaster, just like the original workers."

"Fascinating," Nick said sincerely. The car dealer's indefatigable passion for his church and hometown got even Nick's adrenaline pumping.

Not many people could do that to him anymore. He'd spent too many years covering the courts. His divorce knocked the wind out of him, too. Over the years as a reporter, and as a husband, he'd learned to underreact. His strong feelings for anything had been buried some time ago. Friends accused him of being jaded.

"What about the two statues on the other side?" he asked.

"The one on top is Cecilia. Her head is missing. She's better known as the patroness of music. She was forced to marry Valerien, but she converted him."

Nick didn't bother to take notes. He could get the names later if he needed them.

"On the bottom is Lucy, who was denounced by her fiancé for being a Christian and was forced to work in a brothel. I've heard that her martyrdom included being boiled in urine, having her teeth pulled out and breasts torn off, and having her eyes cut out and her throat slit. Heavy stuff, huh?"

"Yes, it is," Nick said, himself now swatting at a fly pestering his cheeks. He hadn't shaved since early in the morning, and his face felt like sandpaper. He thought about the violence Christians have had to endure through the centuries, from Lucy to Father John. Killing people for any reason never made sense to him. Men were like flies. Pester and get swatted. Be in a spot you shouldn't be and get smashed. Men had always killed, and far too often in the name of God. Centuries changed. So did ethics and desires, but men had never lost the knack for fighting to the death.

As the two men spoke, dozens of people walked slowly into the church, most of them ignoring the exterior statues, some of them having to bend a little because the plank doors leading into the church were so narrow and short.

"Why don't we go inside the church and meet some of the other people?" Nick said.

"Sure," Carl added, waving his left hand to a group of elderly tourists who were speaking German and posing for a photo in front of the entrance. He offered to take the picture and happily took the camera from one of the men.

"*Diga queso*," Carl said. "Better yet, say Limburger cheese." He snapped the photo and handed back the camera, smiling broadly and watching the Germans slowly enter the church. He didn't move until all of them were inside. Then he stood next to the door, bowed slightly, and motioned for Nick to go in first.

The writer wondered if the car dealer knew that Limburger cheese came originally from Belgium, not Germany. He could overlook the indiscretion.

Chapter 6

My *God*, Nick thought when he walked into San Xavier. *It's more spectacular than I imagined. It's not the beauty of gold and diamonds. It's dark, European beauty. There's nothing gaudy about it.*

He always thought like a reporter, taking mental notes of his observations. He had walked through time, into an age when art offered education, and he wanted his intoxication with this unique building to seep in slowly.

The plaster interior walls and ceilings of San Xavier presented a massive canvas of subtle colors. Huge paintings and statues blanketed each wall. Rich, dark, antique wood adorned the spots without art.

Scores of people were inside the cross-shaped cavern when Nick entered, yet no one spoke. Like him, most people stared at the beauty before them.

Some people prayed for loved ones, and the candles flickering everywhere yellowed their sad faces.

Overwhelmed by the grandeur around him, he had to remind himself of his assignment and the guide in front of him. He tried to record his thoughts quickly as Carl led him down the narrow center aisle toward the chancel and two transept chapels. He scribbled in his notepad:

- *Florescent lights but pretty dark.*
- *Natural light pouring in through 8 or*
  so windows high in the ceilings.

- *Cracks in the plaster, breaks too, that have destroyed some art, but what's left is huge, spectacular.*
- *No white walls showing in chancel because statues, paintings everywhere.*
- *Easy to tell which artwork has been cleaned. A dull beauty to it.*
- *Uncleaned stuff is shiny, like it's been painted over with oil.*
- *Cleaned stuff is soft, colors knock your socks off.*
- *Eyes in the art seem to be looking into space. Not at me or anyone else.*
- *Corona's still talking.*

"Nick Genoa, let me introduce you to Rosa Zizzo, chief conservator of this project," Carl said, gently jarring Nick from his notepad.

He looked up and into two beautiful eyes. She moved close enough to him so that he could smell her sweet breath. She'd been chewing peppermint gum. Her teeth were bright, her smile sincere. Her lips moved and she said something to him, but he couldn't hear it. He stood frozen, swallowed by her eyes.

She's as beautiful as the angels above me.

He didn't realize for several seconds more that her outstretched hand waited to shake his. He began to make out the words coming from her small mouth, something about "glad to have you at San Xavier." He saw only warm eyes, a smile framed by a hint of lipstick, her light brown face, lovely skin, and wavy long hair.

"Welcome to San Xavier, Mr. Genoa," she said, yanking him from his brief trance. "You'll be spending some time with us?"

"Yes, yes I will," he said quickly, trying to put on his professional face. Heat rushed though his body. "What do you think of San Xavier?"

He felt like a fool for asking such a dumb question.

Her smile let him know she'd been asked the question too many times. "You have an Italian name," she said.

"I'm Italian-American, but the emphasis is on American."

"Your face reminds me of one of my cousins."

Oh, great, she thinks I'm family. Does that put me in the do-not-touch section?

"Thank you." He didn't know what else to say.

"This is a beautiful church, something America should be very proud of," she said, getting around to his dumb question about her thoughts.

"You think it's worth restoring?"

"Oh, this isn't a restoration." Her tone instructed Nick not to use the term again. "It's cleaning, conservation, integration, preservation. We're doing a little re-stuccoing, but not much."

Nick took notes as she spoke, but he continued gawking into her eyes. He probably wrote on his hand and sleeve, but he didn't give a damn. He couldn't care less if his pen touched anything at all. The warmth of her stare felt like a wool blanket, and he hadn't felt such a rush in a long time.

"We're painting in a neutral color in the areas where there is no paint left or where we've re-stuccoed," Rosa added, obviously feeling comfortable with the writer's sleepy hazel eyes upon her. "That way the bright white won't show. We have had. . . ."

Carl interrupted her. "Centuries of dirt, birds, and candle soot have damaged the art," he said, nodding in agreement with himself. "This place is just like your home. You can't let it go. It requires constant upkeep, and it's never had maid service."

He laughed heartily, and suddenly Nick and Rosa paid attention to him, although neither understood the cause of his laughter. They turned their heads slightly toward him but still stared at each other.

Nick wondered if he should say something about Father John and the gold. He wanted to get it over with, to let her know that he shared some of the pain, but the words weren't forming in his mouth.

"We've had to remove a lot of overpainting before we could clean the original paintings," Rosa said once Carl quit laughing. "Over the years, some people have tried to fix the art by painting over it with fresh colors, including oil paint. We'll get rid of that. When we're done, the people will see the church today as its people saw it two centuries ago."

"Amazing," Nick said, feeling as silly as a schoolboy for not thinking of anything more intelligent to say. He recovered quickly. "I'm already impressed by what you've done. It's clear which paintings have been cleaned and which ones still need to be. The colors are unbelievable."

"Thank you," she said.

He could tell she liked the compliment. *Damn, I'm flirting with this woman. I think she might be flirting, too. Get back on track, Nick. Keep your cool. Stay calm.*

"I understand that you're also training some Tohono O'odhams so that they can take over when you've finished," he added, sounding much more like a reporter now.

"Oh, yes. We train the locals and then they can continue the work. We hope that two centuries from now the church will still have its original feeling of wonderful Catholic art."

"Should we take him up the scaffolding to meet the others?" Carl said, his right arm already outstretched as though he were a tour guide rushing people along.

"*Non c'é più tempo oggi.*" Rosa responded in Italian but repeated herself in English. "There's no more time today. We need to quit early. I'm sure Mr. Genoa can wait until tomorrow to meet everyone."

"No problem," Nick said, now seeing sadness in Rosa's eyes. "But will you please call me Nick?"

And then he needed to say one more sentence. "I know about Father John."

Rosa nodded her head *yes* without speaking. She turned and headed back toward the giant scaffolding at the back of the church.

As he watched her walk down the aisle, Nick felt alone and needy for the first time in years. He'd told himself since his divorce that he wouldn't get serious about a woman again. Play the field, don't get trapped, don't get tied emotionally, no commitments. He'd said it over and over, but at this moment, he floated in the air with the soot, wondering if he'd been ignited by love at first sight.

Chapter 7

During his first days in Tucson, Nick asked questions and tried to get to know the conservators. They spoke proudly of their work and talked about it eagerly, but they were hesitant to discuss Father John or the missing gold. Nick sensed the foreigners' confusion and frustration whenever the murder came up. Each one had said that, by now, the police should have arrested someone.

Nick's interest in Rosa deepened beyond her involvement in the San Xavier project. Although he remained too shy to ask her anything about her personal life, he purposely directed most of his questions at her.

He believed she felt something, too. He fantasized about her making the first move, but also reminded himself to get over such thoughts. She smiled warmly when he caught her glancing at him. They'd passed each other at the apartment building where everyone stayed, but they'd only said hello. So far, their conversation remained focused on the mission.

He also reminded himself that Rosa, the professional from a foreign country, was dedicated to her work, the reason she was in America. And he had an assignment for an international magazine. Still, he couldn't keep his eyes off her, and he knew in his heart that something percolated between them.

Rosa's bright eyes urged him to say something, but his insecurities delayed him. *What should I say? What if she rejects me? Slaps my face? Avoids me? All that would be worse than if I never say anything and simply look at her and grin.*

"You are a good man, Nick," she said one morning after everyone had started working and she and Nick were standing on the lower level of scaffolding.

Her unexpected comment felt great.

"Thanks, but how would you know that?"

"You ask tough questions, but you also know when to stop. You are conscious of our feelings. I and the others appreciate that. We're becoming comfortable with you."

That's what he wanted. It would make his reporting job easier, and help him get closer to Rosa.

"Do you ever do anything but work at the mission?" he said, knowing he'd just asked his boldest question yet.

"I am a far distance from my home," she said. "I try to stay focused on my work."

She did a good job of not answering his question, and he knew not to push.

Later that day, when Nick was sitting alone on a bench in an outside patio, going over his notes, Elizabeth walked up to him and asked if he'd like to join the conservators for dinner at a Mexican restaurant in northwest Tucson.

"You want to go to Sanchez's with us?" the Englishwoman said. For the first time, one of the conservators suggested that the writer be part of their lives away from the church. He hoped that Rosa had asked Elizabeth to invite him.

"Sure," he said. As she started to walk back into the church, he added, "Did Rosa send you out here?"

She didn't answer, but her smile said yes.

A few minutes later, Ali walked out of the church and lit a cigarette. Nick had spoken to the Turk only a couple of times, and he didn't consider him overly friendly. He also had a problem with the guy's constant smoking. His New York friend, Phil Mitchell, smoked but always considered the non-smokers around him. Ali didn't give a damn about others; he lighted up anywhere but inside the church and seemed to enjoy blowing smoke in people's faces. He inhaled deeply and could talk while he was blowing out the smoke.

Ali's smoke drifted with the slight breeze that teased the pages of Nick's notepad. The cloudless afternoon sky resembled lightly tinted glass, and the reporter enjoyed the desert warmth. Even with visitors meandering in and out of the church, he could hear birds singing in the background.

"You going to Sanchez's?" Nick asked the Turk.

"Yes. They serve good burritos. Nothing like our *borek* stuffed with meat or *dolmas* with rice, but this is Tucson, and we enjoy going there for spicy food and a few drinks one day during the week. Time to relax and maybe try to understand Mexicans."

Ali inhaled his Camel and blew out small rings. He held the cigarette between his fourth and fifth fingers, and the rest of his hand covered his nose with every drag. The sockets containing his deep-set eyes were much darker than the rest of his face. His cheeks revealed scars from what must have been severe teenage acne.

Ali managed a quick smile when Nick said he looked forward to the evening. It evaporated quickly when the writer asked, "Is everyone going? The Indians, too?"

"No, just you, me, Franny, Beth, and Rosa. The Indians are good people, but they aren't the people we socialize with. They work for us, not with us, and don't stray far from their reservation."

The Turk dropped his cigarette and dug it into the patio's brick floor with his tan deck shoes. They were well worn, with paint drippings on them. He didn't wear socks.

Nick disliked Ali's arrogance. "Don't all of you conservators actually work for the Indians of San Xavier?" he asked, knowing the Turk wouldn't enjoy the question.

Ali's stare was ice cold. "Bullshit," he said. "We're not here for the Indians. We're here because no one else in the world could save this church.

Look at it. You think these people have taken care of it?"

Nick didn't like the comment, nor could he answer the question. "I'm ready for some Mexican food," he said instead. "I've heard there are some great places for it in Tucson."

"Sanchez's is good," Ali said with the confidence of a food critic for a major newspaper. "Nothing fancy, but I like the *machaca* and egg burritos."

Nick made a mental note of *machaca*. He had no idea what the word meant.

Hours later, the group loaded into two cars, the conservators in one and Nick in his own, and drove across town to the Sanchez Burrito Company, which claimed to be "Home of the Famous Giant Burrito." People packed the restaurant's single, large room and its metal tables lined up against the walls and down the middle of the restaurant, each furnished with four red plastic-covered metal chairs.

The long counter at the back buzzed on both sides. It reminded Nick of a Manhattan deli. Dozens of customers stood on one side, most straining their necks to read the poorly lit marquee displaying the menu. On the other side, a half-dozen workers, five women and one man, shouted in Spanish and worked feverishly over large pots and a steaming grill. A pimply teen-aged girl worked the counter, writing orders quickly on plain pieces of paper before hanging them on metal clips behind her. When she took an order, she gave the customer a number.

The list of burrito types seemed endless and included *carne asada*, *carnitas*, *barbacoa*, *chile colorado*, *chile verde*, and *machaca*.

Nick ordered *machaca* and eggs, "Sanchez style," which, according to the sign, meant the dried-beef burrito came with cheese, sour cream, guacamole, and swam in enchilada sauce. The girl behind the counter did not look up before she said, "You're number seventy-one." He also asked for a Budweiser.

Nick walked back toward the front door to the two tables the group had pulled together. He sat between Francesca and Elizabeth, across from

Rosa. "You like here?" Francesca said to him when he sat down. He couldn't tell if she meant the restaurant, Arizona, or the United States, but he didn't want to ask for clarification and embarrass her. The chubby brunette hadn't spoken to him before. She seldom talked when she worked, and whenever he asked her a question, she normally just smiled and shook her head. When she did answer, she ended her broken-English sentence with a giggle.

Her irises were so dark that it was impossible to tell that her eyes contained pupils. She wore too much makeup, and the powder on her face made her olive skin look ghostly. She had narrow lips, a pug nose, and thick eyebrows.

"I've been to Arizona before, but mainly in the northern half where there are mountains and pine trees," Nick told her. "I'm enjoying the desert and Tucson. How about you? You like Tucson?"

"Oh, nothing like I imagine." She spoke slowly, and Nick knew that she initially said the response in her head in Italian and then tried the best she could to translate it into English. He enjoyed her perfume.

"I thought desert like Sahara," Francesca continued. "Nothing but sand. But this beautiful. Green. Purple mountains. Beautiful big cactus. They called *Saw-whore-oh*. Look like man with big arms. Not whore. And people nice."

She giggled.

She talked with her hands, and Nick couldn't help but notice her ugly nails. Francesca chewed them and never bothered to use polish. But what the hell, she worked in a profession that required persistence, preciseness, and patience, not pretty nails.

Nick liked her, wanted to help her with her English, and wished that he could understand and speak the language of his ancestors so he could carry on a better conversation with her. He knew cuss words in Italian, but not much more. When he was a child, his older relatives spoke Italian. His parents knew it, too, and spoke it occasionally, but after his father died, his mother seldom used it. He'd forgotten nearly all of it.

"Do you know where Mount Graham is?" Elizabeth asked Nick when Francesca took a break from talking.

He turned to look at her just as the teenager behind the counter shouted "Seventy-one."

"That's me," he said, feeling somewhat silly for speaking. The teenager called other numbers, and nearly everyone at his table stood up.

Nick picked up his burrito, which came on a red plastic tray with a small paper dish of tortilla chips. He ordered another Bud.

"Mount Graham is in southeastern Arizona," he said to Elizabeth when she sat down with her tray. She hadn't made a stop at the salsa bar like he had, and he wondered if he'd made a mistake spooning on so much red and green stuff onto his meal. "Francesca asked me the same question yesterday and I looked it up on my road map when I got home. I forgot to say anything to her today, but now I'm puzzled. Why are all of you are so interested in it?"

"That's where the Vatican is involved in building a giant telescope, and we'd like to go see it. Rosa and Francesca, of course, are interested in the project because they're from Rome."

"I read about it in the Tucson paper," Nick said, trying to remember the story. "Something about the Apache Indians protesting because they consider Mount Graham to be sacred. But I don't recall reading anything about the Vatican. The story said the University of Arizona was building it."

"It is, it is," she said defensively. "But, believe me, the Vatican is a big partner. The Vatican observatory is based in Rome, and it has telescopes south of there, but most of its astronomy is done at the university and atop Mount Graham. The Vatican always has been interested in the stars and other planets. Two things excite the mother church—astronomy and gold."

Nick liked looking at Elizabeth's brightly painted red lips when she talked. They curled strangely and the mole above them moved up and down. She had bleached hair but the dark roots had grown out. Her face vaguely reminded him of Marilyn Monroe. She looked younger than the other conservators, perhaps only twenty-three or twenty-four. She'd told him earlier in the week that she had finished her classroom work in the art conservation program at the University of London and had come to Tucson to serve her postgraduate internship on the San Xavier job.

Ali had told him to ignore Elizabeth because of her youth and inexperience, but Nick liked her. She answered his questions helpfully and cheerfully, while the Turk hardly acknowledged his presence.

"Maybe they'll find some hidden Apache gold up there on Mount Graham," Nick said jokingly, hoping to get Elizabeth to talk more about the precious metal. He still hadn't found out much about the treasure the conservators found inside the mission, how it got into Father John's living quarters, or exactly how it disappeared.

She took him seriously. "Probably not, but if they did no one would ever know it," she said. "The treasures of the Vatican are private. It doesn't talk about its riches, and it would never actively look for gold where there might be some publicity. Besides, the Apaches already have caused too much controversy over Mount Graham."

"What about the gold your group found at San Xavier?" he said, pushing harder now. "That has caused plenty of controversy, too. And a murder."

His question struck out. Once again, no one opened up to him about the killing or the gold. Elizabeth looked at him strangely and kept talking about the telescope.

"Several universities have pulled out of the telescope project because of the Indians and a group called Earth First!, but not the Vatican. It will be in it forever, along with the university. You've heard of Earth First!, haven't you?"

"Oh, sure," he said, frustrated because Elizabeth refused to talk about the murder. "They're radical conservationists. You know, the kind of people that chain themselves together and sing songs to halt the tractors of development. Real tree huggers."

"Can they stop Mount Graham?" Elizabeth asked.

"No. I'm sure the Vatican has plenty of money and clout to fight the battle, until the second coming, if it has to."

Nick smiled, but not Elizabeth.

He turned and met Rosa's eyes. They comforted him. She sat next to Ali but they didn't speak.

"What's your interest in Mount Graham?" he asked.

"No strong interest, really," Rosa said as she patted her mouth with a napkin. "We've worked for the Vatican in Rome and we're intrigued by its worldwide projects, not only as Italians but as Catholics. We're also interested in the treasures of the Vatican, but this is not the time to talk about them."

Nick got the message.

"You look full," he said, trying not to agitate her.

"I'm stuffed. No matter how hungry I am when I come here, I can't get through an entire burrito."

He thought he could eat all of his. The *machaca* tasted terrific, but he needed the beer to wash down its heat. He wished that he hadn't put so much of the damn green salsa on his food. Heartburn would surely attack by morning unless he popped a pill or two before bedtime.

She gently scratched her left ear. Her fingernails were unpolished but neatly trimmed. Her fingers were thin and elegantly long. Nick remembered their softness from his first day in San Xavier when they shook hands. She wore no jewelry, not even a watch. He thought about holding hands with her.

"It does seem strange that the Vatican would be involved in a project so far away, doesn't it?" he said.

"Be careful," she responded. "You don't have to be a reporter tonight. I complimented you today for being sensitive to our feelings."

"I didn't mean to . . ."

"Relax, Nick," she interrupted. "I don't mind answering questions as long as you don't remind us about what happened at San Xavier. As for the Vatican, it always has been interested in peering into the unknown. That's why it sent its missionaries to such far-off places like this more than two centuries ago. It's always trying to conquer new frontiers. And that is now space, and this telescope will be one of the world's largest, or perhaps the largest. It will help the Vatican delve deeper into untapped opportunities."

"Want another beer?" he said to her, changing the subject. The booze had relaxed him and he tried hard not to be a reporter. "I've got to have another one to make it through this burrito. You didn't tell me they were so hot."

"Sure," she said. "You also put the green salsa on your burrito. That's the hottest one."

"Now you tell me!" Nick said as he slapped his forehead mockingly with his hand.

They both laughed. Nick felt as though he'd finally connected.

They were social with the rest of the group during dinner, joining in on conversations that ranged from favorite shows on television to what projects would come after Tucson. Ali traveled the most. His wife and two children remained in Turkey and never accompanied him. He hid his unhappiness and bitterness in this small social setting and spoke enthusiastically about his next project. He would be in Spain after Tucson, working on a four-century-old wall painting and not see his family for at least another year.

When everyone finished eating and headed for the door and the cool night air of Tucson, Nick decided to be brave. The three beers, his usual upper limit, had helped.

"Would you like to go for an after-dinner drink?" he asked Rosa. He said it quickly and quietly, and before she responded, he said to himself, *please say yes, please say yes.*

"Sure," she said, casually looking toward Elizabeth and adding, "Nick and I are going out for a drink."

As they walked out of the restaurant, Elizabeth asked Ali for a cigarette. Nick didn't know she smoked.

"Only when I've been drinking," she said to him, acknowledging his surprise. She seemed embarrassed. "I've had a few drinks and I'm ready to party, but this will be another typical night in Tucson. Home and to bed. The smoke calms me."

"Let's go to Famous Jim's," Nick said as Rosa turned and looked at him. "Carl Corona told me about it. Said it's a fun place to unwind, and not far from here."

She smiled, so relaxed and composed. He hoped his nervousness didn't show, but right now his stomach felt as though it had been mixed in a blender.

Chapter 8

"I hope this place is safe," Nick said as he and Rosa neared the open front door of Famous Jim's. Pickup trucks filled its parking lot, and twenty or more "hogs" cluttered a small motorcycle-only area close to the tavern's entrance.

Nick looked at his watch. 9:30 at night. Loudness blasted from inside the building.

"Carl recommended it?" Rosa asked.

"Kind of weird for a conservative car dealer to suggest a biker bar," Nick said as he gently held her arm to slow their pace. For the first time, he'd touched her beyond a hand shake. "Want to give it a try?"

"OK." He sensed her nervousness about going inside, and wondered if she sensed his.

The smell of cigarettes rushed up their noses as soon as they walked inside. The smoke that clouded the tavern's air penetrated their hair and clothes instantly.

A black-haired woman with large breasts and stomach examined Nick with her eyes. She moved her mouth into a counterfeit smile. He ignored her and took Rosa's hand. She grabbed his without reservation. They sat in front of the pool tables at the rear of the building, the brightest spot in a dark bar.

"Whad'll you have?" an anorexic waitress who didn't look twenty-one asked them when they sat. He ordered a Bud, she a glass of chardonnay.

It was impossible to ignore the band about thirty feet away from them.

Four long-haired, tattooed men made up the group, two on guitars, one drumming, one on a keyboard. The two who sang and played guitars wore their baseball caps backward and jeans with torn-out knees. They were screaming a ZZ Top song, off key. The dance floor was empty, except for the large-breasted woman, who'd moved closer to the band, twisting slowly in a fake dance without a partner.

Nick could tell Rosa was uncomfortable. They had to shout at each other to be heard. "Right now I'm wishing for Vivaldi," he said.

She nodded without talking. He studied her pouty lips and thought about what it would be like to kiss them. Everything about her enticed him.

The waitress brought the drinks. Nick put a ten-dollar bill on the table. "I'll start a tab," she said, looking at the ten but not touching it. The band started to massacre another song.

"It's a little loud in here," Nick yelled. Rosa's eyes flitted around the bar, as though she'd never seen anything like it before.

"Yes, it's loud," she said. "I'd hoped to talk."

"Want to finish our drinks and go someplace quieter?" he said.

"Let's go back to our apartment building. I have some beer and wine in my refrigerator and we can sit out on the deck and talk."

Nick, tired of shouting, nodded yes. He called the waitress over with his arm and handed her the ten dollars. She said "thank you" and walked away. No smile. No look. No change.

The full moon illuminated Tucson's cloudless sky. He sat on the redwood deck outside Rosa's apartment, waiting for her to bring him a beer and herself a glass of wine. She walked out smiling, moving her body in a flirt. Her Levi 501s fit snugly. The maroon sweater she wore hugged her chest.

He wore Levi's, too, and a tight long-sleeved green and white rugby shirt that outlined his muscular chest and arms.

She slipped out of her leather sandals and sat cross-legged on the chair across from him. Everything about her was titillating. Nick wondered if she felt the same tension as he did.

"I have to ask you a question," he said when she settled in her chair. He unscrewed the top of his beer and took a swallow. "Why did you send Elizabeth out today to invite me to dinner?"

"How do you know I did?"

"Come on, Rosa, don't tease me."

She laughed. "*Mio amore, é colpa mia.* I did it. Does this mean life in an American prison? Does this mean you're always a reporter?"

"No, I'm off work now. I'm happy that you asked me to come along. And that you wanted to go for a drink with me. Could this be our first date?"

Rosa laughed again. "It's hardly a date."

"Not good enough for you?"

Rosa took his joke seriously. "You're a handsome man, Nick. I like you. You're easy to talk to. But I'm not interested in collapsing into a relationship. I'm not here for that."

"Fair enough. I want you to know that I admire your work but am also guilty of thinking about you when I'm away from San Xavier."

"It has been a long time since a man paid attention to me. I am honored. An Italian would have moved very quickly, but you're reserved and careful. I appreciate that. I'm cautious, but I must be."

I wonder what that means? I'm not going to be pushy, nor am I going to tell you that at this second I'm wishing we were in bed.

He was watching her every move. "Surely men pay attention to you," he said, his eyes wandering away from her tight-fitting clothes. "An intelligent, good-looking woman like you must have to fight them off."

"With a stick? Isn't that what you say? In truth, men are not at my door every night." She blushed.

"How do you handle men who want to go beyond conversation, beyond professional contact?"

"I've become good at not paying attention to it. I change the subject. It's hard to understand men. Most of them are interested in only one thing."

"I was hoping you were interested in me," he said.

"Who wouldn't be? I'm sure women find you romantic."

"Very few women find me at all. Maybe I should put a neon sign on my forehead that says Open For Business."

They both laughed and for several minutes gazed at the stars. Rosa spoke first. "An affair with an American might not be good for my career. It could complicate things."

"How would you like me to proceed? Should I act on my feelings? Should I make a move?"

"I won't slap your face, if that's what you're worried about. Right now, I'd just like to get to know you."

"It's a deal. I guess I've been asking you about everything you do but haven't revealed much about myself. Sorry about that."

"Don't apologize. Let's just see where we go from here."

"Will you go out with me again?"

"Of course."

They glanced at each other without speaking. "Are you happy you're here?" he said finally.

"*Sì, sì*. I never realized such a place existed in the United States. There are spectacular churches in Europe, and I have worked in many of them, and I've seen photos of some of your astonishing cathedrals on the East Coast, but San Xavier is unique."

"I interviewed the Guggenheim guy, Edward Newton, before I came here, and he told me he chose you because you were the best. He worked with you on a project for the Vatican."

Rosa smiled broadly. "He's a nice man to say that. Anyone can learn to do what we do. It just requires training and patience. And, an appreciation for art."

"I keep hearing about the Vatican," Nick said. "It's certainly expanded beyond religion. Art. Telescopes. Gold." He regretted saying the word. He could tell instantly that she felt awkward.

She said nothing for the longest time. A gentle breeze flowed through her hair, and she carefully swept it from her eyes, a few strands at a time. She crossed her arms, looking chilled. In the background they could hear wind chimes. She sighed deeply.

"The gold in San Xavier had been there for centuries," she said sadly, choosing her words carefully.

"You don't have to talk about it now if you don't want to," he interrupted.

She looked at him, leaned over, and patted his hand. He longed for her warm, soft, sensuous touch and he wanted to lean over and kiss her deeply. *Not now. Not now. Move slowly, Nick. This isn't the right time.*

"It was the practice during the Spanish colonial period to store gold in the missions, and usually it was hidden in some secret place to protect it from Indian attacks or robberies," Rosa said.

"Hidden where?"

"In a compartment someplace in the walls. Or maybe even in a statue."

"Why would it still be there?"

"*Mio amore*, I can't answer that. But if it wasn't needed, there was no need to move it. Of course, the gold religious artifacts such as the crucifix or a gold chalice were a permanent part of the church and wouldn't be taken out. The priests lived a simple life. They rarely needed gold ingots or coins. And the Franciscans moved often. Over many decades perhaps they forgot about it. Perhaps over generations the compartment was plastered and replastered until no one knew where it was. Maybe a priest at some time decided the gold was so valuable that it needed to be hidden. No one really knows why the priests ignored such a treasure, but like I said, they lived a simple life. Gold wasn't important to them."

"Did you know there was gold at San Xavier before you came here?"

"I think so," Rosa said. "Before I came here, I went to Spain to research the art in the mission. Spanish authorities were good about keeping records on their projects in the New World. I became fascinated by the journal kept by a priest who spent some time at San Xavier. His name was Hernando Díaz. It was quite obscure, and I don't think many people have seen it. I had the San Xavier portion of his travels translated. He talked about gold."

The captivated journalist sat on the edge of one of the two white wrought iron chairs that decorated the redwood deck. She sat comfortably in hers, Indian-style.

"What do you know about Díaz?" Nick asked.

"He didn't like the heat of Arizona and didn't spend much time at San Xavier. He was on his way back to Spain but was killed in an Indian attack at a place called Yuma Crossing. His party carried gold from San Xavier, but more remained inside the church. His journal ultimately ended up in a historical library in Madrid. I have no idea how or when. Do you know about Díaz?"

"No, but I've read about the uprising at Yuma Crossing. I've never seen any mention of gold."

Rosa uncrossed her legs and sat rigidly. "I didn't know what I would find in his journal, but I was fascinated with it. In one entry, while on his way to Yuma, he wrote that some gold had been left behind at San Xavier."

"Did he mention how much was left, or where it was?"

"I didn't find anything like that."

"Could anyone have read that journal? Is it possible someone came to Tucson because of it?"

"Possible, but remember, it was written more than two centuries ago in a language different from today's Spanish. A researcher would have to understand the writing or have it translated as I did. There's no way of knowing if Díaz was accurate, or if the gold we found was what he described. Maybe all of that gold was spent or used by a goldsmith under contract by the church. I never found any record of what happened to it. We found the treasure by accident. None of the conservators spoke of it before we found it."

"Let's just say someone read the journal and also found the record of the gold. If we know who that person is, and let's say that person ended up in Tucson, then we probably would know who killed Father John."

"My, my, you're amazing. The mind of a journalist is never at rest," Rosa said. "Such fantasies. I have to admit that when I read the entry about the gold, I was intrigued. But I think the killer learned about the gold after we found it. The way news travels around here, that could be anyone."

"Who was there when you found the gold?"

"All of us. The only other person we called in after we found it was Carl."

"No one but you, the other conservators, the Indian workers, and Carl?"

"I think so. What are you getting at, Nick?"

"I think you know."

Rosa closed her eyes, took a deep breath, and said, "Let's forget about the mission right now. Tell me more about Nick Genoa."

He agreed, at least for the moment. *Forget about being in Tucson on assignment. Dammit, forget it. I'm not a cop, nor am I an investigative reporter on the trail of a Pulitzer Prize. I'm with a woman, a glorious woman.*

They visited through the night. By the time they left the deck and separated to go to their apartments for a couple hours of sleep, the sun had crawled over the Rincon Mountains to the east. And the brown mourning doves of Tucson were cooing.

Chapter 9

"You're not like most men," Rosa said to Nick just before he took a bite of his chicken sandwich. "Of course, I haven't known many American men, but I've never met a man like you anywhere."

The more they talked, the more they had to talk about.

They were eating lunch at a small sidewalk café near the Park Avenue entrance to the University of Arizona. Nick called it a quaint "sprouts and veggies joint." Rosa liked it because of its location away from the mission. She told Nick that before he came to Tucson, she and the other conservators had eaten here and enjoyed it.

He worked slowly on a pita sandwich filled with grilled chicken, guacamole, sprouts, and some walnut pieces all topped with a yogurt dressing. *Not bad for an imitation gyro. Oh, if only we had time together in New York.*

She picked at a Greek salad, again nothing like the real thing she could get in New York.

"I don't know whether to take your comment as a compliment or an insult," he said, using a napkin to wipe away yogurt from the side of his mouth and mustache. The large sandwich presented some navigation problems, and he had a tough time picking it up with his hands. He decided to use a fork. As they spoke, one of Tucson's restored trolleys rambled on the street in front of them toward the university's entrance.

"I'm not trying to insult you. The men I've known, they're Europeans and different. They're more forward with women. And they don't express their feelings, particularly to women."

"Most American men are like that, too, but years of education and working with women have helped me. Marriage to an attorney helped, too."

"You also have passion."

He smiled. "That's nice to hear. Some of my friends have told me I've lost it. Are you talking about my passion for work or for you?"

She reddened at the question. "I see it in your eyes. And whenever you talk about your writing."

"You're complimenting me."

"Of course."

"It's you, Rosa. I've known plenty of women, and not one has made me feel like you do. You're in my heart."

"*Mio amore*, I feel the same way."

"I have wanted to tell you that for some time. Also that I want to hold you in my arms."

"Why haven't you?"

" 'fraid you'd slap my face."

"I told you before I wouldn't."

"How'd you react if I became romantic? You told me that you don't want intimacy in your life right now."

She froze, sorting her next sentences in her mind. "I miss not being with you. I wouldn't reject you in any way." She said the words slowly, carefully.

Neither spoke for the next awkward moment. They turned at the same time to look at a student scurrying past them on the sidewalk. He stored his pencil behind his ear.

Nick smiled again. "Ah, the good old days. I remember when I was a college journalism student and put my pencil behind my ear. The only worry I had was who I'd be partying with, or where I'd get my next smoke."

"You're a smoker?"

"Everybody was."

"When did you quit?"

"Years ago. Cigarettes, at least."

Her forehead tightened. She looked confused.

"Pot," he added. "That took longer to give up."

"You Americans and marijuana. Is everyone in this country addicted to it?"

"Not everyone. But it's popular among young people. In Europe, too, I'll bet."

"Yes, but we'd rather drink wine."

"Did you ever smoke?"

"Never smoked cigarettes or marijuana."

"Not even as a kid?"

"I had asthma. I outgrew it, but it prevented me from doing what other children did, such as experimenting with cigarettes. Even after I outgrew it, I was afraid to smoke for fear that it would bring it back. I had to work hard to be athletic, and I never wanted to add risks by smoking."

They were too busy talking to do much eating. They didn't notice the people cluttered around them at the cafe's tight tables.

"Have you had a lot of girlfriends?" Rosa asked.

"I don't know what you would call a lot," Nick said. "I dated before I was married and have since, but I haven't had many steady girlfriends. Until now, there hasn't been one that I'd like to spend a great deal of time with."

"Would that be me?" she joked.

"Let me think for a second. Uh-huh."

"How flattering."

"I mean it, Rosa. If I'm not like other men you've known, you're certainly different from any woman I've been with. When I think of you, I think in terms of companionship, partnership, love. There is a great deal of lust there, too, but my feelings for you are much deeper than that."

"Do you need a woman with you all the time?"

"I would like to be with a special woman, but I don't think I need a woman at my side all the time. As a writer I enjoy and need the solitude of working alone. But I want to share my life with someone."

"Did your wife satisfy your needs?"

He didn't enjoy talking about his marriage, but now the words flowed easily.

"No. When I was married, I still felt alone. I know it sounds strange, but being alone was one thing. Being alone and married was another. It was horrible. What about you?"

"I've been alone most of my life. My schooling and career always came first. There has been little time to develop a loving relationship."

"But you've had boyfriends?"

"Of course, *mio amore*. I'm not a virgin."

Before Nick could respond Ali walked up to their table unnoticed.

"You two lovebirds want to be alone?" he said too loudly. Other people turned and looked at the trio briefly.

Rosa's and Nick's faces flushed. "You startled us," Rosa said. "We didn't see you."

"Obviously. I ordered a bowl of soup while I watched you two talking."

"You're pretty good at sneaking up on people," Nick said as he pushed the green plastic chair next to him toward the Turk.

"I didn't need to sneak. You two wouldn't hear a military tank rolling up to your table." He sat heavily and within seconds slipped off his stained deck shoes and began slurping his hot lentil soup, which was served in a plastic bowl.

"How did you get here?" Rosa asked. "Where are the others?"

"Don't know about the others," Ali said. "I caught a ride into town with Carl. I can wait for him to come back by here or catch a ride back to the mission with you two. Do you mind?"

Nick nodded no, although he wanted Ali to disappear.

"Goddamn Americans don't know how to make soup," Ali said after nearly inhaling his lunch. "Or how to serve it. It should be a crime to eat soup from a plastic bowl with a plastic spoon."

Rosa rolled her eyes as though she'd heard all of the gripes before. "Can anyone on Earth do anything as well as the Turks?" she asked.

Nick felt an argument coming. "There's probably not much of a demand for hot soup in the desert," he said, hoping to calm things down. "I'm sure when it comes to tacos and burritos, Tucson cooks can top anyone in the world."

"There's no challenge to making Mexican food," Ali said, his voice still tense. "All it takes is lard, corn, and beef. These people are primitive in everything. No sophistication in their lives or diets."

"If you're so sophisticated, what are you doing here?" Rosa said.

"I like the lentil soup."

"No, I mean America or Arizona."

"It's all about money. You know that, Rosa."

"And gold?" Nick said, knowing he should keep his mouth shut.

"What do you mean by that?" Ali's voice turned unfriendly.

"*Oro*, as the Spanish say. You're being paid an excellent wage because you're one of the world's top conservationists, but that's nothing compared to the gold treasure you folks found and then lost."

"It'll be found again, and we'll have a claim to it because we're the ones who found it," Ali said.

"Excuse me, but I'm the one who found the sheet of paper in Fidelis," Rosa said. "The gold was stored inside San Xavier. We didn't discover it or dig it out of the ground. We merely uncovered it. It wasn't ours to begin with."

"The police will find it when they find the Indian or Mexican thief, and then we'll see," Ali said.

"What if the bad guy is someone much closer to you?" Nick asked.

"Are you suggesting that one of us is a thief and murderer?" Ali responded. "People have been killed for much less."

"Anyone in the church when the gold was found certainly would have a motive," Nick said. "What's your theory on who killed Father John and stole the gold, Ali?"

"My theory? As I've repeatedly told the police officers, there's no reason for any of the conservators to steal gold and kill a priest. We're well off. Look at the Indians, or Carl Corona, or perhaps the young intern, Elizabeth Smythe. They're poor people. Any one of them could be fueled by greed."

"You don't consider Elizabeth a conservator?" Nick said.

"Of course not. She's just out of school. She has a long way to go before she can work shoulder to shoulder with any of us."

"Would you ever consider a woman an equal?" Rosa spoke quietly, but Ali heard her. He didn't answer.

Nick added, "Carl isn't poor. Anyone who owns a large auto dealership is probably rolling in money. But greed should not be confused with wealth. Everyone to some extent has greed. Some would kill because of it. Come on, tell the truth. Don't both of you wonder if someone you're working with every day could be a killer and thief?"

"Gold could breed a killer," Ali said. "It also could get people killed. The point I was making, which you ignore, was that Rosa and I, and even Francesca, have been around treasures our entire professional lives. We're not interested in stealing them. If we were, we wouldn't be doing it in America. Even though the gold found at San Xavier is a treasure, it's nothing compared to some of the treasures we've touched over the years."

Chapter 10

Police arrested Jimmy Longfellow inside the mission shortly after he arrived at work. They found him in the west transept chapel, gently cleaning part of the entombed statue of the church's patron saint, San Xavier. Already, dozens of tourists milled about in the building's aisles or were sitting on its wooden pews. Most stared at the gallery of art that surrounded them. Two elderly women, on their knees in front of one of the back pews, prayed with their rosaries. Their lips moved rapidly but no one could hear any words from them.

The conservators and other Indians busied themselves at different levels of the scaffolding. No one noticed when the three uniformed police officers, two from Pima County and one from the reservation, walked into the church.

Jimmy's callused hands moved slowly over the lines of blood painted on San Xavier's neck. He used cotton swabs to clean the candle soot stuck to the wooden statue's pointed beard and mustache and wide open eyes. He couldn't repair the cracks on San Xavier's cheeks and head caused by constant touching from the adoring faithful. Nor could he halt the never-ending rope of people who wanted to touch the gessoed and painted saint and pray for a loved one or ask forgiveness.

The county sheriff's deputy with the nametag of Bennett spoke first. "Excuse me, are you Jimmy Longfellow?" he murmured, trying not to cause a commotion. He recognized Jimmy, but he asked anyway. His large hands were at his side, the right one not far from his black holster.

"*Heu'u*," Jimmy said, dropping his chin to his chest. Embarrassed, all he could say was yes and in his own language. Why argue? He'd been asked the same question by police before and knew the routine. Cops never wanted any trouble. Neither did he.

"Jimmy, please speak English. We need to take you down to the station and ask you some questions about what happened to Father John Duvall." Bennett spoke firmly but calmly.

"What are you talking about, man? I already talked to the cops. I don't know nothing more about it."

"We just need to ask you some questions. You don't need to raise your voice."

"*Ñe: nanta ñ-ku:pas?*"

"What did he say, Ben?" Deputy Bennett asked reservation police officer Ben Johnson.

"He wants to know if he's under arrest," Johnson said after glancing at Jimmy.

"Yes, you are, but you haven't been charged with any crime yet," Bennett said.

Jimmy grew louder in his defiance. "*Pegi, pi int sa'i i hi:, pi hebai,*" he shouted.

Bennett looked at Johnson. "He said he ain't going nowhere."

Jimmy couldn't have been more wrong. Before he had any chance to resist, the officers had him turned around and in handcuffs. One of the deputies frisked him quickly before ushering him out the door and into a waiting Pima County sheriff's car.

By now, people inside and outside the church gawked at the quick-moving scene before them. As Bennett pushed Jimmy's head down so it wouldn't strike the roof of the car, the suspect yelled, "What the hell is going on, man? I don't know nothing."

Within seconds, Rosa and the others rushed down the scaffolding and out the front door of the church. They stood powerless, staring as though they'd just watched a tragic ending to a movie and weren't ready to move from their seats.

The arrest of Jimmy Longfellow became an instant major story and played well over the radio and evening news. The next morning, Nick read the front page above-the-fold article in the *Daily Star*. The story had developed further throughout the day and night.

A 23-year-old Tohono O'odham man who learned to fight with knives while serving in the U.S. Army confessed late last night to the brutal stabbing death of Father John Duvall at San Xavier Mission, Pima County Attorney Thomas Clausen said.

"Jimmy Longfellow will be formally charged this morning with first-degree murder," Clausen told reporters in a quickly called press conference shortly after midnight at the county jail. "He has told officers that he killed the priest and stole an undetermined amount of gold bars and coins from the priest's residence behind the mission."

Clausen said the 18th century Spanish gold ingots, coins and an emerald and gold crucifix, which were discovered in the mission by art conservators the day before Father Duvall's killing, were not recovered. However, he added, "We did find a couple of ingots inside Longfellow's home during a search after the confession."

The 52-year-old Franciscan priest was found slain in the kitchen of his residence 11 days ago. Investigators said that he was stabbed through the eye with a six-inch-long sharpened screwdriver.

"It is difficult to kill a man by stabbing him," Pima County Sheriff's Detective Ashton Anderson said two days after the killing. "Whoever did it knew he could do a lot of damage quickly by stabbing the victim in the eye and hitting the brain. It was a heinous crime. The killer also probably knew Father Duvall because there were no signs of forced entry."

Longfellow, who lives on the Tohono O'odham reservation near San Xavier Mission, served in the Army for two years and received special training in guerrilla tactics, Clausen said. He also said that the sharpened screwdriver used to kill the priest belonged to Longfellow and had been found inside Father Duvall's home after the slaying.

Clausen refused to disclose other evidence that police had to link Longfellow to the crime.

Meanwhile, Tucson car dealer Carlos Corona, president of Patronato San Xavier and spokesman for the church, said he was relieved that police had made progress in their investigation, but he expressed dismay over the arrest of Longfellow.

"He is such a gentle man," Corona said. "We all are shocked by what has happened. Somehow, the discovery of gold caused the death of a wonderful priest, and now it has led to the arrest of a fine young man who was trying so hard to put his life back together."

Longfellow was on probation after spending 18 months in prison for assault. Clausen said the suspect

also had a criminal record in his teenage years
and had spent a year at the Adobe Mountain School for
delinquents after he was convicted of robbery.

The missing gold ingots and other items were
found by a team of European art conservators who
are in Tucson to work on the interior of San Xavier
Mission. The treasure was found in a hidden compartment
inside the two-century-old Catholic church and was being
stored in Father Duvall's residence.

Longfellow will be arraigned this morning in
front of Pima County Superior Court Judge Marie
Ketchum.

Nick hurried to Rosa's apartment and knocked on the door. She opened it instantly, as though she recognized his knock. In his three weeks in Tucson, he'd been to her apartment often to pick her up for dates. Their relationship bloomed slowly. They spent most evenings together, eating, talking, going to movies, dancing. Their minds and bodies grew ever closer, but he hadn't spent a night in her bed yet.

Nick walked into the apartment and grabbed a tissue from a box on the pressed-wood coffee table in her living room. Rosa wiped tears from her cheeks as she walked into the kitchen and sat at the white and chrome metal table. He sat close to her.

"None of us knew Jimmy had a criminal record or that he was an expert with knives," she said. "Those weren't questions we asked when he applied for the job. He was such a quiet, peaceful man who learned quickly and did his work. None of us knew he was a killer."

Nick stood up and began to gently massage the taut muscles in her neck. "Take it easy, honey. We don't know for sure that Jimmy did it. All we know is that the cops said he confessed. In America you're innocent until proven guilty."

Rosa looked at him with surprise. "You think he didn't do it?"

"I didn't say that. Actually, I don't think anything. I barely know the guy, and he could be guilty as hell. Usually, police do arrest the right guy for a crime. All I know is that I have seen how minorities are handled in New York City by the cops. It's always possible that a man could confess to a crime he didn't commit."

"But an Indian officer was there, too, when Jimmy was arrested."

"Clearly along for the ride. He wouldn't have said anything if he wasn't asked to translate Jimmy's comments into English."

Rosa thought deeply about what to say next, Nick sensed it. He quit rubbing her neck and walked to the front room window. The brilliant desert sun splashed through the mini-blinds and onto the floor. He squinted his eyes and looked outside, where a breeze gently rustled the palo verde in the courtyard and sent its straw-like droppings to the ground. A radio in the bedroom turned out a Dean Martin love song, but neither of them paid any attention to it.

He turned back to face her. "I came here to do a feature for *Smithsonian* magazine. Instead, there's been a brutal killing and now this. And, I've fallen in love with an Italian who is going to be leaving the country before long." *There, I've finally said it. I hope my timing is right. Probably not, but I couldn't hold it in any longer.*

She heard him, but said nothing.

"I'm not sure I want to get into this Jimmy Longfellow thing any deeper," Nick continued. "Let the American justice system deal with it. I just keep thinking it's a hell of a story, and I might try to get a jailhouse interview with him. He may or may not talk to me."

She pulled her bare feet onto the chair and sat quietly, resting her chin on her knees. Her jeans hugged her thin legs. She wore a loose red T-shirt. "You think you can talk to him? Why would he tell you anything? He confessed. He must be the killer."

Nick sighed. "I think I'll make a phone call today after Jimmy is arraigned. There's no way the cops will let him talk to anyone other than a lawyer before he has his initial appearance in front of a judge and hears the charges against him. Then it's all up to Jimmy. He may not want to talk to anyone, especially a journalist."

She stood and walked to him and hugged him tightly. He thought she mouthed "I love you."

Nick stroked her hair.

"I have worked very closely with him," she said. "It's all so hard to believe."

"Let's see how things unfold over the next couple of days," Nick said. "Maybe we should go to the mission now."

"Not yet. I don't know who to be angry at. Jimmy for killing Father John or the police for arresting the wrong man."

He bent his head to hers and kissed her deeply. They had kissed several times before, but those were pecks compared to this one.

"I do love you." He heard her say it for the first time.

"Why did it take us both so long to say it?" Nick asked.

"I don't want my heart broken."

"You're not married, are you? There's not someone waiting for you in Italy?"

"Of course not."

"I love you, Rosa. I think I have known that from the first second I saw you in the mission. I can't tell you how good it makes me feel that you are telling me that you love me."

"I know, Nick. I know."

Chapter 11

The red numbers on the bedside alarm clock brightened the time—11:59. Rosa and Nick lay naked under the covers of the queen-size bed in her apartment with their heads deep in the pillows.

What started out as dinner at an upscale restaurant in downtown Tucson had turned into a night of wild passion. They had waited long enough for this night, talked about it, even tried to avoid it by using logic, but each had finally given in to desire and chemistry. Nick told himself but not Rosa that Jimmy Longfellow's arrest and confession had drawn them closer together.

"Tell me about your wife," she asked without moving her head or eyes.

He didn't respond. He let the words pass over him, hoping they would get stuck someplace on the bedroom wall. They'd spoken deeply about numerous pieces of their lives, but she hadn't yet asked him about his ex-wife.

He began gently rubbing her forehead. The numbers on the clock slightly illuminated her soft face.

She asked the question again. He watched her without blinking, debating how he should answer. He knew she wouldn't let the question die.

"My EX-wife," he said. "I've been a bachelor for nearly five years now."

"I'd like to know about your wife, I mean your EX-wife. Is it too painful to talk about?"

"It's not," he said, not being completely truthful. The breakup of his marriage had scarred him, much of it caused by his family's belief that a marriage should last forever. As a child, his elders told him that people who divorced were too weak to deal with the natural ups and downs of a marriage. The break-up of his marriage had been particularly tough on his mother. She refused to begin a relationship with another man after Nick's father died. She believed in one life, one marriage, and expected her son to be the same way.

He didn't know where to start with Rosa. "There's not much to tell," he said. "We were married five years and then we split up. We had nothing in common. It's hard for me to understand why we got married in the first place."

"You must have loved her."

"I don't think I did."

"Oh, come on. There must have been love there, at least in the beginning."

"There could have been, but then maybe it was only lust that didn't last long. Don't you love me differently from any man you've ever loved?"

"Yes, *mio amore*. You may be the first man I've ever loved. I never had the time. Too involved in my work, I suppose. I wasn't expecting to fall in love."

The nighttime temperature had cooled to the 40s. The ceiling fan above the bed churned slowly on reverse, pushing down the warm air of the apartment's heater. The remains of two Diet Cokes on the night stand next to the bed had warmed during Nick and Rosa's two hours of passion.

He had the covers up to his neck, but they were barely chest high on her. He looked quickly at her breasts. They were full, not too large. The clear line between her white breasts and top of her chest revealed that she'd spent some time sunning near the pool recently.

"Oh, come on, Nick. You have to tell me more." She sat up in the bed and pulled the sheet up to cover her chest. "I have questions. First, what happens when you and I are done in Tucson? Are all of these feelings just temporary? Second, I've never been married and you have. What does that mean to the two of us?"

"OK, Rosa, take it easy," he said, lifting his hands to calm her. "I don't want to make you angry. Talking about my ex-wife to the woman I love is not easy. I guess I've never dealt fully with the pain." He smiled. "Believe me, I've fallen crazy in love with you. My feelings are anything but temporary."

"Why did you divorce?" Her voice had an edge.

"The question is why did we marry. We met and dated in college and went our separate ways after we graduated. I worked at a couple of newspapers and she went to law school. We kept in touch, mainly through Christmas cards, and then got back together when we both ended up in New York City. We were two lonely people in the big city and we wanted company. We wanted sex. The relationship was convenient."

"I still think you must have loved her."

"Maybe I only thought I did. As time went by, I began to believe that I didn't understand love or wasn't capable of it. I guess I thought that living with someone meant you were in love. Not true. I simply never developed any strong feelings for her. Truthfully, we were married to our jobs. She wanted to make partner in her law firm by the time she was in her early thirties. I was consumed by *The New York Times* and thought I could win a Pulitzer by the time I was thirty."

"Pulitzer?" Rosa interrupted.

"Pulitzer Prize. It's probably the top award that a journalist can win here. Once you've won the Pulitzer, you can go anywhere, do anything."

"Oh, yes, I remember. I know what it is. They give it for fiction and art, not just to journalists. And you didn't win it?"

"No. But that's something we can talk about another time. My wife and I were so tied up with our careers that we ignored our marriage. We ignored each other. We were both selfish and self-centered. There wasn't time for building a deep relationship. There was no companionship. No partnership. Both of us worked long hours, and when we did see each other we would inevitably end up arguing. The adversarial relationship between journalists and lawyers spilled over from the professional world into our apartment. Near the end we bickered constantly."

"And no children?"

Nick couldn't tell if she asked a question or made a statement.

"Hell, there wasn't time for children—or anything else. After awhile, there wasn't even time for sex. We spent all our money on stuff. We came home to great sound and video equipment, the latest gadgets. Nothing but stuff. What we didn't come home to was each other. We'd gone our separate ways long before the marriage ended. The split was simple. She took half the stuff, and I took the other half."

"If I asked her, would she tell me the same story? Maybe she'd put all the blame on you."

"She'd probably tell you I'm a villain. By the time we split up, I believed I was. I had no patience with her. Quit believing in her. I think the marriage failed mainly because of me. Even when she told me that I could quit working full-time at a newspaper and become a free-lancer, I fought her. I thought I needed the security of the damn newspaper. The *Times* became my family, my home. I was more comfortable at my desk. And look at me now. I'm a free-lancer who quit the news business."

"You're being too tough on yourself," Rosa said. She began rubbing his shoulders. Her gentle hands relaxed him.

"I didn't change until after the divorce," he said. "I quit my job, left the city, and bought a small house on Long Island. Then I began free-lancing. I guess I'll always feel guilty for not listening to her. She made plenty of money. I could've taken a big hit in my income while I built up my business. Maybe our marriage would've worked if I'd paid more attention to her. Or if I'd only wanted a roommate instead of a companion."

"You'll get back together then."

Question or statement? Again, he didn't know.

"Not a chance. We haven't even talked for the last couple of years. And why would I go to any woman after being with you."

Rosa brightened. "Are we getting serious?" She teased him.

"I want to spend every minute with you. Forget journalism. Forget art conservation. Forget San Xavier. Let's run off to the forest and never come out. I'll give you nothing but attention. Take me to Europe."

They laughed. He reached out for her and hugged her tightly. He felt himself hardening.

"Are you sure you're not just in it for the sex?" she asked.

"I might be. You're just about as good at that as you are working with a painting at San Xavier."

"Maybe better," she said.

He grabbed her arms and put them around him. The sheet between them fell. Their bare chests touched and they kissed wildly. Their hands moved all over each other, and within a minute she was on top of him. He gently pinched her hardened nipples as she rocked back and forth.

When they relaxed again, Nick wanted to ask questions. "Rosa, you wanted to know about my marriage. Now I want to know something about you."

"Haven't I already told you everything? I haven't hidden anything from you. My parents live near Rome. We never had much money. I was closer to my father than my mother, even though he drank too much. He worked as a minor official in the government. My mother did not have a career. I did fine in school, but was more interested in athletics when I was a teenager and over my asthma. I have a younger sister and an older brother. Both live in Italy and are married. No children yet. We have lots of cousins, but few close friends. I became fascinated with art in college and wanted to spend my career studying it. I have had lovers."

"That's not quite what I meant."

"You want to know something else? Is this for publication or are we still two lovers in bed?"

"I promise not to take notes."

"You can ask me anything."

"The gold, Rosa. I want to know how and where it was found."

"Unfair. I thought you were talking about our personal lives. You are a reporter now, aren't you?" Her body tightened.

"I won't really know you until I find out about the discovery of the gold and its connection to the killing."

"Are you a writer or a policeman?"

"I'm a curious reporter who wants to know the entire story. I'm also a man in love who is concerned about the woman I love. She could be in danger."

"OK, Nick. I'll tell you everything I know, which isn't much. If I'm in danger, maybe you are, too. The more you know, the worse it could be."

She got out of bed and put on a plain white V-neck T-shirt and light blue bikini panties. She sat at the edge of the bed, her legs crossed, not touching him. She had such flexibility that her knees rested on the sheets.

"I had spent several days on St. Fidelis," Rosa said. "It's a wood and plaster statue of the saint who was martyred in 1622."

Nick sat up, too, careful not to touch her. Her deep thoughts had moved her back into the mission.

"Jimmy walked up the narrow scaffold to where I'd moved Fidelis. He said he was interested in the statue because it has a two-inch gash on its forehead with painted blood gushing from it."

She stood up and walked to her bedroom window, looking out into the desert night. She opened the mini-blinds slightly and the moon-lit night lightened her body. She turned and looked at herself in the mirror over the dresser. She swept the hair from her eyes. The movements were quick, impatient, nothing like the Rosa he'd watched before.

Nick saw a tear running down her cheek.

"I said to Jimmy, 'Can you imagine this work was made in Mexico 200 years ago? It took experience. It wasn't a simple work. Nice silver gilding, too.'"

She turned and looked at Nick. "Until I cleaned the bird droppings off Fidelis, no one even knew there was a gash in his head. All I knew about him was that he joined the Order of Friars Minor Capuchin, a severe offshoot of the Franciscans, in 1611. He was a lawyer and an interpreter and was assassinated during a Calvinist-Catholic dispute in Switzerland. He was canonized in 1746, I think." Her voice apologized, like she should have known about Fidelis' gash.

She walked toward the bed, her intense eyes focused on Nick. "Then I found a small piece of paper hidden in the back of the statue. It was old and brittle, but not yellowed. It was on paper made from rags. I carefully unfolded the paper, which spread out into a five-inch square. It was written in old Spanish and gave directions to the secret compartment in the walls of the church."

"Old Spanish?"

"The language of that era is different from today's. I learned about languages in my studies, at least enough to figure out the words on the paper. It wasn't as complicated as the Díaz journal."

"So you're the one who found the treasure map?"

The creases in her forehead deepened. "I'll never forgive myself for that. It wasn't a map. It was step-by-step directions of where to walk from Fidelis to find the compartment."

"Did you walk it?"

"Not at first. Jimmy and I made enough commotion over the discovery that the others came up the scaffolding. We all huddled around the piece of paper."

Rosa laughed. "Francesca was jumping up and down and speaking Italian. No one understood her but me, and I started to speak to her in Italian. Jimmy said, 'English. Use English. We all want to know. Don't talk no Italian right now.' It was quite a funny moment."

She sat on the bed again and picked up her can of Coke. She didn't take a drink but circled the top of the can with her finger. "Ali was angry.

He said the paper could be a great discovery. He wanted to begin walking immediately, but I said no."

"Why?" Nick asked.

"Because, as I told everyone, Fidelis probably wasn't in the same place now as he was when the church was built. If San Xavier is like other churches, most of the statues have been moved, and we could've been going on a silly chase. Besides that, we needed to tell Father John before we did anything. He was in charge of the mission and anything inside it, not us."

"So how'd you find it?" Nick asked impatiently.

"You need to let me tell you everything the way it happened. Please."

"Sorry."

"Father John had told me when we first got to Tucson that he didn't have the early records from the church, but Carl did. I reminded the others of that and said that besides Father John, we also needed to talk to Carl. That got Ali even angrier. He said it was our discovery and we should be the ones to uncover the gold. I finally shouted at him that it wasn't *our* discovery. I was cleaning Fidelis. *We* didn't find the piece of paper. I did. Anyway, it wasn't ours to argue over. It belonged to the church. Then he said 'shit' and walked down to the next level of the scaffolding. On his way down he said, 'You're making a big mistake. We need to find out where the instructions lead, then we can tell the priest and Carl. The more people know about this, the more dangerous it can become.'"

Nick looked at Rosa and cocked his head. "Why do you think he was so angry? And why was he talking about danger?"

She shrugged. "He's always angry at everything. I told Elizabeth to call Carl, and I went to see Father John, with the paper. Oddly, he didn't seem excited. By that afternoon, Carl came to the church to show us the plans of San Xavier from the late 1700s. They showed Fidelis in a different spot in the east chapel."

Nick sat next to her on the bed and put his arm around her shoulders.

She stroked his hand. The rhythm helped relax her, and her breathing slowed.

"Ali walked the steps according to the instructions but found no compartment," she said. "We were all confused. We thought maybe Fidelis had been in a different spot. But then Carl reminded us that the people of the 18th century were much smaller than we are today. He guessed Ali's steps were too long."

"Smart guy," Nick said. He hoped he could remember most of what she said.

"So I took the steps," Rosa continued. "I moved precisely the way that the instructions said. They led us into the sacristy. Sure enough, there was a hollow area behind a heavily plastered wall on the south side. It took a large hammer to break through the wall."

"And you found gold?" Nick said with anticipation.

"We found about one hundred small ingots, neatly stacked. The ingots were beautiful. I'd say one hundred percent pure gold. They had small Spanish markings on them. There were also twenty or so gold coins. Big, like American silver dollars. And a gold crucifix that had emeralds and pearls on it. It was more than a foot tall."

"That's where I would have made my break," Nick said, joking.

Rosa beseeched him, "Don't be cute. That was the last thing I was thinking about. We just stood there for several minutes staring into the compartment. We'd found a treasure, for sure, but it didn't belong to us. We knew that the gold and the crucifix were worth a great deal of money, but none of us knew how much."

"How old were the coins?"

"Most of them were dated in the 1760s. They had beautiful imprints on them. I sent Jimmy to get Father John because he might know more about them, also because we needed to give everything to him. He strolled into the church, looked at the gold, and didn't say much. It was like he already knew it was there, or he was sad because we found it. Then he went back to his quarters and returned with a large black leather suitcase. We loaded everything into it. Father John wrapped the crucifix with a large handkerchief, but he crossed himself first. He whispered something in Latin. The gold made the suitcase too heavy to carry easily. Father John said he'd drag it, but Ali wouldn't let him."

"Why Ali?"

"At first, Elizabeth started to help, and Father John looked at her like he wanted her help, but Ali waved her back. Father looked at Elizabeth and rolled his eyes, but he didn't argue with Ali. All he said was that he would keep the gold until he got instructions."

"Instructions from whom?"

"From his Franciscan order, I guess. Again, he was sort of mysterious. None of us knew who he was talking about. They just carried the suitcase out of the church, like it was no big thing."

"Ali was right. What you found became very dangerous," Nick said.

Rosa began weeping. "The gold caused the death of a wonderful human being," she said slowly as she put her face in her hands. "I found it. I found the instructions in Fidelis and I took the steps. I turned the gold over to Father John not even thinking that maybe his life would be in danger. My God, what have I done?"

He gently stroked her head and let her cry. He touched her wet face with his hand, gave her a tissue he grabbed from the nightstand. "Don't punish yourself for doing what anyone else would have done with a treasure map," he said. "If you wouldn't have found it, someone probably would have. You were honest enough to do the right thing when you found the gold. You turned it over to the priest."

"Do you think the police will find the gold now that Jimmy has confessed?" she asked through her tears.

"I'm sure they will."

Chapter 12

Jimmy's eyes were desperate. He'd been in jail before, but not like this. He didn't want to see anyone, particularly the writer from New York. He gave in after the third request.

"So, you're here to see the killer Indian," he said angrily before Nick could sit in a wooden chair inside the visitor's cubicle at the Pima County Jail. They shook hands, Nick's grip firm, Jimmy's limp.

The two men sat facing each other. Nick occupied the chair on one side of a pitted pine table in a dirty, stark room with industrial white walls. Jimmy sat on the other side. Neither spoke. They examined each other like two cocks just before the fight.

"Why are you here?" Jimmy said finally.

"Everyone at the mission is concerned about you."

Jimmy smirked. "*Sí woho ap am s ha-oidahim.* You know what that means?"

"I haven't had my Tohono O'odham lesson yet today."

"It means you worry too much. You should concentrate on old paintings in San Xavier, not on what's happening in the politics in Tucson, Arizona. This shouldn't concern none of you. I'm from the rez. You all come from someplace else and will be leaving Tucson. None of you can change life here."

Nick let Jimmy's statement pass.

"Is there anything you need?" he asked.

"A dead man don't need nothin'."

Irritated by the Indian's bitterness, Nick said, "Jimmy, look, I'm on your side. You'll get a fair trial."

Jimmy's raven eyes narrowed, like those of a predator. "A fair trial?" he said too loudly. "No Indian gets a fair trial here. It don't matter if he did something or not. He gets fried. I've already told you none of you can change life here. In my language we'd say, *Pi ampt hedai o sai gawul ju: g ki:dag.*"

Nick regretted being there. Jimmy sounded like a sleazy criminal convinced that everybody else had to shoulder the responsibility for his actions. One more poor guy bashed by society.

"Jimmy, am I mistaken or did you confess to the crime?"

"Confessed, shit. The fucking cops did it to me, man."

"Come on, Jimmy, settle down. Do you want to talk about this or not?"

"What's to talk about? The cops got me in that room and they had me guilty before they even talked to me. I couldn't say nothing but what they wanted to hear. Everything I said, they turned around. You ever been interrogated, man? It don't make no difference how many times you say no. They hammer you until you say yes."

"You didn't?"

"Look, Mr. Genoa—"

"Call me, Nick."

"*Nt o m-ce:c 'Nick' s hab-a wa pi o sa'i t-naopuc,*" he spat out.

"Which means?"

"I'll call you Nick, but that don't make us friends."

Nick's face reddened. "Who the hell said I want to be your friend?" he snapped back angrily. "Call me whatever you want. I had enough of jailhouse journalism while I was in New York, and I never could quite figure out the bad guys from the good ones. I'm happy that part of my life is over. I'm in Tucson to do a story on art conservation at San Xavier, not to try to save your life. You want to communicate, fine. You want to hate the world and blame everyone else, fine."

Jimmy paused to size up the journalist. He took a deep breath and slowly brushed his long black hair back from his face. Nick got a clear look at the tattoo of a spider on the bottom half of the Indian's right thumb.

"*Pi int hekid o sa'i mau g pa:l John.* I would never kill Father John," Jimmy said. He uttered the words slowly. "I may be no good, but I'm not stupid enough to kill a priest. He did good things for my people and for San Xavier. He gave me that job when there were plenty of guys from the rez who wanted to work at the mission. I'd never hurt him."

"Not even for a treasure in gold?"

"For nothing, man. I don't know nothing about the gold. Everyone in the church wanted the gold when Rosa found it. Any one of us would've been happy to split it right there and run. But she said no and gave it to Father John. Besides, what would an Indian do with a treasure? Indians already are watched by whites everywhere they go. An Indian with a lot of money would automatically be in trouble. He'd be arrested for something. No white man could put up with a rich Indian."

Jimmy's intense expression persuaded Nick to believe him.

"Why'd you confess?"

"You've got to understand this place, Nick." He tacked the name onto his sentence as though he wanted to practice its pronunciation. "I'm an Indian. I drink. I've been in jail before. These cops hate people like me. They look for a reason to kick my ass."

"You're also trained in knife fighting. And it was your screwdriver found near the body."

"How do you know that?"

"It was in the newspapers and on TV. You're big news, Jimmy. They all say it was your screwdriver found next to the body. And it takes skill to stab someone to death. The killer had to know that the right placement through the eye would reach the brain and kill the person immediately. The eye is a small target, but a trained knife fighter could get to it."

"Shit," Jimmy said, drawing the word out until it sounded like "sheet." He stroked his chin with his brown fingers. "I told the cops that the screwdriver had been stolen, but why the hell would they believe me? When they were grilling me, they told me the media would hang me and say I killed Father John. They says to me that if I didn't tell the truth I'd look like a piece of shit on the rez. So I told them the truth. I didn't kill no one, but that didn't make no difference because they didn't believe me. Everyone will believe the stories. Including my family. They'll think I've disgraced them again."

"Have you talked to anyone in your family?"

"They ain't gonna come down here. Not with what the reporters are saying. And because they're afraid of it here."

Jimmy slid down in his chair. His chin fell. His depression settled in like a fog. "Why don't you start from the beginning?" Nick asked. "Maybe the police coerced you into a confession. That's illegal."

"I don't know nothin' about coerced. All I know is that they got me in there in the morning. This one detective named Anderson and another one named Leigh. They were nice to me, but they never let up. By the end of the day, I would have confessed to anything. I wanted out of that room. I wanted a beer. I needed some peace."

The Indian's eyes inspected the room. "It makes no difference if I did it or not," he said sadly. "The cops think I did. My family, my friends, my people probably think I did. Even if I was a free man, people would talk behind my back about me. I could never walk proudly among my own people."

He repeated his last statement in his language. "*Pi int hekid o sa'i s-gimaim hi: am ñ-O'odham sa:gid.*"

"Jimmy, let's get back to Anderson and Leigh. Tell me what they said to you. I'm sure they know the legal way of doing things. But cops know how to manipulate the words so that they aren't accused of coercing a suspect. They have to play fair and square, but they have a way of letting accidents happen. I'm sure there are cops who have had problems with Indians before, and now they think you're all criminals."

Jimmy said nothing. Nick added, "You think it's bad here; you ought to see how the cops treat blacks and Puerto Ricans in New York. If you confessed to a crime you didn't commit, there's a way to fix that."

"I still think I'm headed for the chair, man, but I'll tell you what I remember."

"Start from the beginning."

"Like I said, they were pretty nice guys. Anderson did most of the talking. Leigh sat on the other side of me. He just kept his arms on his knees, kind of bent over like this."

Jimmy demonstrated, then began talking again. "The Leigh guy mostly nodded at what Anderson says and every now and then added his two cents. It was easy at first. Anderson asked me what time I got up in the morning. I told him six o'clock. He asked me what time I got up on the day of the murder. I says six o'clock. He says where'd I go when I got up. I told him Rositas for breakfast. He wanted to know what I ate. I told him eggs and sausage. He says what did it cost. I tell him. Then what I was wearing. Who I seen. It was real easy stuff. I got real comfortable with these two guys."

"That's usually how it's done," Nick said. "They want to make you think they're your friends, trying to help you out. But they're skilled interrogators. First they ask you simple questions that they know you'll tell the truth about. That's when they see how you respond to questions. Then they'll ask you stress questions, like did you do it, where is the weapon, where is the gold? It's their way of giving you a lie detector test without hooking you up to wires."

"That's how they did it, man. They suckered me in. I've been questioned by police before, but I was guilty then. These guys was something else. They just wanted me to say I'm guilty. I wasn't this time."

"What did you tell them when they asked you if you were guilty?"

"I'm not sure they ever did. Anderson just kept saying he wanted to find the truth. He asked me if I have any weapons of any kind. Sure, I have weapons. I've got a .22. I got a shotgun. But he wasn't asking me about my guns. He wanted to know about the screwdriver. So after I tell him about my guns, he asks about the screwdriver, like it's one of my weapons."

"What did you tell him?"

"I told him my screwdriver was stolen. He says when was it stolen? I says I don't know. He says, then, how do I know it was stolen? Now I'm pissed. I says I don't know, I just can't find it. Then he says so my screwdriver could be lost and not stolen. So now I believe maybe it was lost, when I know damn well it was stolen. Shit, the guy had my brain going like a see-saw. Everything I says, he asks another question. He didn't care about my answers. He just had another question."

"I know I sound like a cop now, Jimmy, but how do you know it was stolen?"

"Same way I'd know a dove from a quail. I keep my screwdrivers in my leather pouch made by my uncle just for my tools. He's great with leather. I'd never lose my tools. I had the screwdriver in the pouch when I worked in the mission. Then it's not in the pouch. Someone in the church took it. I figure they want to borrow it. But it wasn't returned. Now that ain't lost, man, it's stolen. But the cops weren't believing me. They think I killed Father John so they keep pushing."

He mumbled the last few words and just stared into the corner. His head stayed glued to his chest.

"Jimmy, keep talking. Maybe I can help. I've been a reporter long enough to know what cops can do when they're looking for a confession. And I know about the cops in Arizona. I read about the murders a couple years ago at the Buddhist temple west of Phoenix. Six monks, a nun, and two helpers were killed and the cops arrested some Hispanics from Tucson. They confessed and then recanted. Finally, they were released and now they're suing the shit out of the cops."

"Yeah, man, I heard about one of those guys. He's gonna clean up. Get millions, probably."

"He's going to score big time because the cops coerced a confession from him, Jimmy. They deprived him of food. They threatened physical and emotional harm. They're not allowed to do that."

Jimmy held his head higher and looked at Nick. He grimaced. "That won't work for Jimmy Longfellow, man. That guy is a Mexican, not no Indian. Mexicans have it better around here than Indians. You might think Mexicans are low-lifes. And you'd be right, but Indians are below them. They hate Indians as much as white guys do. Mexicans are big shots in Arizona, especially in Tucson."

"Quit beating yourself up, Jimmy. You can't be afraid of the cops. That's why so many police misconduct incidents go unreported. Minorities are intimidated by police or fear retribution if they speak up."

"You can't help me, Mr. Nick from New York City. It don't make no difference where you're from or who you are. You can't help me. *I: ya o wa'i ñ-oimelkuc i:ya, gm hu'i na'a.*"

"You lost me again. What'd you say?"

"My future is in the eyes of my people now."

"Jimmy, look at me. I want to help you. Let's get back to the interrogation for a minute. Tell me more of what they said to you. How'd they get you to confess to something you didn't commit? Actually, forget that for a minute. Did they tell you that you had the right to an attorney?"

"Of course they did, but what the hell did I need an attorney for? I didn't do nothing. I'm innocent. Why pay money for an attorney? They told me right off that I have a right not to talk to them, and I have a right to ask for an attorney at any time. They asked me if I understand that. I said yes, and then they asked me to sign a card that I agree to talk to them without a lawyer."

Nick shook his head in frustration. He presumed that the interrogation had been taped. He'd check it later. He could see Jimmy being swallowed up, manipulated, kneaded like bread dough by an excellent interrogator.

"Did the cops say they'd pay for an attorney for you?" Nick asked.

"I think so, but I didn't think I needed no lawyer. The cops told me they didn't want me to spend the rest of my life in prison if I didn't do the crime. Then they says if I did do it they was going to prosecute me to the full extent of the law. Before long they says if I didn't intend to kill the guy, they needed to know. Shit, how can I answer a question like that? They kept saying prove to them I didn't do nothing."

"What other forms did they ask you to sign?"

"Like I says, Anderson was a nice guy. He says to me that he wants to believe me and asks me to sign some kind of form to gather evidence off a human body. I don't understand what he means and he says if I got nothing to hide then I won't mind lab people coming down and doing tests on my hands. That ain't no problem to me, so I sign."

Nick thought for a second. "They wanted to add as much time as possible to your interrogation, to keep you in there as long as they could. They were willing to go as long as it took to break you down."

"Uh-huh. They did that."

"Did they ask you to sign any forms?"

"Anderson looks at me and says, 'You didn't commit that crime, did you? You've got nothing to hide, right?' After I shake my head *yes*, he says he wants me to sign a consent form allowing the cops to look inside my house. I couldn't let them do that. If I signed it, they were going to go in my home. I've got some pot in the top drawer of my dresser. They'd find it, and then I really would be in trouble. I told them I didn't want nobody in my home. They asked why. I says I don't want nobody in my home when I'm not there. Then Anderson says that's fine, if I refuse to sign the form he'll get a search warrant. That's when I lost it and called him a fucking bastard. He can't do that without my permission."

"'fraid he can. And by your refusal to sign that consent form, Anderson probably felt more sure that you were guilty. He had no idea that you were trying to hide some dope. He's not even interested in marijuana."

"Bullshit, man. They would find that pot, and I'd go to jail for sure, even if I didn't kill Father John."

Nick knew he would get nowhere trying to convince Jimmy that a homicide detective couldn't care less about a bag of pot in a drawer. "What questions did Leigh ask you?" he said.

"He got off on my bedroom, man. He kind of interrupted at one point and asks me who lives with me. I says no one. I live alone in a one-bedroom apartment I rent from a friend. He says who's the friend. I say Nancy Burrell. He asks how many times has Nancy been in my bedroom. I says never. He asks who the last person was in my bedroom, other than myself, from the time my screwdriver was stolen until Father John was killed. I says nobody has been in my bedroom. He then asks me if I don't have no girlfriends. Then I know they got me again. My girlfriend's been in my bedroom plenty of times. If I tell them the truth they know I lied. Now I got to tell them the truth about Wendy—that's my girlfriend."

"Does she have a key to your apartment?"

"She don't need it. I'm not real good about keeping the back door locked. In that area, it don't do no good to lock doors. Locks don't stop nobody. They want in, they get in."

"How long were you in the interrogation room before you confessed, Jimmy?"

"All day, man. They told me I could take breaks to eat or rest or go to the bathroom, but I kept thinking it was going to end. But it didn't. I got up to take a couple of leaks, but that was it. I got so scared and tired. They kept pressuring me until I told them I'd sign anything they gave me just so long as they'd leave me alone."

"They probably didn't have a lot to go on. They were fishing. They knew it was your screwdriver. You know how to use a knife, and you've got a record. That could be all they had. No one has placed you at the scene, I don't think. Have you ever been in Father John's house?"

"Lots of times, man. The last time was when Rosa sent me to get him when she found the piece of paper. He was real relaxed. Gave me a drink of water."

"What do you mean relaxed?"

"Like he wasn't real excited about us maybe finding a treasure. He got a lot more fired up when Elizabeth discovered the seven arrows on a high ledge. Did anyone tell you about that?"

"No."

"They were real old arrows with stone tips. Elizabeth found them when she was way up on the scaffolding. The feathers were still on them. They'd been up on that ledge for a long time. Father John said they probably were from someone trying to shoot roosting birds. He was real excited over them arrows."

"Back to when you went to Father John's quarters. You say he gave you some water?"

"Uh-huh."

"The cops might have found your fingerprints in the kitchen where Father John was killed. Did they ask you any questions about being in the residence?"

"Yeah. They asked me that when they interviewed all of us the day his body was found."

"They push you on that?"

"Sort of, until Leigh asked me which watch I was wearing when I went into the house. I told him I don't wear no watch. Ain't that weird?"

Nick's eyebrows arched. "That might be something important," he said. "I'll look into it. Anything else weird?"

"That Anderson was weird, man. He kept saying, 'Let's have the truth right now. Tell me how the priest died.'"

"Seems to me he had you convicted before you started, or something you said during the interrogation convinced him," Nick said.

"*D o wa ñ-cu'ij'g, ñe:.*"

"Say what?"

"I'm guilty, man. You and I don't have to believe it. But *D o wa ñ-cu'ij'g*."

"Don't give up yet," Nick ordered. "Tell me where you were late that Thursday night when Father John was killed?"

"Same place I'm at lots of nights. The Bushwhackers closest to the rez. Drinking beer."

"Did you tell the cops that?"

"Sure I did. But they kept asking what time I got there and what time I left. I wasn't sure, but I was probably asleep in bed or in my truck when Father John was killed."

"OK, Jimmy, let's just for the hell of it say that I'm going to do a little more digging. Can you promise me that you won't talk to the police anymore unless you have a lawyer present?"

"What's left to talk about, man? I'm going to fry. This ain't New York. It's Tucson, Arizona, and these dudes are just waiting to send one more Indian to the chair. Then they can close their books and not even worry about who really killed Father John. Who gives a shit if a murderer goes free? What's important is one more Indian goes to the chair. Like I says, *D o wa ñ-cu'ij'g*."

Chapter 13

Nick rubbed the sleep from his eyes as he tried to take the rubber band off the newspaper and turn on the Mr. Coffee at the same time. At six in the morning, he wasn't good at much. It had been two days since he'd spoken to Jimmy.

The coffee pot started gurgling. He needed the caffeine to give him a push start. The aroma of the chocolate almond gourmet blend glided from the kitchen and into the living room. Nick picked up the remote control and aimed it at the television. He started thumbing through the *Daily Star*.

On TV, a blonde anchor said, "Here are the stories we are following today. The president announces he'll go to Israel and Jordan to continue his push for Middle East peace. Another shuttle launch is postponed. The suspect in the murder of a Tucson priest is found brutally murdered in his jail cell. Details after we check in with Connie and the weather."

Nick felt nauseous. He unfolded the *Star* to get a full view of page one, but nothing on it reported a murder suspect found dead in a cell. He dropped the first section. The top headline on the front page of the second section slapped him like a flat palm on the face.

SAN XAVIER MURDER SUSPECT KILLED IN CELL

Instead of reading the story, he went right to Rosa's apartment. She'd given him a key and had one to his apartment, too. They spent a lot of nights together and weren't hiding their relationship from the other conservators, but they'd decided, at least for now, not to move in together.

Nick enjoyed waking Rosa up with a kiss on the forehead. He loved to look at her as she slept, her mouth usually open, her breathing so quiet that he wondered at times if she took in air at all. The thin cotton nightie she wore left no secrets. She slept on her stomach or in the fetal position. When the morning sunlight blended in with her hair, he could see streaks of red in it.

This morning started differently. He knocked loudly on her door and then used the key. "Rosa, get up," he said even before he reached her bed. "You're not going to believe what's happened now."

"What's wrong?" she said, sitting up quickly and trying hard to focus. She didn't like being jarred awake. She much preferred waking up with his gentle hands stroking her head and then arms.

"Read this story. I'm going to go turn up the television and watch it. Jimmy's dead. Someone killed him in his cell."

"He what?"

Nick didn't respond. He'd already walked out of the bedroom.

Rosa began reading the story in the *Star*.

> The Tohono O'odham man who confessed to killing the parish priest at San Xavier Mission was found slain early today in his cell at the Pima County Jail, police said.
>
> Police are calling it a gang killing and blaming it on a gang of Mexican nationals known to be operating inside the jail.
>
> Jimmy Longfellow, 23, who lived on the San Xavier Indian Reservation, was stabbed and bludgeoned repeatedly inside his cell, according

to Sheriff's Detective Ashton Anderson.

"We have had problems in the past with
Mexicans and Native Americans in the jail,"
Anderson said. "We keep trying to keep them
separated, and in this case we have no idea
how people got into Mr. Longfellow's cell. Gang
activity is growing in the Pima County Jail, and
this incident could indicate that some guards are
involved, either because they are being paid or
out of fear."

Anderson promised a full investigation. He
said no murder weapons were found.

"At 3 A.M., detention officers did their
normal walk-through and talked to Mr. Longfellow,"
the detective added. "At 3:30, they did their
walk-through again and he was found dead on the
floor of his cell."

She didn't get through the entire story. She got out of bed, put on her
robe, and walked into the living room. Nick was leaning over the couch,
listening for the pretty face on TV to report Jimmy's death. Rosa stood next
to him, her hand on his shoulder. Neither spoke.

The Longfellow story came on about five minutes after six.

Police say a murder suspect was found
stabbed and bludgeoned to death.

Jimmy Longfellow apparently was killed by
members of a Mexican gang operating in the jail.
Police say they have no suspects.

Authorities say Longfellow's death came in

between regular checks of the cells in the Pima
County Jail.

Reporter Sonja Lewis is standing by at the
jail with a live report.

The TV reporter talked to Detective Anderson about the killing. The
cop defended security in the jail, but admitted some guards may be involved.
He called it a senseless death and promised a full investigation.

"What'll happen next?" Rosa asked.

Nick turned off the TV. "Come over here and sit down," he said, patting
his lap. "Even if Jimmy didn't kill Father John, the police and the media
seemed to have convicted him. If he was guilty, his killers have done the work
of the courts. Even if he was innocent, the cops won't be in any hurry to keep
working on the case. They think they got their guy. They may never find the
killer. And you saw how the newspaper and television treated Jimmy's killing.
It wasn't even the top story. Just a scumbag Indian killed. There are more
important stories to follow."

Rosa turned away and asked, "What about the gold?"

"That's what will keep this story going. The cops will be looking for a
break on that. But if it was Jimmy, and he was the only one who knew where
the gold is hidden, it may never show up."

Rosa smiled, and that surprised Nick. "What do you find funny in all
of this?" he asked.

"How ironic that the gold was hidden for more than two centuries and
then it was revealed for only one day. Now it may be hidden again for the
next two centuries. Perhaps justice came to Jimmy and the gold."

Rosa moved off of his lap and onto the couch next to him. Then she stood
abruptly and said, "I need to brush my teeth. Make some espresso for me, please."

Nick went into the tiny apartment kitchen and filled Rosa's espresso
machine with her favorite Italian coffee, which she was able to find in a small

shop in downtown Tucson. He feared the cops would do a quick investigation, rule the Indian's death an unfortunate homicide and not their fault, and then shut down the case. They might arrest one or two Mexican scapegoats in the jail, but the gang activity would likely continue.

"We don't have a lot of time before you need to get to the mission, but let's just go over a couple of things again," Nick said as he walked into the bedroom with a cup of espresso made the way Rosa liked it with a squirt of skim milk.

"I can be late today," she said as they met at the door. "In fact, I should go tell everyone to take the day off. We don't need to be working today. Too much has happened for us to continue working."

He'd never seen her this nervous before. He wanted to scoop her up in his arms and protect her.

The ringing phone startled both of them.

Chapter 14

"I'll get the phone," Nick said to Rosa. "Why don't you take a shower and we'll talk when you get out." He watched her walk slowly into the bathroom and shut the door. She drooped as she walked, and that worried him.

By the time Nick picked up the phone, it had rung five or six times. "Hello."

On the other end, silence. Nick could hear someone breathing.

"Hello," he said again. The hesitation on the other end of a phone line made him suspicious. He moved his finger toward the phone to disconnect.

"Is this Rosa Zizzo's residence?" the caller said before Nick could push the button.

"Yes it is."

"Oh." The caller seemed surprised. "Is Rosa there?"

"May I say who's calling?"

"Carl Corona."

"Carl, it's me, Nick. I'm here with Rosa. We just heard about Jimmy."

"That's why I'm calling. I was . . . ah . . . wondering if perhaps she and the others would prefer not to work today."

Nick knew Carl called for another reason, although he had no idea what it could be. *He's stalling. What's up with that?*

"Rosa and I were just discussing that," Nick said. "I was thinking that it would be a good idea if she took the day off. She's pretty shaken up right now. She's in the shower. Can I have her call you when she gets out?"

"OK, sure," Carl said. "Let me give you the number."

Why the hell was he calling? Nick said out loud this time as he hung up the phone. *Rosa would make the decision on whether or not to work. Carl knows that. He wanted to give her some news that he didn't want to share with anyone else, particularly a journalist. What could that be? Has something else gone terribly wrong?*

"Who was that?" Rosa asked as she toweled her wet hair and walked into the living room. Unlike other times when she got out of the shower, when she teased Nick by keeping her peach-colored bath robe loose and revealing, her robe was pulled tightly around her thin waist.

"Carl."

"Really?"

"Yes, and he wants you to call him back. He told me that he wanted to talk about whether the group should work today, but I'm sure there was something else he wanted to say. He hesitated when I answered the phone. He knows about us, so my answering the phone couldn't have been such a big shock."

Rosa shrugged her shoulders. She dialed Carl's number.

"Carl, it's Rosa."

"Good morning, Rosa. Sorry to bother you, but obviously you've heard about Jimmy."

"Yeah, Nick woke me with the news."

Again, hesitation.

"Rosa, can you talk for a moment?"

"Of course I can, Carl. I wouldn't have returned your call if I wasn't prepared to talk."

"Sorry."

"You American men are funny. You apologize for everything."

"They still haven't found the gold, Rosa, but they did find some of it in

Jimmy's apartment." He blurted out the sentence. "Jimmy may have been the only person who knew the location of the treasure. It could be lost again."

Rosa rolled her eyes. Nick watched her every movement. He didn't know what Carl had told her, but he could see her agitation.

"Who searched Jimmy's apartment?" she asked.

"Sheriff's deputies. They got a search warrant and went through his place. They found two gold ingots in the top drawer of Jimmy's dresser. That's why they called me. They wanted me to identify them as some of the gold we found in the church."

"You know for sure the gold ingots in Jimmy's apartment came from the church?"

Carl kept talking in a whine. "I was there when we found it, remember? The two ingots were definitely part of the San Xavier treasure. They had the same markings as the rest. Of course that means there are still ninety-eight out there someplace, along with the coins and crucifix. Jimmy probably hid all of them and left two in his dresser."

More hesitation, wheels turning, thoughts being organized.

"Rosa, do you think Jimmy didn't do it?"

"He must have done it. The police arrested him and he confessed, but when Nick talked to him two days ago, he said the police made him confess. You say the police called you when they found the gold in Jimmy's house. When did they find it, and why did they call you instead of me?"

"Yesterday afternoon. I guess they know that I'm an expert on the mission," Carl said, his voice condescending. "A Detective Leigh called me last night, hours before Jimmy was found dead, and asked if I'd come down and look at some evidence that officers found in Jimmy's apartment. When I got there, they showed me the ingots. Each was in a plastic bag. I asked them if they found only two, and they said yes. That means a lot of gold worth a lot of money is still out there someplace."

"How do you know how much it's worth? I thought you sold cars."

"It's worth a heck of a lot more than just the gold value, that's for sure," he said without acknowledging her comment about his sales expertise. "I think each ingot weighs about a troy pound. That's twelve ounces. That means just the gold is worth nearly a half million dollars. But the value in those ingots isn't in the gold. It's in their value as antiquities. There's no telling what collectors would pay for those bars. I've seen Spanish gold come up for sale before, and there's always someone willing to pay the asking price. The coins could be worth thousands of dollars each, depending on their rarity. And who knows about the crucifix? It's engraved with the Madonna holding the Christ child. The emeralds and pearls make it priceless, maybe worth a million or more."

"Do you believe Jimmy was guilty?"

This time, he didn't hesitate. "There was overwhelming evidence against him. The gold in his apartment convicted him."

"You seem to care only about the missing gold. What about the people who killed Jimmy? Do you care if they're brought to justice?"

"I'm not sure I like or appreciate your attitude. Try to remember who was responsible for bringing your team here."

"How can I ever forget," Rosa said, trying hard to hold back her anger. "Did you say they found the gold in Jimmy's kitchen?"

"Kitchen? I told you they found it in his dresser. Top drawer."

"Oh, yes, his dresser. Why do you think he would leave only two in his dresser?"

"Maybe he kept two just to show them to people. You know, he was looking for a buyer. Who really knows? He had two ingots in his dresser. Ninety-eight are missing. We should be concerned with those ninety-eight."

"Maybe we also should be concerned about the deaths of two people we knew and loved. Why should we care about the gold?" she added. "Isn't it up to the police to find it?"

"Yes, of course it is, but what if they don't find it? You know that gold and the crucifix are part of San Xavier's history. They belong to the mission, to the Franciscans. They belong in Tucson, in our hands."

"I don't care whose hands the stuff should be in," she said, her voice rising. "I don't care if the gold is found or not. It will just cause more harm if it is. I'm sorry I ever found that damn sheet of paper."

Carl changed the subject. "Rosa, why did Nick answer the phone when I called today?"

He should've stuck with the gold. He would've been better off.

"Because we're fucking each other," she said, quickly turning and looking at Nick. "Any other questions?"

Nick sat rigidly on the couch, suddenly feeling embarrassed and self-conscious. He knew she only wanted to prod Carl, but her language surprised him. He snapped to attention.

Carl didn't know what to say. "I just thought perhaps—"

She interrupted him. "It's not important what you think about my private life. It's none of your business."

"Of course it isn't, Rosa. I'm sorry."

Both of them stalled.

"Maybe it would be a good idea if you and the others didn't work today," Carl said. "I'll go to the church and tell the Indians. Why don't you spread the word at the apartment complex? Just take a couple of days off and we'll begin working again."

Rosa slammed down the phone. "How about that son-of-a-bitch!" she shouted. "He thinks that gold is his."

Nick hadn't seen her this angry before. He stood up and took her in his arms. He could feel the tightness in her body.

Chapter 15

The conservators returned to work after two days. Nick stayed in his apartment and made phone calls. His work in Tucson had turned into an investigation of Jimmy Longfellow's death and the missing gold. Even though he hadn't uncovered anything, he pushed himself to keep going.

The sunny Tucson morning sparkled, compared with the gray and cold afternoon in New York. Nick wanted to catch up on some big city gossip as well as ask his reporter pal Phil Mitchell for help. He also needed to call his editor at *Smithsonian* in Washington, D.C., to give her a progress report on his story. She would know about the deaths and missing gold, for certain, but Nick believed she would tell him to keep his story focused on the conservation project.

He dialed New York.

"*Daily News*, Mitchell."

"Hey, Mitch. Hello from Tucson."

"Is that you, Nick? What the hell's going on?" Mitch always began his conversations with questions. "You sweatin' out there in the desert? Do I need to tell you what you're missing here?"

"You wouldn't believe it," Nick said. "There have been two murders, a stolen treasure of gold, and, oh yeah, I'm in love. I hope you have time to talk."

He knew he could entice Mitch by starting the conversation like a news story. Get the murder and theft up-front. Then hook him with the romance.

"Wow, buckaroo, slow down a damn second. Hold on while I send my budget. Damn city desk is always on my ass. You've got to tell me what you've gotten yourself into out there in the wild West. Obviously, you're into more than the cactus."

It was a good time for Nick to call. Mitch still had hours before his deadline for tomorrow's paper. His daily budget would tell his editors what to expect.

"Back with you, Nicky boy," Mitch said after a moment of phone silence. "So what the hell's going on? Actually, just get right to the woman. Murder and theft is routine stuff I deal with every day. Love is something else, especially for you. Who the hell is she? You doin' her? What'd they say in *Lonesome Dove*? You pokin' her?"

Nick enjoyed his brash pal. "Settle down, Mitch. She's the lead conservator that I told you about before I left New York. Name's Rosa Zizzo, she speaks great English, and she's beautiful inside and out. I'm head over heels. She feels the same way about me, I think. I'm spending as much time as I can with her."

"Sounds serious. Congratulations. But what happened to the man who vowed never to get mixed up with a woman again? To remain independent? To explore? And what happens when it's time to come home?"

"You know the old fiction bullshit about love at first sight? It's not BS. It happened to me, and for the first time in my life. It feels great. The bigger problem is what happens to us when the job is over here. We're talking a lot about that, and right now, I'm figuring on taking a long vacation to Italy. I can take my laptop and produce copy from anyplace. There are plenty of magazines in Europe screaming for stories about the American West."

"Sounds like you're trying to convince yourself."

Nick nodded. "Maybe I am, but I feel like I can do anything I want, as long as Rosa and I are together."

There was a pause while Mitch lit another cigarette. Nick thought of bars, small cafes, and newsrooms, traditional havens for smokers, and journalists.

"Any broads for a stud like me out there? Tell me true, Nicky boy?"

Nick pictured his friend. Overweight. Balding. Ashes on his tie. He was a good guy, but no one would consider him a stud.

"You know Jenny would never let you leave, even if it was just to visit me," Nick said. "By the way, how is Jenny?"

"She's crazy. Always on my butt. Shops 'til she drops. Never listens to me. Can't get her to do a damn thing I want. God, I love her."

Mitch laughed riotously into the phone. Nick did too. He had heard it all before. Mitch joked about his wife to get a laugh, but he and Jenny had found and put to use the elusive formula for a successful marriage.

"So what's with the murders and gold?" Mitch asked after a deep drag. When he talked, he had the raspy, wheezy voice of a longtime smoker. Deep breaths were impossible.

"While they were working in the mission, Rosa and the others found a hidden cache of gold ingots and coins. Also a spectacular gold and emerald crucifix. That happened before I got here. Then a day later the priest-in-charge at the church was found murdered and the gold was gone. He'd stored the gold in his living quarters. It's probably worth millions."

"Sounds like one hell of a story," Mitch said. "Maybe a pro like me should come out there and cover it." He paused long enough for effect and then added, "Just joking."

"Not funny," Nick said. Like any former newspaperman, he had to suffer through the comments of those still at it. He'd discovered that there is life in journalism after *The New York Times*, but he knew he couldn't convince his reporter friends. He hated the question so often asked: "How's it feel not to be in journalism anymore?" It was a stupid question, always asked by newspaper people who thought they were the only ones practicing journalism. Little did they know that journalism went far beyond the walls of a newspaper.

"The cops arrested one of the Indians working with the conservators in the mission, and he confessed to the murder," Nick added. "I think his confession was coerced, but he was killed by Mexican gang members in his cell before I could help him. The hatred between Mexicans and Indians extends even into the jail here, particularly when the Indian is believed to be a priest killer. That's another story, though. I'm planning to do the conservation piece for *Smithsonian*, but I might also produce a story for someone else on lost treasure, murder, and greed. You know, the stuff you poor reporter slobs thrive on. Talking about slobs, how's your weight?"

"Nice segue, Nicky, my boy. If only you could see me. I'll bet I'm skinnier than you. I'm embarrassed to look in a mirror I look so gawd-awful beautiful."

"And you've quit smoking, too?"

"Right after this drag, Nicky. I promise."

They laughed again.

"Let's talk serious here," Mitch said. "You think we'd be interested in the piece? I haven't seen anything on any of that stuff in Tucson yet, not even from the AP."

Nick was sure that the Associated Press reporter in Tucson covered the story of Father John's murder, Jimmy's killing, and the missing gold. A few hundred words probably went all over the country, but that doesn't mean any of the New York papers used it. At best a few inches would be buried in the back under a one-column headline. Front page news in one city is often worthless in another. To most New Yorkers, Arizona might as well be in Australia. They seldom hear about the desert Southwest.

"I might try to sell an investigative piece to the big newspapers or a major magazine," Nick said. "I'm not sure yet. It has been such a whirlwind down here the last month that I haven't come up for breath. A few reporters have been asking questions about the gold, but I don't know if anyone is pursuing the police coercion angle. I think everyone has concluded the Indian did it and then hid the treasure someplace."

"What do you believe?" Mitch asked.

"I interviewed him after he confessed, and he had me believing that the cops coerced him."

Nick could hear another line ringing at Mitch's desk. His friend was polite enough not to interrupt him in mid-sentence. "Hold for a second, will you, Nick?" Mitch said quickly. "I've got to get this call."

Nick had time to look over his notes. His news instincts told him to work from the outside in, interviewing people on the fringes before he moved in close. Before he would confront the police, the conservators, Carl Corona, or deal with the Tucson legal system, he'd learn more about each of the conservators and Spanish gold.

It seemed logical to him that one of the people in the mission killed the priest. Someone connected to the conservation project, someone who had seen the gold, probably did it and surely must now be relieved that Jimmy Longfellow confessed and died.

Mitch came back on the line. "Sorry, Nick. That was a call from a New York Supreme Court judge. He wanted to compliment me on a story that ran yesterday. Can you believe it? Someone called a reporter to pay a compliment."

"Good work. Now for the real reason I called. I need some help. Would you mind going down to the Guggenheim and talking with Edward Newton? I'd like to know what he knows about each of the San Xavier conservators. Specifically, I'd like to know if any of them conducted some research in Spain before coming here. He might know that. I want to question each one of them, as well as the Tucson car dealer who brought them here."

"Sure, pal. No problemo. I can do that in the next couple of days. Should I tell him about what's been going on down there?"

"I'm sure he knows. You can tell him you're doing some reporting work for me, or you can give him your usual line of bullshit and make him think his words and picture will be on page one of the *Daily News*. I think a face-to-face, particularly with your friendly mug, will work better than me trying to do a long-distance phone interview."

"OK, asshole, what is it you don't like about my face? Ah, forget that question. I don't have time to hear your answer. Anything else you need?"

"Yeah, will you check to see if there is any kind of gold association or dealers group in New York? There's got to be something. I want to find out if there are any Spanish gold experts living someplace in Arizona. I looked up gold in the phone book and there are plenty of dealers. There's also the University of Arizona here, which may have an expert or two. But I'd like to save the trouble of making dozens of calls and getting dead-ends. I need someone who can educate me about Spanish gold, its value, and how someone with a lot of it could sell it. Maybe even melt it down."

"So you think the murderer might still be out there?"

"That seems to make the most sense right now. I don't want to make my investigation public yet. That could get my throat slit. I just want to make a few calls and begin to understand some things. Meanwhile, I'll stick around the mission as much as I can and continue to work on my *Smithsonian* story."

"Let me check on the gold thing, Nick, and I'll call you back in a day or so. By the way, where do I send my bill?"

"You want to know where you can put it?"

Mitch's long-distance chuckle seemed to be coming from the next room. Nick liked that his friend never took things seriously. Maybe that's what made his marriage to Jenny work so well.

"Call me as soon as you can," Nick instructed.

"Aye, aye, cap'ain. But I'm not going to let you go until you tell me something more about the lady."

"She's incredible." Nick's grin widened. "I want to spend as much of my time with her as I can, perhaps forever. We're just taking it kind of easy and keeping it low-key right now because of everything that has happened and because I'm from New York and she's from Italy. But I'll tell you, I love her."

"Love's blind, man, so be careful. Don't forget you're working on a story about murder and stolen gold. A lost treasure could make people crazy. And I notice you didn't say to check out all of the conservators except your girlfriend."

"I'm not quite as jaded as you are, my friend. I don't think I'm having an affair with a killer, but I want to learn more about each conservator. Rosa already told me she was in Spain before she came here and read a reference to the gold in a 200-year-old journal. Right now, I can't accuse or eliminate anyone."

"Just be careful, Nicky boy. Things could get dangerous for you, particularly if the Indian didn't do the priest."

"Don't worry about me. I'll be fine." The words came out of Nick's mouth but he really didn't believe them. Of course he was scared, and his friend could tell it.

Even after saying goodbye, Nick held the phone for a moment and thought. *I do need to be careful. And what about Rosa? I think about her constantly. Will our love endure, or are we merely in lust? Will she leave once her job in Tucson is complete and forget all about me? Could she somehow be connected to a murder and theft?*

That thought terrified him.

Chapter 16

Luckily for Nick, one of seven certified coin appraisers in the world and an expert on Spanish gold owned a shop in Phoenix. Phil Mitchell had called him a day earlier with Robert Clarkson's name, and the gold dealer had said over the phone that he'd be happy to talk to a writer for *Smithsonian*.

Mitch found Clarkson's name through a New York-based professional association for appraisers. He hadn't interviewed Edward Newton about the conservators yet because the Guggenheim official was out of town for a week.

Nick was so deep in thought during the boring two-hour drive from Tucson to Phoenix that he nearly missed the Camelback Road exit off Interstate 17. Clarkson Jewelers was near Camelback and Seventh Street.

To be admitted into the shop, which was protected by a locked black iron gate over the front door, he had to ring a bell. A woman behind a glass counter buzzed him inside.

Robert Clarkson was a short, rotund man whose Coke-bottle glasses kept sliding down his flat nose. His handshake was soft, too soft, and his pale skin needed some Arizona sun. He reminded Nick of one of the villains from an Indiana Jones movie, the one who spoke with a German accent and enjoyed killing.

Clarkson ate the end of a donut as soon as Nick walked into his shop. Even after swallowing the last of the pastry, he continued to lick his left index finger and then stab at sugar specks on the glass display case that separated him from Nick. When he sat, he had the annoying habit of letting his right thumb dance on his thigh.

"After you called, I brought in a couple of books on Spanish gold from my library," he said after several minutes of pleasantries. "They should help us. I read about the Tucson murder and theft, but not much was said about the quality of the gold."

He had a soft voice, as though he tried to hide his words, and his responses were methodical. He made Nick uneasy.

"There were one hundred gold ingots, probably weighing about twelve ounces each," the writer said. "Would they be worth just what their gold value is?"

"There could be historic value there, which would make them extremely valuable as antiquities," Clarkson said. He looked down when he talked.

Nick listened and took notes. So far, he had no reason to bring out and turn on the tape recorder in his pocket.

"Were there any markings on them? Mint marks or the stamp of the monarch?" Clarkson asked.

"Yes. No notes or photographs were taken when the ingots were found, but I was told there were Spanish markings on them."

"Oh, then they'd be worth much, much more than their gold value," Clarkson said with excitement. His thumb danced faster on his thigh. His face lit up like a cherub's as he heard more about the gold.

"Can you tell me about the coins that were found with the ingots?" Nick asked. "I know you haven't seen them, but they were the size of silver dollars and dated mainly in the 1760s."

"Those would be the coins from the reign of Charles III, and they're worth a lot of money. I've seen an eight *escudo* piece from Charles II that was worth twelve thousand dollars."

The only other person in the shop, a clerk Clarkson called Lucy, walked up slowly to the two men and interrupted. She had straight brown hair and wore blue plastic-framed glasses that were out of style. She talked as softly as her boss. Nick hadn't heard the phone ring, but Lucy said something about a call from a man wanting to sell some gold jewelry.

The creases on Clarkson's forehead tightened. "Not today," he told Lucy sternly before turning back to Nick.

"Gold and silver coins were made in New Spain for many, many years," he added as Lucy walked back to the phone. "The gold was mined in Mexico or South America, and rather than shipping it back to Spain, the dies were sent this way. The Mexico City mint ran for nearly three hundred years. Can you believe it? Three hundred years, and our country is struggling after only a little more than two hundred."

Clarkson squinted his eyes and gritted his teeth. Nick thought the man had a sudden stomach cramp. "It's probable that the coins in Arizona were from Mexico City," the gold expert said even quieter than before.

Nick blamed the donut. He knew a reporter once who became this quiet just before having a heart attack. The reporter walked into the newsroom without talking to anyone, sat at his desk, started to sign onto his computer, and slumped over. Nick saw the whole thing and never forgot it. The reporter died before paramedics got there.

Nick hoped that the jeweler wasn't having a heart attack. "You OK?" he asked.

"Top shape, top shape," Clarkson said, straightening himself. "What else you want to know?"

"The coins were made in Mexico rather than in Spain?"

"Oh heavens, yes." Clarkson laughed, as though Nick had told a joke and rejuvenated him. "Mexico had several mints. Coins were made in all sizes, some rough, some very nice. Their markings changed with the kings."

"Those in the 1760s would've been from the reign of Charles III?"

"Yes. Those from 1760 and 1761 came in different sizes, from one *escudo* to eight *escudos*. On one side was the bust of the king. On the other was the king's coat of arms. There were also other markings, such as the date, the mint location, maybe an assayer's mark. There are many things that could add to their value. In 1762 the bust was enlarged."

"Any idea what they would be worth now?"

"It's difficult to say without seeing them. But I appraised a Spanish gold doubloon not long ago. Let me get the paperwork on it."

Nick watched as Clarkson walked slowly into a back room. The jeweler, in terrible shape, waddled more than he walked.

Nick speculated about the riches stored in the back room. Bigger diamonds? Millions in gold? It didn't make much difference to a free-lance writer with inexpensive tastes. The jewelry in the display cases dazzled him enough. Every piece had a price with too many zeros. He couldn't afford any of it. He thought about Rosa. Would she like something in one of the cases? He'd love to buy it for her. He didn't even know if she liked jewelry. She didn't wear any while she worked, nor had he seen any in her apartment.

Clarkson remained in the back room for several minutes. Nick thumbed through one of the books on the display case but read nothing in particular. He glanced at the clerk to make certain she didn't mind him picking up the book. She busied herself by working on her bright red nails and didn't even look his way. She had a ring on almost every finger.

The book he skimmed had color photographs of priceless religious items that were in a treasure brought up from a Spanish ship that had sunk off the coast of Florida. The gold, emerald, and pearl crucifix found at San Xavier probably resembled one of those pictured in the book. He thought about how excited the jeweler would become in the next few minutes as he described the gem-filled golden cross. He hoped Clarkson's heart could take it.

"Here we go," Clarkson said as he plopped his body heavily into his chair. His left leg started hopping almost immediately. "The coin I appraised was an eight *escudo* piece minted at the Lima, Peru, mint and bearing the mint mark *L* and the assayer's initial of *H*. The date on the coin was 1708. It was well struck and in uncirculated condition. The coin weighed 27.06 grams and was 22-karat gold."

"Isn't 24 karat pure gold?" Nick was proud of himself for knowing at least that much about gold. He didn't tell Clarkson that he'd just read it in a book.

Clarkson wasn't impressed. He continued to speak quietly, with head down. "Yes, that's right. This one was rounded, about an inch wide, which would make it a little smaller than your coins. I valued it at three-thousand, four-hundred and fifty dollars. The value of the gold in the coin was less than three hundred dollars."

"So the chances are that the thief wouldn't want to steal the coins just for their gold?"

"Not unless he was desperate."

"Would you buy a coin from someone if he walked in and tried to sell it to you?"

"He'd have to be twenty-one and show his ID. There are state laws regulating it. I'd have to fill out a dealer report for the police. But if nothing looked suspicious, sure, I'd buy it."

"If a report has to be filled out, the likelihood is that the person would not try to sell the coin, at least not in Arizona." Nick wasn't asking a question. He knew the answer.

"I'd say anywhere in this country," Clarkson added. "Of course, fake IDs are easy to get around here or anyplace else. If the person has some time and money, he or she can get a driver's license in any name possible. Someone like me would have no way of knowing if the ID was real or not. We're not required to fingerprint them. We just have to look at the ID and fill out a report for the police. By the time the police get around to being suspicious, the person could be long gone."

"What about in Europe? Are gold coins easier to sell there?"

"Who knows? That probably would be easier. I'm sure there are unscrupulous buyers all over the world. Maybe your person had a buyer even before the coins were stolen. Maybe it's someone in the Middle East. The Arabic countries love gold, you know. I've never been there, but I've seen photos of bazaars laden with gold. Everyone who goes to the Middle East always comes back with a gold necklace or bracelet. I appraise plenty of them, often for much less than their cost. The people doing the selling have a never-ending appetite for gold. It might be easy to sell in the Middle East in any form."

"How would someone get the gold out of the United States?"

"You can do whatever you want with gold. An ounce of gold can be rolled out to stretch over an acre of land. It can be sent in little fragments at a time. The coins could easily be shipped. The bars could be made into any shape, any size. Someone could make the gold into beautiful golden necklaces and then silver plate them so that they don't look valuable."

Nick had hoped for simple answers that could lead him down a single-lane road from point A to point B. Instead, he got an expressway jammed with traffic, aimed in all directions.

"Let's just for the heck of it say that the thief is going to melt the gold and deal with it in a new form," he asked. "How do you melt it?"

"That's easy, too." Clarkson had no time to elaborate. He was interrupted again by the clerk speaking softly in his ear.

"Tell him to bring it by this afternoon," he said to her, his voice louder than before. "I won't be much longer with Mr. Genoa."

Nick understood. Clarkson didn't have much more time for this interview. "Can anyone melt it?" Nick asked.

"Oh yes, as long as you have the right supplies. A couple of propane torches will do it."

"Could I put it into a kitchen pan?"

Clarkson's eyes rolled. He smiled. Nick felt stupid. "The pan would melt before the gold," the jeweler said. "The person would have to have a steel mold or a smelting pot with a higher melting point than the gold. And tongs to grab the pot to pour into the mold."

Before Nick could say anything, Clarkson added, "Everything you need probably would be for sale at a hobby shop."

"I know you're busy, Mr. Clarkson, but I wanted to ask you about the crucifix."

"Oh, yes, tell me about it."

"It was about fourteen inches tall, with emeralds and pearls, and with an engraving of the Madonna holding the Christ child."

"Wonderful piece, I'm sure," Clarkson said. "And priceless. Great historical value."

Nick could tell his source was getting fidgety. "One quick question," he said. "The gold was in a large suitcase. Could one person carry that?"

"Maybe, but I wouldn't think very far. All that gold in one box would weigh somewhere between seventy-five and a hundred pounds, maybe more depending on the size of the coins. That's pretty heavy for one person. Most people get tired just carrying a heavy bag of groceries. I would think that with a suitcase, the handle could break. Maybe your thief had a set of those rollers that you see on some suitcases."

"So it would have to be a strong man who could carry the suitcase alone?"

"Mr. Genoa, I think you should be looking for more than one thief. Maybe there was an inside person and an outside person. Yes, one person could lug that suitcase someplace. But it would take some effort. I don't want to spoil any of your theories, but it just seems to me that you should be looking for two people instead of one."

Chapter 17

When he returned from Phoenix, Nick called the Pima County Sheriff's Department to speak with Ashton Anderson, but was told the detective was unavailable. The response didn't surprise the journalist. Cops too busy fighting crime never seemed available to talk on the phone when a reporter called. Appointments were allowed, but any cop in any city would rather have a reporter talk to the department's PIO, public information officer. To journalists, the PIO is a flack, the person who sanitizes, cushions, and releases only snippets of the truth.

Nick wanted to avoid talking to a flack. He made an appointment with Anderson for the next morning and then decided to spend some time catching up with the conservation project inside San Xavier.

Each time he walked into the mission, Nick saw significant changes. He watched from below, with his head up, admiring the conservators' ability to coax beauty from such murky walls. He believed that one of them was a murderer, but he had no idea which one. Each arrived on time, worked all day long, answered tourists' questions, explained things to the steady flow of journalists. None aroused suspicion. He loved the one in charge.

He didn't think Jimmy Longfellow was the killer. Perhaps it was Corona, who knew about the gold discovery soon after the Europeans. He had a motive. He knew the priest better than anyone. Maybe it was one of the other Tohono O'odhams helping in the project. Except for Bahadir, everyone trusted them and welcomed them with open arms.

Nick felt helpless, frustrated. He searched for clues, a facial expression, a slip of the tongue, something that would reveal a killer. He got nothing.

Minutes after Nick's arrival, Carl walked into the church with a dozen people. He noticed Nick and nodded but didn't speak. He strolled over to Ali, the only conservator at ground level, who said the group was from the U.S. Park Service. They were interested in learning how a historical building handles large daily crowds.

Nick waited until the visitors were at the other end of the church and Corona sat alone on a pew before he approached him. "Can I ask you a few questions?" he asked. Carl had taken on much of the public relations duty for San Xavier since Father John's death. A new pastor had not been named yet, or at least a name had not been announced yet from the powers above.

"Sit down," Carl said as though he commanded an army and Nick, a lowly foot soldier, sought an audience with him. "I'm tired today and don't have much time. It's been a busy and stressful time." He spoke coldly to Nick, nothing like the first time they met.

The car salesman wore a tan cotton shirt covered by a green tweed jacket with elbow patches. Nick wanted to make a joke about the bolo tie with a large, highly engraved silver saguaro cactus, but he knew he shouldn't. Carl must have eaten Mexican food for breakfast because when he spoke, Nick smelled onions. As always, he looked freshly ironed and casual. His tall frame fit awkwardly into the wooden pew.

From where they sat, both men could see the conservators at work. A minute passed. "There have been interior projects over the years, but none like this one," Carl said. "Anything done in the past was done by local so-called experts or amateurs. They did more to hide the beauty than they did to enhance it. People have even covered the original colors with glossy oil paints. They thought they were improving them. This is the first time anyone has thought to raise the money to bring in the best people in the world to do something to this church. Seems funny we waited so long, huh? On the other hand, this is a church, not a museum. It's a place where people come to express their faith. They want to pray. They want to light candles for their loved ones. They don't want to worry about the impact of those candles on the artwork. Father John used to say that the candles would never be banned."

Nick wanted to ask about Spanish gold and perhaps uncover a clue or two, but he knew if he probed too hard in the beginning, Carl would walk away. He must keep it simple, at least for now, and he had to listen without interrupting.

"Why don't you tell me more about Padre Kino, the first priest here?" Nick said. He pulled the Sony mini-cassette recorder out of his back pocket and sat next to Carl on the pew. Nick wore acid-washed jeans and a long-sleeve yellow button-down cotton shirt. He had on a new pair of Reebok walking shoes, which he'd bought earlier in the week at a Tucson mall.

"Kino first visited this valley in 1692," Carl said as he watched a bent old woman use a walker to shuffle to the entombed statue of San Xavier. She lifted her crinkled hand slowly and rubbed her weathered, bent fingers over its wooden face. Carl's eyes were glued on the woman as he spoke. "There were about eight-hundred Indians here at that time. In the Pima tongue this place was called Bac, a spot where water emerges from an underground flow. Kino showed the native people a world map and told them where the padres came from. He baptized their children. He came back to the area several times, and by 1697 when he visited, there were more than six-thousand people at Bac, all living peacefully in this fertile valley with livestock and wheat. Kino had brought cattle, sheep, goats, and horses here. The Indians had developed a good canal system, which brought ample water from the Santa Cruz River."

As Carl spoke, dozens of people filed past him to get to different areas in one of the three altars. The conservators seldom looked down from their perches on the scaffolding. The old woman rubbing her hands on San Xavier cried softly, as though the memories of her life were before her and she'd been ordered to confess her sins and reveal her regrets.

"In April of 1700 Kino laid the foundations of a large church," Carl continued. "Until then he worked out of small adobe houses. But he died nearly a century before this church was built. There were other Jesuits here through the mid-1760s, but the grand church was not built until the Franciscans came in after the Jesuits were expelled."

"Expelled?" Nick interrupted. He wanted to steer Carl away from the lecture.

"Hey, politics were alive and well even in colonial Spain. The Jesuits were thrown out and the Franciscans became the religious keepers of Alta California. Garcés was the first Franciscan here. He came in 1768."

"He built this church, didn't he?" Nick asked.

"No. He just got it started. The Franciscans used the adobe Jesuit church parallel to this church to the west. That Jesuit structure stood until 1810, when it was torn down for its beams and other materials."

"What happened to Garcés?"

"He went to Yuma in 1779 to establish another mission, and he was killed in the massacre of 1781. Work on this structure began in 1783 and was completed in 1797. Father Juan Bautista Velderrain took over the job of building a new church at Bac after Garcés left. San Xavier was already the patron saint. Velderrain had worked in Mexico and was familiar with the Mexican baroque design. He also had worked with skilled artisans down there. But he died in 1790 and Father Juan Bautista Llorens took over. He completed the church."

Nick glanced at his tape recorder to make sure it was functioning properly. Carl had gotten to a point of talking freely. The reporter wanted to tighten the noose ever so slightly.

"Carl, back to the massacre of 1781 when Garcés was killed. That's when the Quechans at Yuma Crossing revolted and killed the Spanish soldiers as well as the priests. Why'd they do it?"

Carl's eyes narrowed to slits.

Don't stop now, Nick thought during Carl's silence. *I don't want you to suspect anything. Just keep talking like you have been. Come on. Come on.*

"The Spanish soldiers treated them like crap," Carl said finally. "Took their best land. Tried to destroy their lifestyle in the name of Christianity and civilization. These Indians who initially welcomed the Spaniards with open arms couldn't take it anymore. After so many years of abuse, they were willing to attack the well-armed conquistadors with their stone clubs. They overwhelmed the Spaniards with their numbers."

"I've heard about a Padre Hernando Díaz who also was killed in that massacre," Nick said. "Was he killed with Garcés?"

Carl stood up. His belt was too loose and he needed to adjust his pants. "There were several priests killed. How'd you know about Díaz?"

"Rosa told me about him. I've read about the strong connection between San Xavier and the missions in California."

"Sure there was. There were a string of missions stretching throughout New Spain. They were there to colonize the Indians."

"Did you know that Díaz wrote in his journal that his party was carrying gold from San Xavier to Yuma Crossing when it ran into the massacre?"

Carl snapped his head as though a sharp pain had just shot through his side. "I don't know what Díaz wrote in his journal."

Carl, a consummate politician good at handling adversarial questions, was lying, and Nick knew it.

"Rosa told me she read Díaz' journal in a library in Spain," Nick said. "Somehow, it survived through the years and ended up in Madrid. The journal said that a load of gold was being taken to California, but half of it was left at San Xavier."

"And Rosa knew that before she came here?"

"Yeah. Do you read something into that?"

Carl sat again, much closer to Nick than before. His onion breath seemed to have grown in intensity.

"Don't you think it's odd that Rosa should read about the gold and then also discover it?" Carl spoke quietly, suddenly conscious of being in a cloister.

"How so, Carl? Seems to me that she discovered the piece of paper describing the location of the gold. You all discovered the gold together."

"Now don't get me wrong, Nick. I know you and Rosa are more than colleagues, but if I were you I'd be a little careful of her. She may know more than you think."

You slimy son-of-a-bitch. You're trying to shift the focus to Rosa.

Nick pretended to be unfazed by Carl's statement.

"Don't you agree that anyone in the church when the gold was found could be a suspect?" he asked.

"Don't go there, Nick, particularly if you're suggesting I had something to do with it. I'll just presume you're defending Rosa right now."

"If the massacre at Yuma Crossing was in 1781, and this church wasn't built until after that, then the gold you and the conservators found inside the church may not be the same stuff Díaz was talking about, right?"

"Because the coins we found were dated in the 1760s, there's a good likelihood that they were part of what Díaz described," Carl said. "The cache could've been moved from the Jesuit chapel to the new church upon its completion. The statue of St. Fidelis wasn't here before the current church, which means the sheet Rosa found was inserted some time after 1783 and very likely closer to 1797."

"Could it be that the cache described by Díaz is still buried with the old church?"

"Possible but not likely. We did major excavating of the old Jesuit structure and never found gold. You can go outside and still find parts of the old building's walls between the church and the school."

"But some of the old church is underneath this church, right?"

"Yes."

"You ever been to Spain, Carl?" Nick knew the abrupt question might anger Carl even more, but he didn't care. He still boiled inside over what the bastard had said about Rosa. Of course Carl was right. Nick was defending Rosa, but he also wanted to question a man he considered a suspect.

The car dealer took the question in stride. "Yes, Father John and I went two years ago to do some research on San Xavier."

Before Nick could ask a follow-up, Carl said, "Any other questions? I need to get back to my group. Sorry to cut this short, but I think you're out of line."

Nick unloaded. He had nothing to lose. "How can I be out of line?" he said. "You were ready to convict Rosa just because she's been to Spain. You've been there, too."

"Jimmy Longfellow confessed to the crime after the police arrested him. Why would I blame anyone else? You're the one who came here for a story for *Smithsonian* on the conservation effort and are now trying to do the police department's job. Stick with your job."

"No chance that Jimmy might have been framed by someone who knew about the gold before it was found and then panicked once it was?"

Carl stood and walked away without responding. Nick knew he'd just made an enemy.

Chapter 18

"Detective Anderson, thanks for seeing me," Nick said as the two men shook hands. Anderson's fishy grip surprised the reporter. His eyes revealed neither welcome nor hostility. Although he stared intently, he looked through Nick.

The well-built cop with red hair and a bushy mustache stood about five-feet-eight. Papers and notebooks cluttered the top of his gray metal desk. The desk, single chairs on each side, and a small bookcase filled his small office inside the headquarters of the Pima County Sheriff's Department. Brown industrial carpeting sure to hide years of coffee spills covered the floor. Nick had seen similar places countless times before.

"I'm here doing a story on San Xavier Mission for *Smithsonian*, but obviously my focus has changed because of what's happened there. I'd like to ask you a few questions about Jimmy Longfellow."

"Sure," Anderson said in a husky voice. Nick wondered if the detective would unfold the interview as a talker or a nodder. He hated nodders.

"I was hoping I could take a look at the transcript of his interrogation. Was it videotaped?"

Anderson cleared his throat and grinned sarcastically. Lately, a lot of people smiled that way when Nick asked them questions. "This isn't New York," the detective said. "Departments our size can't afford to use video, even though the county attorney would like us to."

Anderson had done his homework. Nick didn't mention that he was from New York.

"What about an audio tape?"

"If there's one left, you can listen to it. But we usually recycle them quickly, particularly in a situation like this where we don't need the evidence anymore. We do, however, keep the paper transcript."

"I'd like to see whatever I can. It's good of you to make it accessible," Nick said, politely. He'd learned long ago how to patronize sources, particularly cops, even though he realized they usually saw through it.

Anderson scratched his ski-slope nose. He didn't care for journalists and needed time to think of a response. He cleared his throat again.

"We wouldn't release anything to you other than the incident report if there was still an ongoing investigation," he said as though he'd rehearsed frequently on other journalists. "It wouldn't become public record until after the trial, but this case has been adjudicated. When Longfellow was killed, he turned his case over to God."

"So you really believe Jimmy was your man? You talked to everyone who was working at the church at the time. Other people were there, too. Why Jimmy?"

"Why not? We had probable cause to believe that he was the right man. We had evidence to support that. The murder weapon was his. He knew the priest and had been in his home. There were fingerprints. Jimmy had a record. Didn't he tell you that when you interviewed him at the jail?"

"Yes, but I'm not sure he killed Father John. Where were Jimmy's fingerprints found?"

"Inside the priest's quarters. It hasn't been disclosed, but you'll see on the transcripts that we asked him about that. He said he'd been in Father John's earlier in the day and had a drink of water."

"That could be the truth. He went to tell Father John about the map."

"I think it is the truth. But I also think he came back later and killed the priest."

"So there were additional fingerprints?"

"As I said, we think we got the right guy."

"What about the missing gold? That part of the case isn't closed, is it?"

Anderson's face reddened. "We have an ongoing investigation. We're hoping a witness will come forward or some of the gold will turn up. We're doing the best we can. I can't ask my detectives, who already are overworked, to spend much of their time looking for a killer when we think we found him, nor for a suitcase of gold that so few people ever saw. There's little to go on."

"The gold is worth millions. Doesn't that make the suitcase important to your detectives?"

The phone rang. "Let me grab this before voice mail kicks in," Anderson said. "I'm expecting an important call."

The detective swiveled and put his back to Nick. He spoke too softly to be overheard.

Anderson turned and hung up the phone. "If something turns up that we didn't have the right guy, we'll jump all over the case," he said angrily. "Or if something turns up on the gold, that would make us look aggressively at this case again. But it would be hard to convince a detective with ten other cases on his desk to keep looking into one where we have a confession and the guy is killed before he goes to trial. We need to go after the people who killed Jimmy, and we're not getting much on that. No one talks in a jail, and I can't tell you what we've uncovered so far. As for the gold, all we can hope at this point is that something surfaces."

"How did Jimmy's killers get into his cell?"

"No idea, although I wouldn't tell you if I did. Someone might have had a key. Was it a guard? A prisoner? We don't have a lot of chatty people in the county jail. Everything's pulled tightly. The folks in there know they could end up like Jimmy if they say anything."

The room became silent, the only sound coming from people talking down the hall. Both men wanted to think. Nick's fishing trip for information had little to do with his story on art conservation. Anderson wasn't going to provide any more than he had to under the state open records law. They looked hard at each other, both savvy enough to know each other's thoughts.

"How do I get the transcript?" Nick asked.

"I'll send you to records. You pay for the copy of the report, and it's yours. Just one thing, though. Tell me why you're so interested in the murder of the priest and Jimmy's confession."

"I'm trying to learn as much as I can about everything connected to San Xavier. My story is for a natural history magazine. That's my main job here. But as you probably know, Jimmy told me some interesting things after he confessed. He said you and a Detective Leigh did the interrogation."

"And?"

"And what?"

"Cut the shit," Anderson said harshly. "What did Jimmy tell you about the interrogation? I know why you're here. You're nosing around for a story that has nothing to do with the San Xavier restoration project." The cop's anger showed.

"It's a conservation project, not restoration," Nick said with irreverence, angering Anderson even more. "Jimmy told me that he figured he was convicted when you brought him to jail. He didn't say much about the interrogation."

"We brought him in to talk to him. He talked. Once he confessed, he was arrested for murder. We did nothing illegal."

"I'd just like to see what he told you during the interrogation."

"Be my guest. Records is down the hallway and to the left."

"One other quick question. Is Detective Leigh a reservation officer?"

"No, he's not."

"Why didn't the reservation police handle this one?"

"San Xavier is on land that belongs to the Diocese of Tucson. It's surrounded by the reservation, but the church, its buildings, and the grounds around them are excluded. Any crime in the church is under the jurisdiction of the Pima County sheriff. As a courtesy, however, we had an Indian officer with us when he arrested Jimmy."

"Why wasn't a reservation cop in on the interrogation?"

"One watched from the back side of a two-way mirror."

"Could you tell me his name?"

"Johnson."

"Does he have a first name?"

Anderson hesitated. He cleared his throat again. Must be a habit. Nick wasn't sure he'd answer.

"Ben," he said finally.

"Thank you, Detective Anderson."

"One thing, Mr. Genoa. If you turn up anything that we might have missed, will you let me know?"

"Be happy to." He lied.

Nick returned to the couch in his apartment by midday to read the transcript of Jimmy's interrogation. He would go to Rosa's apartment later, after she returned from San Xavier for the day.

Jimmy had told him pretty much what happened. The transcripts showed that the two police peppered the Indian with questions. They tried like hell to confuse him. He tried his best to answer them, until he became so tired and frustrated that he simply gave up.

Two things about the questioning perplexed Nick. He couldn't figure out why the police kept asking Jimmy about a watch. Even when the suspect told them he didn't wear one, Anderson continued to press him about it.

Leigh also asked several times if Jimmy knew anyone with the initials T. K.

"Who's T. K.?" Leigh said.

"I don't know," Jimmy answered.

"Do you go by those initials?"

"Huh? What you talking about, man?"

"Think about them, Jimmy. Who has those initials?"

"I don't know, man."

"Are you sure?"

"Yes."

"Do you have any friends with those initials?"

"No."

"Think, Jimmy."

"I am, man."

Leigh had been the most aggressive over the initials. *Why were they and a watch important to the police? Did Jimmy tell the truth when he said over and over that he didn't know a thing about them?*

After Jimmy confessed, Anderson asked him if he meant it. "There's no reason for you to confess unless we've got you," Anderson told him.

Jimmy probably didn't respond to the question. Maybe he shook his head. Whatever happened, Anderson asked him again if he understood. "Do you know that you just confessed?"

Jimmy answered this time. "Yeah."

Nick pictured the interrogation in his mind. Jimmy had been arrested in the morning and confessed late in the afternoon. He got tired, probably had the shakes. He wanted a beer. He said whatever the police wanted to hear.

The next step was to learn more about Father John. Nick called Carl late in the afternoon and asked if he could look in the priest's living quarters in the morning. Until a new priest arrived, the car dealer controlled just about everything at San Xavier.

Carl questioned his intentions. "The police don't want us to know everything they have," Nick told him. "They might know that Jimmy didn't kill Father John."

"I'll call the church office and tell the secretary to give you the key. If you turn up anything, will you let me know?"

"Be happy to."

Nick lied again.

Chapter 19

Whether he worked full-time at the newspaper, Nick enjoyed being an investigative reporter if he had the time. One of his investigations revealed corruption by federal judges and led to several resignations and a few indictments.

When not delving into an investigation, he worked the court beat, facing daily competition from scores of other *Times* reporters trying to squeeze into the best spots in the paper. The newspaper's pages never offered enough room for everything written. Nick always aimed for a page one story, but so did everyone else. He knew that the editors were the gods, and sometimes they would slice his stuff into a two-paragraph brief or not use it at all.

He thought of his days as an investigative reporter, and the wild cast of characters he'd met, when he turned the key that opened the front door into Father John's living quarters behind San Xavier Mission. He felt as squeamish in this house of a dead man as he did the first time he went to a home to ask a family for a picture for an obituary.

The heat had not been on for awhile. Nick felt the chill and quickly found the thermostat in the narrow hallway leading from the living room to the bedroom. He turned the dial until the furnace, awakened from its sleep, clanked to life. Within minutes, it offered warmth but not comfort. Nothing could make Nick comfortable in a house where a man had been murdered.

As he walked into the priest's living room and looked around, Nick couldn't help but feel that an amazing and unique man had been here before him. To say that John Duvall, Roman Catholic priest, lived a Spartan existence wasn't enough. He was a rotary phone in an Internet world. He'd lived in a box, a white-plastered Spanish rectangle with log beams. It reminded Nick of an unfinished dollhouse decorated by a child who added to its contents slowly, as she got her allowance.

The red Spanish tile floors were covered with worn area rugs that looked Navajo but came from Mexico. The living room recliner and couch were brown, clean, and not tattered. There were two oak bookcases clumsily filled with books and magazines. Bookcases are always an accurate reflection of a man, and these revealed that Father John wasn't well organized, nor did he care about neatness. He stacked his books in piles and in no particular order. He liked reading fiction, mainly mysteries, although he owned about two dozen Arizona history books. He didn't bother to separate fiction and history into separate piles. He subscribed to *Time*, an Arizona historical journal, and several religious magazines.

The simple kitchen contained little: a single row of cabinets and drawers, table and chairs, small refrigerator, and a microwave on an oak cabinet. No garbage disposal or dishwasher.

Inside the priest's bedroom, another lonely box, an old and scratched, never refinished or polished, double poster bed had been pushed against the wall so someone could clean the floor. A white patch quilt, probably made by a parishioner, neatly covered the bed. A black and silver crucifix hung above where the bed's headboard should be and a painting of Christ, in a white robe with his arms outstretched, adorned the white plaster walls.

A Macintosh Classic on a card table in the corner of the bedroom seemed to be the home's only indulgence. Father John also had a Macintosh in his church office, and Nick wondered if the priest brought work home with him at night or if he used his home computer for personal things. He visualized a man of the cloth playing some wild video game on a home computer.

The card table's green plastic top was faded but untorn. Paper was neatly stacked in two piles next to the computer, as though someone recently straightened it. *Nothing like the living room bookcases,* Nick thought. *Anyone who kept his bookcases so messy would never keep his desk so tidy.*

Nick spotted a professional reporter's notebook next to one of the paper stacks. NEWS was printed on the cover in big letters. Nick had used many of these small notepads in his career. They were slim, with a spiral binding at the top, and fit easily into a back pocket.

Seeing the notebook made him think of Rosa, who had taught him how to say "reporter's notepad" in Italian. *Blocco per appunti.* He smiled and said it out loud. *"Blocco per appunti."* She taught him words in his ancestral language, and he enjoyed it, but right now the sound of his voice in this sterile environment gave him goose bumps.

He picked up the notebook and opened it, wondering why a priest would have one. Its pages were blank, although some of them had been torn out. Left behind were thin remains of paper inside the wire spirals.

The only marks on the notebook were three wiggly lines on the back cover, two in blue ink, one in black. Father John must have made sure his pens were working before he began taking notes. They were a dead man's scribbles. Nick didn't like being here.

He dawdled at the computer. In an awkward moment his finger danced at the on-off switch, hungry to push it, not sure if he should.

So much for indecision. He turned on the switch and began rapping his fingers impatiently on the table while the machine whirred and hissed to life. While he waited, he picked up the reporter's notebook and scratched his mustache with its wire spirals. It was an unconscious habit he formed years ago. His ex-wife hated when he did it.

Why would a priest use one of these? How would he even know where to get one? Actually, a priest carrying a small notebook made sense. Such a pad would be great for scribbling down a sermon. Franciscans do give sermons, don't they? He made a mental note to ask someone that question as soon as he could.

His years of not going to church were finally revealing his ignorance about religion. He believed in God, and he had decent boyhood memories of his Sundays in the Catholic church not far from his family's home. But his father made him and his sister, Annie, go, and organized religion became one more thing he tuned out as he grew older and rebellious. Going to church was not important to him when he got into college. By the time he married, the *Times* stylebook had become his Bible. He'd forgotten most of what he learned in his church classes.

Finally, the hard-drive icon appeared on the right side of the monitor. Nick double-clicked it and waited again. He looked at the keyboard. The keys hadn't been soiled from constant pounding by fingers. Even the cleanest hands ultimately turn the keys gray. Either Father John didn't use this computer much, or the keyboard had been cleaned recently along with the room.

There were twelve folders. The fax and modem folder contained nothing. There was a print file folder, even though the priest had no printer in the bedroom. Father John must have used a disk and taken it to his office for any printing he wanted to do.

Nick was interested in two of the files. One was labeled Personal and the other Fiction.

He double-clicked on Personal. Father John kept an address and phone number list in this file, about sixty names, mainly other priests in churches scattered throughout the country and Mexico. Nick didn't recognize any of the names preceded by *Fr.*, nor any of the others. He wished he had a spare disk to copy the list.

Several letters of recommendation written for parishioners and a file labeled Resume ended the file.

Nick opened Resume.

Father John had worked at seven churches in the thirty years since he'd been out of college. He was a graduate of San Francisco State University, where he majored in journalism. While there, he worked on the campus newspaper.

His major and experience at the *Golden Gater* would've made him familiar with reporter's notebooks.

After San Francisco State, he went to the seminary for Franciscans in Santa Barbara, which made him part of the St. Barbara Province headquartered in Oakland. He noted on his resume that he was one of 28,000 Franciscan friars worldwide, one of about 300 in his province.

After seminary, he worked in churches in several western states and at the mission in Guymas, Mexico. He spent time at the Franciscan Renewal Center in Scottsdale, about 120 miles north of San Xavier. His resume described the renewal center as the *Casa de Paz y Bien* (House of Peace and Wellness), where Franciscan friars conduct retreats for adults.

The resume demonstrated that the priest never spent too much time in any one place. Nothing about it aroused suspicion, although Nick wondered if the priest moved because he wanted to or his superiors ordered him.

Satisfied, Nick double clicked the Fiction folder, which contained two items, Outline and Chapter 1. According to the menu, the items had last been modified two days before the priest's murder.

The Outline file revealed that Father John had been working on a piece of fiction about a Catholic priest who'd fallen in love with a woman.

Nick opened Chapter One.

> I'm writing this letter to you, Dear Mother,
> to tell you that I've fallen in love. She has brought
> me the greatest joy of my life, and yet I must now
> struggle with the greatest sadness of my life.

Nick reminded himself about the folder's label: Fiction. Still, he had no idea if the murdered priest was a journalism-trained writer taking a shot at fiction or a priest in love screaming to break out and tell the world his secret.

He felt a stab in his right eye. The pain arced across his brain. He couldn't think clearly. He needed aspirin.

> My Lord knows of this, of course, for he knows
> everything. I know that now He must be able to
> forgive me for letting myself pick the forbidden
> fruit of a woman's loving and touching. He must
> forgive me. I'm hopeful that you'll forgive me.
> My guilt has now passed, and I've forgiven myself.
> She is young and beautiful, warm and
> energetic, sensitive and witty. Oh, my Dear
> Mother, she is everything I've prayed for,
> for so many years. She is my goddess.
> Reefer here to a letter that the priest
> received from his mother a month ago.

Nick could tell that Father John had been trained in journalism. "Reefer" is a common device used by writers to refer to something else, a reminder to insert something later.

He wished now for a nearby printer. He wanted a hard copy of the priest's writing, a more solid record rather than a computer's electronic impulses that could be erased with the touch of a button. There were no spare disks lying around on which to copy the files.

"Shit, damn, shit," he said to himself as he continued reading.

> I met her innocently, and she didn't
> know right away that I was a priest. I could
> not allow myself to tell her initially. Instead,
> I wanted her to look at me as a man. A man who
> wanted to walk hand in hand with a woman. A

man who longed for the body of a woman to caress. A man who so much wanted a woman's love.

Long live Blackpool.

She needed me so much and I gave her something she never had. Her life so far was terrible. She came from a poor home with an unloving mother and a hard-working but abusive and alcoholic father.

I showed her love.

Oh, mother, I have fallen so in love with her that I would die for her, would kill for her.

TK—more on his feelings.

I'll never let her go. I have found my goddess.

"I'll be dammed," Nick said to the screen in front of him. His mind went wild. His head throbbed. The cops had seen the writing, too. They probably thought "TK" was a person, and that's why they kept asking Jimmy Longfellow about it. They didn't know Father John used the journalism abbreviation for something "to come" later.

And who or what was Blackpool? Had the priest come up with a fictional name, or was Blackpool a real person? Why didn't the police ask Jimmy about Blackpool?

Nick had little to go on, nothing but the fragments of a dead man. He couldn't tell if the friar wrote fiction or hid his secret from everyone but his lord and mother. The priest could've labeled his letter fiction simply to mislead anyone trying to pry into his private life. Perhaps he wanted to trade in God and the priesthood for a new-found goddess. It had been done a lot lately worldwide.

Nick looked through every other file on the computer. There wasn't much. He made only a few notes and felt more driven than ever to learn all he could about the dead man.

He thought about Jimmy. *Why did his interrogators ask him about "TK" but nothing else in the computer files? What else did the police know? Did forensics find pubic hairs or other evidence of sex in the priest's quarters? Was there something they found that they haven't shared publicly? Had the priest been with a woman the night he was killed?*

Of course the writing could be nothing but a chaste man's fantasy. Nick stood quietly, staring at the card table, frustrated and confused. A book he'd read years ago flashed in his mind. It was about John F. Kennedy. He remembered the title as *Johnny, We Hardly Knew Ye*. Even if he remembered the title incorrectly, the book made him think of Father John Duvall, a man so few people knew, a man who died too young.

Nick decided to leave the bedroom and look through the other rooms. A hospital smell drew him to the kitchen. The lingering odor of disinfectant told him that the kitchen had been scrubbed clean after the police were finished with it. There were no remaining signs that a man had died on the room's tile floor.

He stood in the doorway, looking around until his eyes stuck on two drawers, one on each side of the sink. He felt compelled to open them. Perhaps like the computer they held unrevealed secrets.

There were only plastic lids and small bowls in one drawer. He opened the other. There were plastic spoons and forks, a few metal ones. A couple of sharp knives. An ice pick. Father John wasn't one to color coordinate eating utensils.

He grabbed for the ice pick too quickly to notice the sharp blade of a knife next to it.

"Ouch," he said out loud when he realized he'd sliced the end of his right index finger. He put the finger in his mouth as he grabbed for a paper towel to wrap it.

Nick turned toward the bathroom, where he hoped to find a medicine cabinet and some type of bandage. The finger was bleeding, but he'd managed not to spill any of his blood in the kitchen or on his clothes.

Inside the cabinet were shaving supplies, a bottle of multiple vitamins, and, luckily, a tin can of Band-Aids rusted at the bottom. It had probably been in the cabinet for years.

"Thank you, Father John," he said as he opened the can and poured the contents onto the sink counter, a badly painted vanity that must have been donated to the church long ago.

Nick grabbed at a bandage so quickly that he almost missed the two Trojan condoms at the bottom of the can. They were stuck there, still in their foil wrappings.

Chapter 20

The phone rang in Nick's apartment. His first thought was to ignore it, but then he picked up the receiver slowly, after the fourth ring.

"You're there?" Phil Mitchell said with surprise. "I thought I'd be talking to your machine. Isn't it only midafternoon in Arid-zona?"

Nick hadn't been to the mission in two days. Instead, he huddled alone in his apartment, with his radio on low, playing light jazz, as he tried to make sense of what he'd discovered so far. He didn't want to conduct any more interviews until he could work some things out in his head.

No luck. No conclusions. No simple paths.

He desperately wanted to find the clues that would clear Longfellow. More important, he wanted to make sure his lover, Rosa, wasn't somehow connected to the horrible crimes. Did someone frame Jimmy and now get away with murder? Did someone plant gold in Jimmy's bedroom and now escape with the rest of the treasure?

He needed to know so many things. The priest's writing, even if it was fiction, had to mean something. And what were the police doing with the information contained in the computer files?

The biggest mystery was the two condoms in the medicine cabinet. What would a priest be doing with them? Maybe they were for someone else. Maybe they were put there before Father John came to San Xavier, and like the gold they had been forgotten, undiscovered, for years.

Bullshit. The more likely story is that they were hidden away in the can for use by the priest during his escapades with the woman in his writing. Nick felt it in his gut. Father John had fallen in love with a woman.

How could a writer from New York prove it? Who knew anything more? Who would talk?

The phone call from Mitch jarred him back to reality. "What're you doing in your apartment in the middle of the day?"

"Working. Why are you calling me now anyway?"

"To tell you about Edward Newton of the Guggenheim. He gave an easy interview. Answered my questions candidly and didn't seem to be hiding anything about the conservators. He wanted to help. He'd been told the Indian named Jimmy Longfellow murdered the priest. I told him you were delving deeper into the crime. Didn't tell him about you and Rosa Zizzo. He said he didn't know much about the conservators other than their professional reputations. He hired Rosa, and then it was her job to hire the others. He called her one of the best conservators in the world."

"He couldn't tell you anything about the others? That's odd."

"He has their resumes and was willing to show them to me, but there's no need for me to see them. You might want to at some point. He said he knows the most about Rosa and also the Turk, Ali . . ." Mitch paused, needing to search through his mind or notepad for the name.

"Bahadir," Nick said before his friend could come up with it.

"Yes, that's it. Newton said he'd worked with Rosa and Bullshit-deer or whatever his name is on a couple of projects. They have excellent reputations."

"They've worked together before?" Nick asked. He didn't like the upheaval beginning to brew inside his gut.

"That's what Newton said. Hold on. Let me find it in my notes." Nick could hear Mitch flipping pages. "Here we go. They teamed up before on several European projects organized by Newton. A couple in Rome and others elsewhere in Europe."

"But she despises him. She told me she thinks he's an asshole."

"Hey, I think my boss is an asshole, but I work with him," Mitch said. "He's a hell of an editor, but he's also an asshole. All I know is that Newton told me that your Rosa and the Turk are two of the best in the world. Maybe they had a falling out at one time, but she still hired him for the project out there in Arizona and hoped that he got his ass bitten by a rattlesnake. Seen any yet, Nicky?"

"Forget about rattlesnakes." Nick was getting testy, and his friend knew to stop the joking around.

"Look, pal, anything's possible nowadays," Mitch said. "Remember, Zizzo and Bahadir knew each other long before you came along. Maybe she dumped him. Maybe he dumped her. Maybe she was a vulnerable woman who had just gotten out of a sour relationship and you came to her rescue."

Nick could feel heat rumbling under the surface of his face, down his neck and toward his stomach. He changed the subject. "What about the others? Did Newton say anything about Francesca Vitucci or Elizabeth Smythe?"

"Vee-two-chee and Smeyeth. Interesting pronunciations. Let me see. I took some notes on them. Newton didn't know much."

More flipping of pages.

"Here we are. Vitucci has a good reputation, although Newton said he hasn't worked with her before. Zizzo recommended her highly. They'd worked together on several projects in Italy. Vitucci has done little traveling, and I sense that the Arizona gig is a big deal for her personally and professionally.

"The Smythe woman is even less known. Newton said she contacted him after she got her degree at the University of London. She specifically wanted to do her internship at San Xavier."

"Smythe contacted him?"

"That's what he said. But he added that's not unusual. She could've heard about the project at her school. Newton was hired by the Tucson group to bring in the conservators. He hired Zizzo, and he also told her about Smythe."

"Did you ask him if any of the conservators had worked in Spain or had been there to do some research before their Arizona trip?"

"I was hoping you weren't going to ask."

"Don't play games, Mitch. What did he tell you? Who's been there?"

"You're not going to like this, pal. Don't get pissed."

"I'm already pissed and about to boil over. Who's been to Spain?"

"Zizzo and her buddy, Ali."

"You're right. I'm not liking this. In fact, I hate this shit." Nick felt nauseous and wished he hadn't started this conversation. He could only muster, "I knew about Rosa, but not about Ali."

"She and the Turk were hired by Newton to do a major project in Spain," Mitch continued. "Newton called the project a huge mural in an ancient church. I have the name of it somewhere here if that's important to you."

"It isn't." Nick wondered why Rosa hadn't told him Ali had been to Spain, too. He did the best he could to ask another question, even though he wanted to hang up the phone and scream. He knew his weak legs wouldn't hold him if he tried to stand.

"Does Newton know if Rosa and Ali were romantically involved?"

"He didn't know, Nick. And I'm telling you the truth. I sort of made a joke about that, and Newton seemed sincere when he told me he didn't believe they were. But like I said, he only knows about them professionally. What people do before or after work is not his business."

Mitch paused, knowing that his last comment had slammed into Nick's heart head-on. "You OK?" he asked.

"No, I'm not. I was already feeling shitty when you called. I'm a lot worse now. It doesn't take Doctor Ruth to know that two people working closely together all over the world could become romantic, especially when one of them looks like Rosa and the other doesn't take no for an answer, and doesn't give a shit about his wife back home."

"If you love her, Nick, you've got to trust her. I know you don't want to hear that right now, but I'm sure you know what I mean."

"You're right. I don't want to hear it now. Let me call you back later. There's something important that I need to do right away."

Chapter 21

Getting into Rosa's apartment was easy. Nick used the key she'd given him. They spent nearly all of their free time together. Always excited to see him, she would embrace him, kiss him passionately, whenever he walked in. They seldom ate dinner until after making love.

He'd spent time with women since his divorce, but none of them compared to Rosa. The other women had been lonely souls looking only for a quick, but ultimately unsatisfying, encounter. When he looked in their faces, touched their bodies, he saw another image. His mother? His wife? A former lover? He could never tell. He felt guilty that he was incapable of getting past an encounter, that he couldn't achieve some level of love. Rosa changed all that. Even when she wasn't with him, her image breathed at his side. He thought of her constantly. He wanted to tell her that she was the love of his life.

Right now, being in her apartment made him feel terrible, like a stranger, a burglar peering into her life before she returned home from work. He stood amid her possessions and felt cheap, insecure, ashamed. He justified his imposition by telling himself, *I'm mad, dammit. Rosa should've told me about her relationship with Ali, or at least told me they'd both been to Spain together.*

Like his, Rosa's one-bedroom, sparse apartment was furnished in green, brown, and orange, adequate but not fancy, and typical in a university town like Tucson.

Nick focused on the pile of unread, untouched, neatly stacked Italian newspapers in a corner on the floor in the bedroom. The subscriber had been too occupied lately to read.

Driven to find something, anything, Nick still had no idea where he should look. Walk here. Look there. Walk, look, stare. He proceeded like a robot in the daylight darkness of an apartment with its drapes drawn. He moved toward the dark, pressed-wood dresser on the wall opposite the bed and window in the bedroom. He wouldn't have hesitated before to throw open the dresser's secret drawers and play with the colorful inner and outer garments that were kept inside. He knew something like that would make Rosa laugh, and it would excite both of them.

No time for that now. I'm an intruder, a man with cat eyes, a spy, a detective rifling through someone's private things. Last night Rosa would've loved it, laughed at me, been turned on. Today she would be outraged. I'm guilty of illegal entry, ashamed of doubting the woman I love, or thought I loved.

Jealousy and anger had consumed him, at least momentarily.

He opened the top drawer and saw panties and bras. She liked red and black. A small clear-glass bowl in the drawer held several pairs of earrings and a watch.

Second drawer, a few T-shirts and sweatshirts. Third drawer, socks, a dozen pairs, all colors.

Nick leaned over to look inside the fourth and bottom drawer. It contained two pairs of neatly folded Levi 501s. He stood up straight and pushed the bottom drawer shut with his foot. So far, he could accuse his lover of owning socks, bras, panties, and folded Levi's. He began to calm down, and he felt stupid.

As he walked toward the bifold doors that weren't quite shut on Rosa's closet, he remembered the glass bowl in the top drawer. The watch. He walked back to the dresser.

He opened the drawer. The Mickey Mouse watch wasn't running. The battery must have died. He smiled, thinking how strange it was that foreigners couldn't wait to visit Disneyland or Disney World when they came to the United States. They loved to buy mouse ears and Mickey Mouse watches. Levi 501s were hot, too. Foreigners loved them, even paid outrageous prices for used ones.

The smile faded when he wondered if she'd been to Disneyland with the Turk.

He picked up the watch and looked at its band. It was black metal, a Speidel Twist-O-Flex, or something like that, one of those flexible stretch things that bend easily and is made up of small sections that fit together over some sort of springs.

Several of the pieces of metal that made up the outer part of the band were missing. The watch band still worked, but pieces of its outer section were gone. *There's no crime in having a broken watch band*, he thought. *Problem is, the police had asked Jimmy about what kind of watch he was wearing, even though he apparently didn't wear one.*

Nick put the watch down and closed the drawer. He kept thinking Rosa's broken watch band and the questions the police asked Jimmy were somehow connected.

He walked to the closet, where she had neatly arranged her shirts, pants, and shoes. He looked at the clock on the table next to the bed, one of those cheap, white plastic electric things with a lighted dial, the ones that begin humming loudly just as you're trying to go to sleep. He'd joked about it a couple of nights ago. Now it screamed at him that his time was running out. It said almost five. Rosa would be home soon. He should've been patient and waited until the morning to do this.

He went back to his apartment to call the sheriff's department. He needed to check on the watch before Rosa got home.

Detective Anderson answered the phone call from Nick right away, unlike the last time.

"Yes, Nick, what can I do for you?" he said like they were old friends.

"I've spent some time reading the transcript of the interrogation of Jimmy Longfellow, and I just have a couple of quick questions."

"Shoot."

"You pressed him on the type of watch he was wearing."

"Uh-huh."

"He kept saying he didn't wear a watch."

"Right."

Great interview. Nick knew why he didn't like Anderson, the typical detective who refused to volunteer anything. He had to be asked a direct question, which he would then manage to muddle through as basically as possible.

"Even though Jimmy said he didn't wear a watch, you kept asking him questions about it. Was there something you were looking for?"

"Yes. We found a couple of pieces of a watch band in the priest's house, and we wondered if Jimmy knew something about them."

Nick's stomach started rumbling again. Pain from deep inside his head jabbed him in the eyebrows. His heart pounded, and he had a tough time asking the next question. "Do you think they were connected somehow to the murder?"

"We don't know. We tried to ask Jimmy about everything. What we had were two small pieces of metal that had broken off a watch band and weren't picked up off the floor."

"Was it one of those gold flexible bands?" As he asked the question, he swiped at a bead of sweat rolling down his cheek. He prayed Anderson would say yes, they were gold.

Anderson paused. Nick knew the detective might not answer the question.

"They were black," Anderson said.

"One other quick question," Nick said, trying not to reveal his agony. "Did your forensic people find anything in the house that would suggest Father John was sexually involved with a woman?"

Anderson paused again.

Nick wondered if he should reveal that he'd read what was in the priest's computer. He decided not to. Besides, the cop probably knew that he'd been in Father John's quarters.

"Pubic hairs were found on the sheets," the detective said finally. "Also traces of face powder."

"What color was the hair?" Nick asked.

"Brown."

Before Nick could say thank you and hang up, Anderson added, "We have no proof that what was found on the bed was connected to the murder. Do you?"

"No."

"Have you found anything that would require a reopening of the case?"

"I don't think so."

"Then as far as we're concerned, Jimmy Longfellow is still the bad guy."

Nick didn't respond to the comment. "Thank you, Detective Anderson," he said. "Good talking to you."

Nick wondered if Anderson would even give the conversation a second thought. *Probably not. He's already on some more important case, or at least something with living people and solid evidence. Not me, though. The watch band. The black watch band. What does it mean. My God, I'm ashamed of what I'm thinking right now.*

Chapter 22

At nearly six o'clock, the sunny Arizona day had surrendered to a starry night with a dim half moon. Nick kept looking at his watch, one of those incessant things New Yorkers and newspapermen do. He'd returned to Rosa's apartment after calling Detective Anderson and waited for her impatiently on the couch.

She should've been home from the mission by now. Something small must have delayed her because she hadn't called. He knew she'd walk in at any minute.

His heart knocked and his mind filled with confusion. His emotions grew more intense by the second. *I can't tell if I'm furious or scared, or both. I should run right now. Get out. Jump on the first flight back to New York and do the story on the art conservation project from there. Forget the murder and the gold. Forget Jimmy Longfellow. Leave Rosa.*

Finally, the bolt lock on the front door turned. He stood up quickly from the couch, preaching to himself. *Be calm. Don't say something stupid the second she walks in.*

"Nick, I didn't know if you would be here," Rosa said when she walked in and saw him. "You weren't at the mission today, and I didn't hear from you."

He remained silent. He pictured himself walking to her, throwing his arms around her, expressing regrets for doubting her. He didn't move. There was nothing he could offer her that would make any sense.

She smiled broadly, displaying her happiness to see him.

Just looking into her soft and lovely eyes stimulated him. She had pulled her healthy hair back from her face. Her lips invited him. Her white T-shirt fit snugly on her round breasts. Her jeans squeezed her long legs. He loved watching her, everything female about her.

She walked up to him and threw her arms around him.

He jerked.

"Are you OK?"

"Sure I am." He lied.

Until today, he hadn't been afraid to tell her the details of his investigation. Now he worried if that could be dangerous.

"Why weren't you at the mission today?" She asked the question forcefully, and he could tell she sensed something wrong. You don't fall madly in love with a woman, spend all your leisure time with her, and then expect to lie to her and get away with it.

"I had to do some paperwork in my apartment."

"You weren't there yesterday, either."

"I know, Rosa. I've been busy doing some other stuff, personal stuff." He could tell his curt response signaled to Rosa that he wanted to avoid her questions.

Calm down. She's already catching on. She knows something's wrong.

"I love you, Nick." She whispered in her erotic way.

Why did she have to say that? I'm slipping here. Hold back, dammit. Don't say something I'll regret later.

He turned and sat on the couch, folding his arms across his chest like an old man on a park bench.

"Rosa, why don't you get comfortable? Get out of your work clothes and come sit down. We need to talk."

"I am comfortable," she said, sliding gently onto the couch. She pried her canvas sneakers off with her feet and then unsnapped her bra. He caught every sensual move. She sat cross-legged next to him, her knees touching his thigh.

"What's going on?" she asked. "You're not happy to see me?"

He tapped her knee with his fingers. He owed her an explanation, but he wanted to delay it as long as he could. He began stroking her knee without saying anything or looking in her eyes. He had a tough time expressing his feelings, although she'd helped break that habit. As children, he and his sister were never encouraged to reveal their feelings to their strict parents. He'd learned to express his feelings through writing, not through talking.

"Want a drink?" he said finally. "I'm sure you're tired."

"I'll take a soda," she said. "I have some in the refrigerator. Why don't you get me one and we'll talk."

He took his time. He rinsed two coffee mugs and filled them halfway with diet ginger ale. He preferred something stronger, but Rosa didn't keep booze in her refrigerator.

Even before he came back to the couch, she asked, "What's wrong?"

His dark eyes betrayed his emotions even when his mouth couldn't put a voice to them.

He spoke softly. "Every time I dig into the mess at San Xavier, I find something crazy. I'm more confused and frustrated than ever, and I'm getting nowhere with the damn case."

"Why are you so worried about it? The police should be the ones worrying. You told me they closed the case over the murder but were still hunting for the gold. Let's just finish our job at the mission. It won't be long before we leave the United States."

Leave the United States. Nick replayed her comment in his mind.

"I can't think about anything else," he said. "Maybe I'm the only person in Tucson who gives a damn about it."

"We all give a damn." Rosa's voice had become tense. "We knew Father John and Jimmy better than you did. But we're not the police. And, I don't understand why all of this is driving a wedge between you and me. You seem angry, like I've done something wrong. What are you thinking?"

He didn't answer. He didn't want to hurt her, or say something based on anger or jealousy, although he knew he would.

"Are you having doubts about us?" she asked.

"Let's talk about the mission. I'm not quite ready yet to discuss you and me." He wanted to, but not yet.

"Remember the gold dealer I told you about? The guy in Phoenix I interviewed?"

"I remember, but what was his name?"

"Robert Clarkson. He said more than one person probably was involved in the killing and theft. That means even if Jimmy did it, there may have been someone else in it with him. That gold is worth a fortune, and the people who killed Father John may have planned everything in advance. They might already have the gold out of the country. I've got to call Clarkson back and find out if he's heard anything."

"How did a gold dealer in Phoenix suddenly get into our conversation?"

"Stick with me for a second, Rosa. It'll become clear."

They inspected each other in silence. Their shortened breathing became the only noise in the room.

"Do you think it was one of the conservators?" she asked finally.

"That's why I need to call Clarkson. If there was a sale or movement of gold, he may have heard about it. Have you noticed anything odd about the other conservators in the last few days? Anyone shipping large packages?"

"Do you suspect me?" She didn't waste time.

Embarrassed, he hesitated, trying to construct and rehearse his sentences before he said them.

"Only you Europeans and the Indians were on the scaffolding when you found the sheet of paper inside Fidelis. Then you all found the gold together. That doesn't convict anyone on the team, but I've got to take a look at each person."

She said nothing.

"Was there anyone else at the mission that you haven't told me about?" Nick asked.

"No." He didn't like the way she said it.

He smiled but it was forced. None of his words came out the way he wanted them to. "My friend from New York, Phil Mitchell, called today. He asked Edward Newton some questions for me."

"Oh?"

"I wanted him to find out as much as he could about each of the conservators."

"Edward might not know much about them. He hired me and I hired them. All I did was send him their resumes. I guess I would've been the better person to talk to about the people on my team. Did you think of talking to me first?"

"I didn't know how well Newton knew the others until after Mitch talked to him. He told Mitch he didn't know them well. I guess the only two he knew were you and Ali."

"Yes." The way she said it revealed her irritation.

He was on the verge of exploding. "Newton told Mitch that he'd worked on several projects with you and Ali, including one in Spain. You didn't tell me that you and Ali were together in Spain before you came here."

"Now I see the problem." She stood up quickly from the couch as though she were going someplace, but then sat again, this time with both feet on the floor. She put her hands on her knees. Her back became rigid and she rocked defiantly. "You've never told me who you worked with before you came to Tucson. Have I asked?"

"No, but . . ."

She didn't let him finish the sentence. "Ali is one of the best conservators in the world. He and I were part of the team that oversaw part of the work in the Sistine Chapel in the Vatican. So you tell me, Nick, why shouldn't I hire him to work on other projects with me, in Spain or anyplace else in the world? If you worked on a story with a great photographer, the best in the world who also happened to be a woman you didn't like, wouldn't you hire her again?"

"You're right, Rosa, but I still want to know if you've been with him."

"Do you mean have I slept with him? Or should I talk like you Americans? Have I fucked him?" Her face reddened. He'd pushed the wrong button.

"Rosa, it's none of my business about the other men you've been with, but, yes, dammit, what about you and Ali? Is he your boyfriend? Former boyfriend? Have you told him you love him?"

She peered into his eyes. "You . . . *figlio di puttoma.*" The right words came to her more naturally in Italian. Nick guessed she said SOB because he knew the Spanish word *puta.*

Rosa shook her head and stood up from the couch. She walked to the window and looked into Tucson's cool winter evening. The dull slice of moon failed to illuminate the desert. The dazzling stars told the truth—there would be no rain tonight.

She kept her back to him. "It seems that you've made my past your business. Ali and I probably could've been romantic in the beginning. He's good-looking." She chose her words carefully. "But it didn't take long before we both realized that our relationship would be purely professional. He's married, you know, although he seems not to care about his wife. You should know by now that I respect marriage. That means hands off a married man. One other thing. In case you haven't noticed, he has no interest in me."

She could see Nick's reflection in the window. He sat at the edge of the couch next to an ugly clay lamp that came with the apartment.

"I love you, Nick, but right now I want to scratch out your eyes. Is there anything else you want to know before we put a stop to this evening?"

"Rosa, I'm sorry. I don't want anything to come between us, but don't you understand that I have to ask you these questions? I didn't even know you a month ago, and for the last few days we've been talking about the rest of our lives. I want to make certain I'm doing the right thing."

"I didn't know you a month ago, either, but I'm not accusing you of anything. I'm not asking you questions about your past. You haven't told me who you have been with."

"You did ask me about my wife." As soon as he said it he realized how ridiculous he sounded. Now he acted like a third-grader on a playground, arguing with a playmate.

She turned toward him.

"Do you know if Ali saw the journal of Padre Díaz while you were in Spain?" he asked.

"I don't know," she said, her answer quick and cold. "I have no idea what he did in Spain, other than the murals in the church we worked in. We weren't together during our off time."

Nick's voice softened. "Please, Rosa, come sit down. I'm just trying to find out all I can about this San Xavier mess."

She moved only slightly.

"Rosa, I need to ask you another question."

"I'm sure you do," she said sarcastically.

"I talked to Detective Anderson today, and he said they found a couple pieces of a broken watch band in Father John's residence."

His statement didn't register with her immediately. When it did, he saw the shock in her eyes.

"Oh, my God," she said, her angry eyes on Nick. "You don't think the police think. . . . You were hunting through my apartment before I got here, weren't you? How else would you know about my watch?"

"Rosa, I. . . ."

"No, Nick, no. Don't say anymore now. There's nothing more to say. Just get out of here."

He didn't budge. "The broken pieces of watch band they found were black, just like yours," he blurted out.

Tears started to flow from her eyes. She sat on the couch and put her face in her cupped hands. A stereo had been turned up in another apartment and its loudness soaked through the walls.

"I spent many hours with Father John before he was killed," Rosa whispered. "In the church and in his quarters. He was a kind man, a wonderful man, and he had a great love for San Xavier and its Indians. He and I could talk for hours about the great art inside the church. I broke my watch weeks before his killing, but I didn't know it. I just happened to notice it one day when I got home. I could've snagged it on something inside Father John's, or anywhere else. I put it away when the battery died and forgot to ask him about it."

Nick put his hand on her shoulder. "Rosa, I surely didn't mean to hurt you in any way."

She wiped the tears from her cheeks with the back of her hand. He handed her a tissue. "You need to leave, Nick. Please go. Right now, I don't want to be with you."

He knew it would do no good to say anything. He walked out, gently closing the door behind him. As soon as he moved away from the door, he heard her turn the bolt lock. She also put the chain on the small lock that would prevent him from getting in even with a key.

Chapter 23

Over the next week, Nick put his best professional face forward, but he did a lousy job of masking his misery. Even though he worked hard on his article, he felt lonely and deserted. He punished himself mentally for the things he'd said to Rosa. If he'd kept his mouth shut, trusted her, respected her, none of this would have happened.

In the last couple of days, he noticed that some warmness returned to her eyes when she looked at him, although the scars remained and she had yet to welcome him back into her life. She spoke to him when she had to, professionally but friendly. He wanted so much to return to her apartment, to be with her, to apologize.

Shortly before lunchtime, he looked at his watch. He had an hour before Don Farmer, the photographer from Phoenix who had been hired to illustrate his story, would be at the church. Farmer had spent the last few mornings there, and now he needed some shots with afternoon lighting.

Nick walked out of San Xavier and started nibbling at a banana and Snickers that he'd shoved into his pocket earlier in the day. He spotted Francesca Vitucci sitting on a bench outside the mission, listening to a cassette tape. She spent many of her lunch hours practicing English.

As she sat quietly, the chubby brunette chewed on her unpolished fingernails. Nick approached her.

He startled her when he sat next to her.

"How's your English lesson going today?"

She smiled. "*Bene*, uhm, fine. Very fine. I pray, too."

"Pray for whom?"

"For everyone. My family. My friends. People in mission. You, too. I pray every night, everywhere. Even when tired, I stay up to pray. Now even when I'm listening to tape, I start praying."

"You must be a strong Catholic."

"Catholic, yes, but not so good. I not go to church on Sundays. But I am spiritual. *Molto spirituale*."

"I am finding a need in my own life to be spiritual," Nick said, believing his statement. He'd thought about it before but hadn't said it out loud to anyone. "But I don't think I could go to church. It's more like I want to find something in the mountains, or the earth, or the sky, like the Indians do."

Francesca's eyes arched and she stared at him. He couldn't tell if she misunderstood his English, his logic, or both.

"I see spirits," she said.

"Often?"

"Yes, often. The other night, in bed, I wake up, see a woman dressed in white. *Una visione*. She at the end of my bed, near the door. Her feet not touching ground, and she is flying through my room."

"Do you know who she was?"

"*Non so*. Don't know. Don't know her. She is someone I will meet."

"Do you usually recognize the spirits?"

"*Si*. My brother. He is with me sometimes. He die in an automobile crash eight years ago. Lose control. Crash into bridge. *Morto*. I was at home with his dog. It started barking even before police officer come to tell us the news. *Terribile*. Policeman who came to door is my brother's friend. He had bloodstains on the arm of his uniform. He tried to save my brother, but *niete da fare*."

"And your brother now visits you?"

"*Si*. He smoke pipe with tobacco that smell like cherries. Sometimes, I am alone and I smell the cherry tobacco. I know my brother is near me. He sends me messages."

"Is the fact that you see spirits the reason you don't go to church?"

"No. No one angry at me because I see spirits. I don't go to church because I let spirits guide me. And because I am not married."

"A lot of single people go to church. Why would that stop you?"

"I no say I'm single, Nick. I say I'm not married. *Ho una compagna*. I have, what you say in English, a partner. She not in America with me. She stay in Rome."

Nick didn't know what to say. He'd learned long ago to expect the unexpected, to be unmoved by practically anything anyone said, to believe that anything could happen with people. *Does Rosa know Francesca is a lesbian? Probably. That certainly eliminates her as a priest's lover.*

"Is your partner spiritual, too?" he asked finally.

"Oh, *si*. She like me. Spiritual. *Visioni preghiere*. Pray every day. We no need church, but we believe."

"Did Father John know you were spiritual?"

"We talk. *Si*. He knows, but he say nothing. He was able to love without conditions."

"Do you think he had a lover?" Nick knew the question might offend or anger Francesca, but he wasn't afraid to ask it.

"He know about me, and we talk, but he not say much about himself. But I can tell in his eyes that he was in love. *Innamorato, molto innamorato*."

"With a man or a woman?"

"Woman. He not a gay man. I know that. But he no interested in young boys. He more comfortable with women. His eyes told me he was in love with a woman. His eyes like the art in San Xavier. They say much. People no understand how much they say."

"Do you think Jimmy killed him?"

Francesca shrugged her shoulders.

"Come on, Francesca. You worked closely with Jimmy. What was in his eyes?"

"Jimmy no kill Father John. He love Father John, because Father John believe in him. And he not go to church every Sunday. He believed. Like me. *Spirituale.* He believed."

"What about the gold? That could drive people to do crazy things, including Jimmy."

Francesca rolled her eyes at what she considered a stupid question. "Jimmy here for the art, the beauty in the art," she said. "He not here for job or money. He like me. We don't know America enough to steal gold. Where we go with it? We love art. The rich here is in the art. We have chance to study it, to learn it, to feel it. People not understand the art like we. Jimmy *non é un assassino.* He cannot kill Father John."

"One more question, Francesca. In your job as a conservator, you have traveled throughout the world, right?"

She giggled. "Oh, no. Stay in Italy. America first trip."

"I thought you've worked with Rosa before."

"In Italy. Plenty of churches, buildings there."

"You didn't work in Spain with her."

"No. *Solo in Italia.* Rosa like me. She bring me to America."

Nick didn't need to ask Francesca any more questions. He sat silently on the bench next to her, listening to the muffled sounds of the cassette. After he went back to work, he remained deep in his own thoughts. *You're innocent, Francesca. Never been to Spain. A lesbian. Spiritual. You have black hair. Police found brown hair on the sheets in Father John's quarters. You're nothing like the goddess the priest wrote about. Nothing about you fits. You're not capable of murder.*

Don Farmer jarred him from his thoughts. He tapped Nick on the shoulder and walked inside the church without saying anything. The reporter followed.

Nick enjoyed Farmer. He was a laid-back, bearded man with thick eyebrows that needed trimming and auburn hair that was combed back and always looked wet. He was in his early thirties, handsome, with turquoise eyes. He wore a tan photographer's field jacket with canisters of film loaded in each of the pockets sewn across the chest. He made his living on Southwestern pictures, and Nick's editor said Farmer was good enough to work for some of the best magazines in the world, including *Smithsonian* and *National Geographic*.

The two men climbed the stairs and walked into the choir loft, a floor above the pews at the back of the church, where they watched the conservators working on the scaffolding in front of them and the visitors below them.

"You have an uncanny ability for the best angles," Nick said. "That's why I like tailing you. You make your pictures, and I take notes."

"Have you seen this?" Farmer said, pointing to an unpainted section of white plaster wall in the choir loft with pencil sketches on it. "The artists were going to cover this back section of the church with art, but they never got to it. They only had time to draw the outline on the wall."

Nick was intrigued. "Are those sketches from the 1700s?" he asked.

"That's what Carl Corona said. He brought me up here to show me where I could set up my tripod and lights."

"Speak of the devil," Nick said. "Carl just walked in the church."

The car dealer marched up to the scaffolding and motioned for Rosa to come down. She did as instructed. They moved away from the scaffolding and the other conservators. Nick couldn't hear what either said.

Carl talked. Rosa listened intently.

Suddenly, she frowned and waved her head no. Carl pointed his finger at her. He spoke too quietly to be heard from Nick's perch.

Nick felt a rush in his blood, a quickness in his breath. He wanted to fly to her side and defend her even though he had no idea if she needed it.

Rosa turned from Carl and started back toward the scaffolding.

Carl raised his voice. "It's not going to happen your way. This church isn't going to change because of what you've done."

At least that's what Nick thought he heard.

Carl walked quickly out of the church. "Did you hear what they were talking about?" Nick muttered to the photographer, who seemed too busy to care about the conversation below.

Farmer shrugged. "You'll go crazy trying to figure out what people are saying down there, unless you can read lips." The photographer laughed and changed the subject, "Hey, Nick, that Kino was some kind of guy, wasn't he?"

His concentration shattered, Nick turned his back to the front of the church and said, "Yes, quite a guy."

"Think about what he started here," Farmer said. "Here was this Jesuit dressed in black who gave up all of the simple comforts of life so he could ride his horse around the frontiers of New Spain. He tried to bring civilization, make that Christianity, to the natives. Incredible. The guy thought people weren't civilized unless they were Christians. He baptized them. Taught them farming, brought them cattle, and showed them how to irrigate their fields.

"Too bad the Spanish soldiers had to get here and ruin things. Getting gold for their government was their chief objective. So was acquiring land. They took the land from the natives and also turned them into slave labor for their mines. They were Christians, too, but they didn't think much of the Indians."

Farmer bent over his camera and tripod, focusing carefully as he talked. "People who walk into this church for the first time aren't quite ready for a place so wondrous, so full of angels, saints, and flying cherubim. There are churches like this in Mexico, but nothing like it anyplace in the United States."

"You need to take pictures during a Sunday Mass," Nick said. "It's a combination of Indians, Mexicans, whites, Africans, Asians, locals, tourists, you name it. For a split second in history, everyone is together, friendly, beautiful. Too bad we can't capture that loveliness and sell it by the bottle."

Farmer studied his camera. There was a lengthy pause before they spoke again.

"It's too bad we didn't know Father John," the photographer said. "I understand he was really loved."

"I'm sorry I didn't," Nick responded. "The Tucson priests who come in to do the Mass now aren't quite like the friar dressed in a brown habit and sandals with a rosary swinging from his side. He remained in the middle ages. They're twentieth century. A new Franciscan priest will be arriving soon."

The photographer changed the subject again, and Nick wondered if his words filtered through the air without being heard. "I've got permission to climb up on the roof next and take some photographs of the domes and towers," Farmer said. "Want to tag along?"

"Sure." Nick hadn't been to the top of the church yet.

The cool afternoon showed no hint of a breeze. The sun's rays danced off the bright white plaster of San Xavier's domes, which reflected the light like mirrors. Nick imagined he had climbed onto a snow-packed hill.

Shiny cars and chatty gawkers filled the parking lot and shopping plaza to the south of the church. A sandwich board at the entrance to the plaza advertised a sale on Indian jewelry and Tohono O'odham baskets.

"Have you heard the story of why one of the towers is unfinished?" Farmer said as he screwed his camera onto the tripod. He used a 40-millimeter lens on his Hasselblad 500 C/M to get a full photograph of the incomplete tower and the desert and hill behind it. He waited for the sun to be in precisely the right place to light his shot the way he envisioned it.

"I've heard it," Nick said. "There were two architects for San Xavier, brothers named Gaona. They were from Mexico and were building a church down there at the same time. Supposedly one of the brothers, Ignacio, fell from the tower at San Xavier during the last months of its construction and was killed. It was never completed. Tohono O'odham legend says Ignacio turned into a huge rattlesnake and lives under the tower to this day."

"Their name had just about the same letters as yours, at least the same number of letters." After he spoke, Farmer laughed. "I've also heard that the builders of San Xavier didn't want to finish the church because as long as it remained incomplete, funding would continue to come from Spain, or at least they could send less of their gold back to Spain."

Nick hadn't heard that story. It seemed to make better sense than a brother falling to his death and turning into a rattlesnake. He promised himself to check it out.

"Know why the church faces south?" Farmer mumbled between photographs. "They all did," he answered, not giving Nick a chance to respond. "Toward Mexico. When they were built, that was Spain, the mother country."

As he spoke Farmer's eyes never left the images in his viewfinder. "This place has had rough times, but somehow managed to retain its beauty. There was a plague here during the 1860s. So many people died at San Xavier that they were buried three and four deep in the old cemetery, around the walls of the church, and under the floors of the cloisters."

The two men spent nearly an hour on the roof. "When are you going back to New York?" Farmer asked as they packed the bags for the trip down the narrow adobe and wood stairway and back into the church.

"I don't know. They'll be finishing this year's conservation project in the next couple of weeks. Probably sometime before then. I've already started writing the piece and should be pretty much done with it before I leave. Then I'll plop the story and a disk down on my editor's desk and forget about this place."

"I heard you and Rosa have a good thing going, and that you might be going to Italy with her."

"Where'd you hear that?"

"Word travels fast."

"Oh well, it's probably better to say we HAD a thing going. I screwed things up."

"Sorry to hear that. How 'bout the other two sweet ladies? Francesca Vitucci isn't bad looking, maybe a little chubby, but she laughs at everything. She's sincerely interested in helping this church and its people. I've promised to send her some prints after I get the transparencies back from *Smithsonian*."

Nick didn't tell Farmer what he knew about Francesca.

"What about Elizabeth Smythe?" he asked.

"She's a bizarre one," Farmer said. "Real chatty, asks a lot of questions, and seems friendly. But there's something about her eyes. There's a coldness there that I don't want to deal with. When she sees you coming, she's nice, but I'm not sure I'd want to cross her."

"Interesting," Nick said. "She's a little aloof at times, but she's in a strange country and is the junior member on the team."

"You know, I take a lot of photographs of people, and I really get into their eyes. Smiling eyes can make a great portrait. Elizabeth's never smile."

Nick said nothing.

"Ali told me to stay away from Elizabeth," the photographer added. "Said we should be getting our information from experienced conservators like him, not from an intern just out of school. I kind of like her little body, though."

Nick agreed that Elizabeth had an attractively small and wiry body. She took care of herself. "What do you think of Ali?" he asked.

"Now there's a piece of work. If Elizabeth is cold, that guy's Siberia. He's supposedly the best at what he does, but he's pompous, arrogant, and believes his shit don't stink."

"Does he seem like a ladies' man to you?" Nick wanted another man's opinion.

"I'm sure if he wanted to scheme on one of these women, he could," Farmer said. "He knows how to turn on the charm when he needs to, but to me he's a typical foreigner in this country. I had lunch with him the last time I was here. The guy ate his food, leaned back, belched and then farted. The prick's a real piece of work. I can just picture him like a wild Turk with one of those long curved knives."

"He doesn't seem to get along well with Rosa," Nick said.

"Man, he doesn't get along with anyone. I'd hate to be competing against him for a job. He'd eliminate anyone in his way."

Chapter 24

Rosa waited for Nick and the photographer to walk back into the church. "Nick," she called softly from the third level of the scaffolding. "Please climb up here. There's something I want to show you."

Surprised and happy that she paid attention to him, he quickly did as instructed. As he climbed the ladders two steps at a time, he wondered if she'd been watching him all day like he'd been watching her. He hoped, no, perhaps he prayed, that she was.

"What do you think of this?" she said, pointing to a statue of a beautiful angel who appeared to be flying out of the wall between the main and west chapels. "I've just finished working on it and am amazed that the linen used on it is so well preserved."

He wanted to grab her, embrace her, swallow her up in his arms and put his lips to hers. He didn't. He felt her excitement about her work and wanted to share it with her. He should expect nothing else. *Patience. Don't move too fast this time. Keep your mouth shut and let beautiful Rosa guide the conversation.*

She held a bottle of the gray coloring that the conservators called dirty water. They brushed it on the areas of cleaned artwork that had chipped away from the bright white plaster behind them. The gray color blended in with the original colors and guaranteed that it would be difficult from the ground level to tell that some paintings and statues had unpainted blotches on them. No matter how careful they were, the conservators couldn't save the areas of art that had been erased after two centuries of abuse by leaking ceilings, animals, and people. Dirty water took the place of repainting.

The youthful angel Rosa described wore an outer garment with red blossoms. There were yellows, reds, violets, and greens on its outstretched wings.

"Notice the hands," Rosa said. "They're positioned as if the angel is pulling a drapery cord to reveal the sanctuary."

Nick beamed. "The artisans thought of everything. Thank goodness you're here to save it."

She studied him and grinned. She caught the compliment but didn't acknowledge it. "I'm impressed with it because of the cloth that has survived all these years. It's gesso-stiffened cloth that is molded so that it appears that the angel is in flight."

"Who is it?"

"It is listed in the records only as 'Angel' and isn't meant to be as great as the statues of the saints. The feeling of movement and remarkable colors have been an exciting experience for me. Working on this angel has made me feel joyous again."

Nick's heartbeat quickened. He could tell her sentences also delivered forgiveness.

"Rosa, can we go somewhere and talk? It's time for us to work out our problems."

Rosa nodded. She swept her hair from her eyes. "*Mio amore*, why did it take you so long to ask?"

"Because I'm an idiot. I thought . . ."

"Oh, never mind," she interrupted. "It has been too long since we talked. I want you in my life. I don't want to think of my future without you in it."

"That's how I feel."

"I feel silly for having to defend myself. I'm not guilty of anything, Nick. Do you believe me?"

"Yes."

"I know you're a reporter and are asking questions of everyone, but your doubts about me hurt me more than you can imagine."

"I know they did. I hope you can forgive me."

"I have. Let me pour out this dirty water and we can go."

She touched his arm reassuringly. "I've missed you."

"Rosa, I can't tell you how sorry I am about the other night." He spoke quickly. He'd rehearsed the sentence a dozen times.

"I love you, Rosa."

"But do you trust me?"

"With my whole heart," he said truthfully. He longed for her company, her smile, her love.

He watched her as she moved around the scaffolding to pick up her brushes. When she bent over, the outline of her body in its tight jeans sent a jolt through his body. Even her simplest actions ignited everything inside of him.

"I love what you say and who you are, and I'm sorry we didn't talk earlier," she said.

He looked at her gently. "I noticed that you and Carl had quite a conversation this morning. The photographer and I were in the choir loft when Carl came in and called you down from the scaffolding."

A crease of worry stretched across her forehead. "We argued about the candles. Whatever we do in this church, it will be ruined in the future if the faithful are allowed to continue lighting candles in here. One day's soot does nothing, but multiply that times many candles and many years, and there will forever be a problem in here. The art will one day be black again. I want the candles taken out."

"And Carl disagrees?"

"He's speaking the word of the Franciscans. They maintain that this is an active church today as it always has been. The candles will stay forever, even if it means ruining the art."

Relieved to hear Rosa's explanation of her conversation with Carl, Nick asked, "Aren't you training the Tohono O'odhams to maintain the church after you're gone?"

"Certainly. But there still will be tiny amounts of damage to this art that will continue to grow slowly, like pollution creeping across the earth until one day everything is choked."

They walked outside slowly. The sunlight assaulted them and demanded that they squint until they adjusted to its glare. Nick put on a pair of sunglasses. She had none. He made a mental note to buy her a pair.

They hesitated nervously. He touched her face with his hand. Rosa tensed but didn't resist. She smiled nervously. He stepped closer and hugged her tightly. She embraced him. They kissed, finally.

Chapter 25

"It won't be long before we're in Italy. A month maybe." Still speaking, Rosa walked into her kitchen and gave her lover a good morning kiss as he poured her a cup of espresso.

"I'm finishing up my story," he said, embracing her. "I can't wait to be in my ancestral country with you. I'll be in New York just long enough to turn in my piece and do revisions. Then it's on to Rome for an extended vacation, Baby."

Everything seemed perfect in their relationship. They now spent nearly all of their free time together. They'd even talked about marriage sometime in the future, perhaps in Europe.

"I'm going to spend the morning in my apartment," Nick said as they sat on the living room couch together and watched a local TV happy talk team.

He hadn't done much investigating since he and Rosa got back together. His gut kept telling him not to give up on the murder and theft story, but for the time being he ignored it. He wanted to finish—and be paid—for a conservation story, not to be a sleuth. He'd play cop when he had a chance, but little could be done until someone who knew something came forward, either to the police or to Nick.

All he wanted to do for now was call Robert Clarkson. Perhaps the Phoenix gold dealer had heard something. If so, Nick promised himself he'd call the sheriff's department in Tucson. Let Anderson and his staff of gumshoes handle it. He'd do them a favor if he found out anything.

He dialed Clarkson's shop a little after nine in the morning. As it had most days, the sun had warmed the desert and Nick's apartment. He'd opened the window in his kitchen to let in the gentle cool breeze. He sat at his kitchen table, in front of his laptop, a Macintosh Powerbook.

No answer. He let it ring a dozen times before hanging up. He couldn't understand why no one answered. Maybe the guy opened at ten?

He went back to his notes and tapes. He also wanted to read two magazine articles he'd found in the Tucson library on the significance of the artwork at San Xavier. Although much had been written on the mission over the years, not much research had been done on each of the statues. He found one old book and the two articles.

He tried Clarkson again in an hour. This time, someone picked up the receiver on the third ring.

"Hello?" The unfriendly female voice asked a question. It wasn't a greeting. She hadn't expected the call.

The question perplexed Nick. It seemed odd to him that the woman didn't answer a business phone with something like, "Clarkson's Jewelry." Maybe he dialed the wrong number.

"Is this Robert Clarkson's shop?" he asked.

"Who is this, please?" Again, the unfriendly, brusque voice revealed no joy over the phone call.

Nick, feeling like an intruder, said: "This is Nick Genoa calling from Tucson. I'm the writer who interviewed Mr. Clarkson a couple of weeks ago for the story on San Xavier Mission. Is he there?"

"No, he's not." She scolded him for asking.

"Any idea when he'll be in?"

"Mr. Genoa, Robert Clarkson is dead."

She said it so quickly that it didn't register at first. Then the word "dead" crashed into him head-on. *What is she talking about? Dead? Clarkson's dead.* "Oh, I'm so sorry," he managed. "What happened?"

The woman didn't answer, leaving only an eerie silence on the phone line. *She must be the clerk who worked in Clarkson's shop. What was her name? Lucy, I think.*

"Is this Lucy?"

"Yes."

He searched through his mind for an image of Lucy. *Dark brown hair and glasses. Plain, unattractive, a lot of jewelry. She worked on her polished red fingernails while I was in the shop. She whispered the day I met her, nothing like her voice over the phone just now.*

"Do you remember me?" he asked hopefully. "I'm the writer who came into the shop and visited with Mr. Clarkson about the gold coins at San Xavier Mission."

"Yes, I remember. There was a murder at the mission, too."

Too? Goose bumps sprouted on his arms. He began to tremble. Another killing? They seemed to be following his interviews.

"Can you tell me how Mr. Clarkson died?" he asked.

"He was butchered," Lucy said without hesitation. She didn't elaborate. The vigor and bluntness in her voice stunned Nick. He nervously began twirling the end of his mustache. "When did it happen?" he asked in the strongest reporter's voice he could manage.

"Three nights ago. I'm in the shop trying to complete inventory. We're no longer open."

"Can you tell me how it happened?"

"It was late at night or early in the morning. I don't know much except that someone called and made an after-hours appointment with him on Friday night. He seemed pretty excited after the phone call because the person had some antique gold to show him. He told me to go ahead and leave for the weekend and that he'd close up after the appointment. That's all I know. I've already told the police all of this. Wasn't the priest in Tucson killed with a knife, too?"

"No, he was stabbed and killed with a screwdriver, but the killer definitely knew how to use knives. Do you have any idea who the caller was?"

She answered, "No."

Nick wanted to keep Lucy talking. He threw out questions quickly because he didn't know how long he had her attention. He'd learned years ago to keep a phone interview going as long as possible.

"Do you know if the caller was a man or a woman?"

"No. Bob didn't tell me that. He never told me much about his customers. All I know is what the police said, and they placed the death sometime between eleven at night and one in the morning."

"Did Bob often work late?"

"Whenever the business needed him to. He met at any hour with people who wanted to buy something or had something to sell. In the six years I worked for him, he never told me much about where he got his gold, but he stayed late or opened early if he thought he could make a good buy. He knew how to get something of value real cheap. That was Bob. He never forced himself on anyone, and he knew how to negotiate."

"How was he killed, Lucy?" Nick still hadn't gotten the answer to that question.

She began crying, and Nick regretted the question. Like any reporter, he suffered at times as a tormented and punished man simply because he did his job. Sometimes he hated being paid to pry into other people's private lives. Death—make that murder—always complicated things.

"I don't know if I should be talking to you," Lucy complained. "Maybe you should be getting this information from the police. You won't use my name in any story, will you? I don't want my name used."

"Of course not, Lucy. And I'll be happy to go to the police if I have to. But I sure would appreciate your help. Mr. Clarkson and I were working together."

"His throat was slit." Despite her tears, she delivered her matter-of-fact response as though she were a prosecuting attorney presenting her closing argument to a jury. "The newspaper story said someone came in here and nearly cut off his head with a knife. It was a big story in the Phoenix papers and on television. I'm surprised you didn't hear about it in Tucson."

Lucy came into clearer focus. *Medium height. Thick glasses. Looks like a woman who lives alone with her cats. Probably a bookworm. Nothing attractive or special, except her fingernails and jewelry.*

"I haven't been watching TV lately, and I've only been skimming the papers," Nick said. He thought of the untouched pile of newspapers in the corner of Rosa's bedroom. Her collection of Italian papers had been supplemented by the Tucson papers he'd thrown on the pile. They would have surely done something on a killing in Phoenix, but it probably wouldn't be a front page story.

"Did you find him?" he asked barely above a whisper.

"No, the police did. His wife called them on Saturday morning after he didn't answer the phone or come home. She gave them the keys. Even when I came in Monday morning, there was still some dried blood on the floor and display cases." She sobbed deeply now. "Bob was butchered by someone and nothing was stolen. Why would anyone do that?"

"I'm so sorry, Lucy. Do the police have any idea who did it?"

"When they interviewed me, they said someone in the neighborhood heard a car screech away from here after midnight. They know that the person who did it was only interested in killing Bob. The killer could've stolen thousands of dollars worth of jewelry but didn't."

"Did any of the stories give a description of the car or any possible suspects?"

"No, but the first story in the *Republic* quoted police as saying the killer knew what he was doing. He simply walked up behind Bob and swiftly slit his throat from ear to ear."

Nick wondered what type of lunatic could walk up behind someone, pull his head back, and slit his throat in one quick motion. Even if the killer knew exactly what he was doing, Clarkson's death would've been slow and agonizing.

"What do you plan to do, Lucy?" he said.

"I have no idea. Mrs. Clarkson asked me to come back in and do the inventory. That will take the rest of this week. Then I don't know."

The conversation ended, and Nick hung up the phone, thinking. *Could Clarkson's murder somehow be connected to Father John's? Had the gold dealer learned something about the San Xavier treasure and died because of it?*

He pictured each of the people involved in the San Xavier project. Could any one of them really be guilty of such gruesome crimes? He felt a chill on the back of his neck.

How would any of the conservators even know about Clarkson? Nick searched his mind for an answer. Then he remembered he'd told Rosa the gold dealer's name. Nick suddenly felt sick to his stomach. *Not again, Nick. Not again.* He tried not to think about Rosa.

He reached into his memory to bring back Friday night, the night of Clarkson's slaying. Rosa had complained about feeling nauseous and weak, and she had told him not to come over that night. She wanted to go to bed and sleep late Saturday morning. As promised, she had called him at midmorning and they went out for brunch. She had said she felt much better after a good night's sleep.

"Dammit," he shouted.

Chapter 26

"Nick, good to hear from you. Where are you?" Clay Branom was a busy editor in San Francisco, but he always took calls from newspaper friends, particularly those with whom he'd worked in New York. The tight bond they formed in a newsroom lasted a lifetime, no matter where they were. Nick and Branom hadn't seen each other in years, since Branom left the *Times* to become metropolitan editor of the *Chronicle*. They traded Christmas cards and talked occasionally on the telephone, when one or the other needed a favor.

"I'm in Tucson, working on a story. I'm trying to get some information on a Catholic priest who spent some time in your part of the country. Your library may have something."

Branom didn't acknowledge Nick's inquiry, at least not yet. He still had questions. "How's life been for you outside the joint?" he asked. Married only to the newspaper, Branom had no concept of what life would be like away from daily journalism. His career didn't start moving forward until he put in a decade in New York. Then he realized that after New York he could go anywhere. Like other New York journalists in the last few years, he landed in San Francisco.

Branom, a quick-talking, good-looking forty-year-old with a mane of rust-colored hair, wore pin-stripe wool suits and wing tips, smoked fine cigars, and shot from the hip. He knew how to coax the best out of reporters, particularly young ones just out of college. He had little time for small talk and always made his point, even if he offended someone.

Nick knew he wouldn't have to answer the question. Talking with newspaper people on the phone never changed. They weren't good about taking or returning a call, unless it was from a source or good friend. When they did talk, they always were in a hurry and had little time to visit, even if they were hours away from the next deadline. As usual, Nick felt like a doorstop, holding his friend open for only a couple of minutes.

"Life's good," Nick said quickly. "I'm checking out a priest by the name of John Duvall. Can I have your library check on a file?"

"Would we be interested in the story?" Branom said. "You're not keeping a hell of a story from us, are you? Plenty of people in the Bay Area are interested in what's happening in Arizona."

"Keep your nose down, Clay. My guy is dead. I'm just looking into his background. He went to school at San Francisco State and worked on the campus paper. I called the *Golden Gater*, but a woman there said the paper's files don't go back to when Duvall was a college student. She invited me to make a trip to the university archives, where all the campus papers are stored."

"Nice of her. You gonna do it?"

"No. I called the registrar's office, too. Another woman told me the only information her office could give out was that John Duvall had attended and graduated with a degree in journalism."

"I'll ask one of our librarians to check it out," Branom said. "Let me transfer you to Katy Dillon. She's our best. Hold on, Nick. Good talking to you. Call if you need anything else."

The phone went silent during the transfer. Nick assumed Branom was telling the librarian to help out, and also ordering her to let him know if the *Chronicle* should be paying attention to anything she finds.

"Library, Katy Dillon."

Nick introduced himself and started to explain why he was calling.

"I can check our databases," Dillon interrupted. "Please hold." She already knew why he was calling.

Once again the line went silent. Nick felt like he was in a fast-moving car and she was a road sign flashing by. He needed information. She offered it, but he had to be quick.

She came back to the line in less than a minute. "There's nothing in the library files on John Duvall. No news stories. But he's in our human resources database. He was a journalism major at San Francisco State and worked here for a summer as a clerk a long time ago."

"Is there anyone there who might have known him?" Nick knew there wouldn't be.

"According to the personnel file, it was a normal hire," Dillon said. "He was let go a little before the end of summer because the wire editor at the time, a John Finberg, put a disciplinary note in the file. Let me look that up."

She was gone for less than twenty seconds. Nick could hear other people talking in the background. The *Chronicle* library was a busy place. "It seems young Mr. Duvall could not keep his eyes off the girls," the librarian said. "Wanted to spend more time visiting with them than working at his job. Finberg suggested the early release and recommended that Duvall not be hired on a permanent basis. That put an end to Mr. Duvall's career around here."

"Any other problems?"

"Nope. There's a note that after college he went to a seminary in Santa Barbara. That's all we have."

So much for trying to dredge up Father John's past in San Francisco. Next stop, Carl Corona's auto dealership. Nick stopped at a Tucson fast-food institution, the Lucky Wishbone, for a burger and fries and then headed for a 2 P.M. appointment at the Corona Pontiac/Toyota Superstore.

The salespeople at the dealership were predictably good looking and well dressed. One of them, a young sandy-haired body-builder with polished teeth and a confident smile, patronized Nick the instant the writer walked in.

"Welcome to our *soup-a-store*," came the greeting from the man with a nametag that identified him as Roy.

Nick glanced at his rented Nissan Altima parked outside the front door. Roy probably viewed it as a trade-in.

"How can we help you today?" asked Roy, a dashing young man who likely had spent most of his morning primping. Nick wanted to ask how Roy's parents felt about him growing up to be a car salesman, but he didn't.

"I'm here to see Carl Corona," he said, ruining Roy's hope of a sale.

"Is he expecting you?"

"Yes. My name is Nick Genoa."

"Please wait here. I'll tell him you're here, Mr. Genoa." The writer watched as Roy aimed for a hallway leading like a tunnel out of a corner of the superstore's showroom.

Nick scanned the place. He hadn't been in an auto showroom in years. Carl had built a cavernous field of dreams with floor-to-ceiling glass and waxed tile floors, and he filled it with shiny cars. People rushed back and forth in the hospital-clean showroom as though they were part of a choreographed movie scene. A speaker tied to an intercom chatted constantly, calling salespeople to the phone. A young man and woman seated in the small cubicle closest to Nick looked at each other pensively, hoping their salesperson would come back with the right number.

A red Firebird convertible parked on a big turntable in the middle of the showroom caught Nick's eye. The impressive, sleek beauty rotated slowly. Its windows were heavily tinted, a giant pair of sunglasses. Nick couldn't see inside the car when he walked up to it and bent over for a look.

"Want to take it for a test ride?" The booming voice from behind startled him.

Not Roy this time, but still another primped salesman with the same smile and look. His nametag said Stan.

Nick straightened. He had an urge to kick the Firebird's big black tires with raised Goodyear lettering. He didn't.

"No thanks. Just looking."

"Mr. Genoa, come this way," Roy called as he walked back into the showroom, rescuing Nick from Stan.

Large and small Western paintings lined the long hallway to Carl's office. As the two men walked quickly, images flashed by: Cowboys. Indians. Buffaloes. Cattle. Mountains. Streams.

Beautiful pieces of art lured visitors to the wood-paneled office at the end of the hall.

"Nick, welcome to my Graceland," Carl announced as he stood from behind his expansive, uncluttered wooden desk and pushed out his large right hand to the writer. "What brings you here?"

Like his sales staff, Carl spoke from the polished and rehearsed script he kept in his mind.

You can't be the same guy I've seen in San Xavier Mission. Too primped and primed. You have a twin brother? Do I know you? "I want to buy your most expensive car," Nick said. He smiled before adding, "Just joking."

Carl laughed energetically, just like he had the first day Nick met him.

What's with the good mood? We're not friends. I'm not buying a car. No deal to close here. How long before you turn into a condescending bully? I can see it in your eyes. I'll be nice, for now at least. All it'll take is one question and you'll suddenly be a rattlesnake poked by a stick.

"I'm still working on my story," Nick said. "It's been a terrific experience professionally and spiritually."

Carl relaxed and sat. "I'm glad to hear that. Your story will be excellent publicity for the project, and I am hopeful it will help increase donations to the Patronato. We're already collecting money for 1994. It takes about a hundred thousand dollars a year."

Nick nodded. He didn't need to make a note of what Carl just said. He'd heard it before on more than one occasion. "As you know, the conservators and I will be out of here in about a week. I'm trying to tie up a few loose ends." *Keep it loose, Nick. Save the tough questions for later. Reel the guy in a little more like a car salesman would.*

"When I visited the mission yesterday and didn't see you there, I figured you were someplace working on your story," Carl said. "Are you happy with how your article is coming along?"

"Yes."

The phone atop Carl's desk buzzed.

Carl said nothing when he picked it up. He listened for several seconds. "Tell him I'll call him back in a few minutes," he said impatiently. "If he needs to talk to someone else, give him to Roy. And please hold my calls right now. It shouldn't be too long."

As Carl spoke, Nick looked at the built-in bookcases that swallowed the wall behind the desk. Like everything else in the office, they were made of rich, dark walnut. There weren't many books, but there were plaques and mementos, including a white plaster replica of San Xavier.

Someone must have dusted. Dust from the desert always presented a problem in Tucson. It settled on everything. Not at the Corona Superstore, however, where workers probably erased dust as quickly as a blemish on a new car. The shelves on Carl's bookcases and everything on them were immaculate, in perfect place, like a still-life painting, or a museum.

Pictures of his family, Nick assumed, as he looked at a brightly dressed blonde and three girls. Carl had never talked about a family or a wife, although he wore a gold band on his left hand.

The white walls jutting from each end of the bookcases were covered with dramatic paintings of Old West cowboys and their horses. Carl's office and the hallway leading to it housed a gallery of spectacular and valuable art.

"Sorry, Nick," Carl smiled. "We won't be bothered again. Now, how can I help you?"

"Thanks for agreeing to see me," Nick said as he looked into Carl's creamy brown eyes to search for an emotion. They revealed nothing. "I wanted to talk to you away from San Xavier. I'm never sure who is listening in when I talk to you there."

"Sounds ominous," Carl said, leaning back in his high-top tan leather office chair and lifting his cowboy boots onto his desk. His black Wranglers inched up his leg enough to reveal the finely tooled leather on the upper part of gray snake-skin boots. "What could I tell you here that I cannot tell you at the mission?"

"I just wanted to ask you a few more questions about Father John."

"Father John?" Carl's words and mood turned cold. The rattlesnake began to coil.

"Yes, I'm doing some research on his life before San Xavier, and I was hoping perhaps you could help me out."

The lines on Carl's forehead curved into small ravines. "And this has something to do with your story about the art conservation project inside the church?"

"My art story obviously has entered some new territory in the wake of all that's happened at San Xavier in the last couple of months. While doing my research, I uncovered some unusual things. And you're the resident expert on San Xavier."

Carl liked the compliment, but remained guarded, tense. "Go ahead, ask your questions," he said.

Nick hesitated. Carl might tell him to go to hell and throw him out of the dealership. In his career, Nick had been told "no" many times and in many different ways by a wide array of people. He didn't like it, but he was used to it, even expected it. He knew the rattlesnake would strike quickly, at any second. He couldn't turn back now.

"You told me once that you and Father John had gone to Spain to do some research on San Xavier."

"Yes."

"How long were you there?"

"I was there about two weeks. Father John had already been in Europe for a month when I met him in Spain."

"Had he spent the entire time in Spain?"

Carl chuckled. "Oh, heavens no. He deserved a rest, and he spent time traveling throughout Europe."

"Throughout Europe?" Nick repeated.

"Yes, why?"

"Just wondering," Nick said while scribbling a few words in his notebook.

The car dealer stood up like he'd forgotten to turn off a light, then he sat down rigidly. "Why are you asking these questions?"

Nick changed the subject. "By any chance, did you ever take a look in Father John's computer files, the ones in his computer at home?"

"Of course not." Carl lied, and Nick could tell it. The car dealer wouldn't look the journalist in the eyes. He nervously rolled up the sleeves on his denim shirt and asked, "What would I be doing looking at his computer files?"

"I looked at them the day I searched his home," Nick admitted. "I turned on his computer and read quite a revealing piece about a priest crazy in love with a young and beautiful woman. She didn't know he was a priest when he met her."

"For Christ sakes," Carl yelled. "That's his story."

"Is that an admission that you *have* seen his computer files?"

"Father John had told me he was writing a pretty wild story," Carl said. "He liked to write short stories during his off time. He wanted to write fiction. There's nothing wrong with that."

Nick looked at the floor. *Carpeting in here, tile in the superstore. What the hell do I say next? How much can I get out of this jerk?* He raised his head and looked into Carl's eyes. "OK, let's just say it was fiction, but how can you explain the condoms I found in Father John's quarters?"

Carl's face crimsoned. "You found condoms?" he asked sheepishly.

" 'fraid so. In his medicine cabinet inside a can of Band-Aids."

Carl's eyes revealed his fear. Now he became a child searching frantically for a missing cigarette just before his mother got home. Nick guessed he was asking himself how he could have possibly missed the Band-Aid can and its damaging contents.

"Why don't you level with me, Carl?" Nick implored. "We both know you're protecting Father John. My story will deal only with the conservation project, but I'm also trying to help solve Father John's murder. I don't believe that Jimmy Longfellow did it, and your protection of Father John could be helping a vicious killer remain free."

Carl rubbed his eyes. "Father John had an affair while he was in Europe," he said. His voice cracked. "I knew about it because he needed to confide in someone. But I swear to you, I have no idea who the woman was. It was a woman he met in Europe. He didn't dress like a priest there. No one knew who he was. It would've been easy for him to meet someone while he was over there. He was a good-looking man and an excellent conversationalist. And always approachable."

"You're sure you have no idea who she was?"

"I told you the truth."

Nick believed him but kept pushing. "Why do you think there were condoms in his home here?"

"Maybe he brought them back with him. No, that would be ridiculous. I don't know why or even think he'd carry them back to Tucson. He certainly didn't tell me about them."

"Could the woman be one of the Europeans working on the conservation project here? Maybe she followed him here."

Carl shook his head. "How could it be? I'm telling you he had the affair in Europe, long before the conservators came to Tucson. I'm sure it had to be a woman he met by chance. She could have been a tourist or a local."

"Carl, when you and Father John were in Spain searching through the records on San Xavier, who found the journal of Hernando Díaz?"

"I did, and then I showed it to Father John."

"What was his response?"

"Same as mine. For years we all heard the legends of a cache of gold being stored inside the mission. Something like that wasn't unusual in the early days of the Spanish missions. The gold came from Mexico. If anything, Díaz only confirmed what many of us believed. And Díaz said nothing about where the gold was hidden."

"Was there ever any indication that Father John was looking for the gold in San Xavier, or that he'd gone to Spain specifically to try to find some information on gold being stashed in the church?"

"Of course not. Like I said, I found the Díaz reference, and quite accidentally. We'd been searching through documents for days. I enjoyed reading the journal, so I kept at it. I understand most of the language. There was no compelling reason to read it other than I felt connected to someone who'd actually been here. I wasn't looking for any secret about gold."

Carl stood to look at the painting on his wall by an artist named Cox. A cowboy and his dog rested under a tree next to a stream while the cowboy's horse drank water. Red and golden leaves glistened in the autumn scene.

"Why would a priest be looking for gold anyway?" Carl asked, his eyes focused on the painting. "His life was simple and dedicated to his religion and other people. He had no need or want for riches."

"How 'bout you, Carl?"

That did it. The rattlesnake struck. Carl didn't need to say anything to signal an end to the interview. "I have a staff meeting," he said, offering Nick his hand without enthusiasm. "I've told you as much as I know."

"One other quick question, Carl. I'd like to know the name of the maid who found Father John's body?"

"Maria Gomez, but didn't you get that from the sheriff's department?"

"Do you know how I can get in touch with her?"

"She doesn't have a phone, and I'm sure she's not interested in talking to a reporter. At this point, I'm through, too."

Nick stood, asking, "How would I find Maria Gomez?"

"She starts back to work tomorrow. She'll be getting the quarters ready for the arrival of the new priest three days from now."

"And his name?"

"Father William McGraw."

Chapter 27

Rosa paused for a moment on the scaffolding and rubbed the small face of St. Elizabeth of Hungary, a robed statue built into a crevice in the wall thirty feet above the floor. The smile on Rosa's face revealed her excitement over seeing Nick later in the day. They planned to go out to dinner and a movie.

Suddenly, Rosa felt Ali's icy stare as he moved up the scaffolding next to her.

"These people are uneducated slobs," he grumbled. Despite the winter coolness inside the church, beads of sweat dripped slowly from his sideburns. "I'm working my ass off trying to teach these Indians how to handle the art, but they don't give a damn about it."

Rosa sighed. Ali always had something to gripe about. She refused to let him grind her down.

She slowly moved her hands to the uncleaned wooden staff in one of St. Elizabeth's outstretched hands. It was coated with what felt like hardened grease. She turned and said calmly, "What is all the commotion about now?"

"They promised me that they'd carry on our work and would care for the art the way we do. But I watch them and they don't take their time. The fat one, Arwood Burnett, is the worst. I watched him a little while ago while he worked on one of the corner paintings. A small flake of paint dropped from it. The paint's so brittle that pieces of it are falling away. Instead of picking up the flake and gluing it back on, he ignored it and covered the spot with dirty water."

"Why don't you just remind him of the proper procedure again? Remember, the Tohono O'odhams are our students."

"Not that fool," Ali complained. "His brain is like his name, made out of wood. What the hell kind of name is Our-wood, anyway?"

The question irritated Rosa, but she ignored it. She didn't want to argue with Ali. Better to just let him have his say. Then maybe he'll go away. "Are you getting along any better with Billy Harrison?" she asked.

"He's another savage to me," Ali said coldly. "A little better than Arwood, but he acts like he's using a machete rather than an X-acto knife. I have no idea how in the hell these people are going to take care of this art once we leave."

Disgusted with his incessant complaining and crudeness, she said, "It's their church, dammit." Her eyes became prism narrow, severe, like a hawk descending on its prey. He'd pushed her too far. "There's nothing we can do after we're gone. Just show them and hope they'll continue. Now quit complaining and go back to work."

"They'll screw it up," the Turk said, ready to fight instead of listen.

"Maybe it won't be the workers who screw it up. Over the years San Xavier's faithful will ruin it. I'm still arguing with Carl over the candles. He doesn't seem to understand the damage that their soot does to the art."

Ali lowered his voice. "He's a Mexican who has suddenly become the king of San Xavier. I don't like the way he's been hanging around and watching us."

Carl bothered Rosa, too, but she needed to defend him this time. "Carl is head of the Patronato San Xavier. His group is paying our salaries, so we need to pay attention to him. He's also the church spokesman until the new priest arrives. And your comments about Mexicans aren't appreciated."

"I don't like the way he butts in."

"Enough, Ali." Now she began to scold him. "Carl's not butting in. His group works for ten months to bring in a team for two months. I'd hate to have to spend so much time begging for donations. And if I did, I'd keep my eye on the work, too. He's had a lifelong affair with San Xavier, and you've been here less than two months. He wants to preserve it as bad as you or I, just not in the same way. It's really none of your business."

"Your love affair isn't my business, either, but maybe it has made you too busy to care about what goes on with your work. Where is your boyfriend today?"

What an idiot, Rosa thought. For a split second she thought about slugging him right in his hateful mouth, slamming him to the floor.

"Ali, go back to work," she snapped. "Nick is working on his project today, just like you should be doing. Until you're put in charge, you're working on my team, and I'm telling you to get back to work."

Ali said nothing. He turned casually and walked down a level of scaffolding, muttering something under his breath. Rosa knew he didn't care what she said, and that made her even angrier.

She needed to take a break. She climbed down the scaffolding and started to walk outside the church for a breather.

"*Ciao, come va?*" Francesca Vitucci asked.

Rosa smiled at the gentle voice, turned, and said, "*Bene, grazie.*"

"I could hear Ali," Francesca said in Italian. "He has no patience with other people, particularly those who don't know as much about his craft as he does. I've enjoyed working with the Indians. Since Jimmy's death, I've gotten closer to Arwood and Billy."

"You've done wonderful work down here at floor level," Rosa said. She touched Francesca's arm maternally.

Francesca's face brightened. "With the help of the Indians, I've cleaned all of the checkered pattern along the base of the walls of the nave. The frescoed pattern of blocks was almost rubbed away by generations of shoulders, but we've brought much of it back. It's the same pattern that was found on the ruined walls of Pompeii."

Rosa looked wistfully at the walls around her. "There is so much beauty in here. Too bad there's also been great sadness."

"It's good that we'll be returning home soon," Francesca admitted. "I think we all need a break. I am anxious to get home to Stefania."

Rosa nodded and walked out into the courtyard in front of the church. She closed her eyes tightly and leaned her head back to absorb the desert sunshine. Its warmth seeped through her V-neck T-shirt and jeans and into her pores. She began to relax. She thought of Nick and this evening's date.

"What's going on between you and Ali?" the English conservator Elizabeth Smythe asked quietly as she walked out of the church and toward Rosa.

"Who knows?" Rosa shrugged. "Ali was just being himself. He lives his own life and is angry at the world."

"He sure doesn't like me, although I've tried to be his friend," Elizabeth said as though she were telling Rosa a secret. "What's with him? He doesn't consider me a valuable part of this team?"

"He doesn't consider anyone a valuable part of the team except himself. He has a problem with all other conservators, particularly those of us who happen to be women."

"Chauvinist swine," Elizabeth muttered, her face flushed with anger. "He is a coarse man whose charm would work only on whores. He believes that men control, men command, and women should stay at home. If they do work they should have no-brain jobs and never wear trousers."

Rosa turned to walk back into the church. She thought the conversation with Elizabeth had ended. She raised her hand to rub her tight neck.

"Where's Nick today?" Elizabeth asked.

"He's at his apartment working on his story. He wants to have it pretty well done before he returns to New York."

"Isn't he also doing some investigating on his own?"

Rosa turned and looked in Elizabeth's gumball-blue eyes and felt a chill. She'd never spoken much about Nick's investigative work and she wondered how much Elizabeth knew. "I'm not sure what he's doing besides the story," Rosa said. "I just look forward to the time we have together."

"I would like to make a trip to Mount Graham in southeastern Arizona to see the Vatican's telescope. Maybe you and Nick would like to go along," Elizabeth said after a pause.

"That would be nice. I'm sure Nick would enjoy it, too. But when can we go? We don't have much time left in Tucson."

"No, we don't, but I'd like to set something up. I was thinking of inviting the others, but I don't know about it now. Ali is such a pig, and Francesca isn't interested in going anywhere else."

"We haven't seen much of Arizona since we've been here," Rosa said. "I'd like to see more of it."

"I've seen as much as I want to," Elizabeth said sarcastically, surprising Rosa.

"Then why do you want to go see more desert, another mountain, and a telescope?"

Elizabeth moved her lips but didn't say anything while she searched for her next sentence. "Oh, I'm interested in that. I just don't want to spend any more time trying to get to know any of the people in this state or doing any of the tourist things."

"We'll go with you to Mount Graham. Just let us know when."

"We can go in Nick's car, perhaps."

"I'm sure he wouldn't mind loaning it out again," Rosa said.

"Yes," Elizabeth said. Her white cheeks blushed.

An hour later, Rosa climbed aboard a city bus and headed home. She wanted to forget her conversation with Elizabeth and concentrate on her upcoming evening. It seemed odd to her that the Englishwoman would get embarrassed over using Nick's car. It had been done before, even without him knowing. She knew he wouldn't care. She usually rode with him back and forth to the mission, but on the days that he worked at home she took the bus or he picked her up. He often left the car keys in her apartment.

She saw Nick walking toward her place at the same time she crossed the parking lot. He whistled at her as soon as he saw her. She smiled and threw him a kiss.

They embraced near her front door.

"Hungry?" he asked.

"Starving."

"Good. We're going to try an old Italian place in downtown Tucson called Caruso's. I hear it's been there a long time, and that the food's terrific. It's an old house on Fourth Avenue."

"I'm sure we'll love it."

On the way, Nick asked Rosa about her day.

"OK, but I had the usual problems with Ali. Elizabeth asked if we'd like to go to Mount Graham with her, and I said yes."

Nick shook his head in agreement without saying anything.

"I still don't know if I'll come back to San Xavier next year."

"Why not? You're the best."

"I'm not sure I'll be asked. Carl did tell me at the outset that he'd like me to lead the team of conservators each year until the job is completed, but he hasn't said anything recently."

"He probably will."

"I'm not so sure. Maybe our argument over the candles soured him. Perhaps he'll look for someone new. There are other good conservators in Europe. He might want to put Ali in charge."

"You're beating yourself up, Rosa. There's no need to feel insecure. You've done a hell of a job. Anyone who looks inside the mission realizes that."

"I know in my heart that any reputable conservator would agree with me that burning candles will only hasten the deterioration of San Xavier's art. No one wants the church turned into a museum with the sole purpose of preserving it for future generations, but certainly it is possible to run the place without destroying it. I suggested that the church use a new glass-enclosed smokeless candle, but Carl is against it. Nothing will make him budge. The most I can get out of him is a promise to discuss the problem with the new Franciscan priest."

"Hey, I'm on your side. No need to convince me."

"You're right, of course. I don't know why I worry so much about the church. I was hired to do a job, which I'm doing as skillfully and professionally as I can. We're not being paid to maintain the church for future generations. Besides, there is plenty of work available in Europe."

"Now you're talking. We can live quite well without ever coming back to Arizona."

They looked at each other in silence, and smiled.

"You're my salvation," she said finally, reaching out and touching his arm.

"You just like me for one thing," he said, smiling and touching the inside of his leg.

"Stop it, Nick. You know you're much more than just a lover. Well, you are good at that, but you've touched my soul. I want to show you Europe."

"I'm ready, believe me. Never been there. Never done that. It's about time I see the hometown of my ancestors."

"Please stay safe until we get there. I worry about you all the time."

"Don't worry about me, Rosa. Nothing will stop me from getting the hell out of here and going with you."

"Promise me?"

"I promise."

Chapter 28

"I wonder why Carl asked so many government and church officials to attend but so few Tohono O'odhams," Nick whispered as he slid over to the refreshments table and Rosa. She'd just eaten a chocolate chip cookie and was washing it down with black coffee. She much preferred espresso, but it wasn't on the menu at the reception for Father William McGraw in the east chapel of San Xavier two mornings after his arrival.

"Only a reporter would notice," she replied. "You should be happy to be invited yourself."

"Come on. This church belongs to the Indians. Why are only a handful here?"

"It's Carl's dog and horse show. He didn't even have to invite me or my colleagues."

He touched her arm. "Honey, you mean dog and pony show."

"Sorry, *mio amore*. I knew it was something like that. Anyway, Carl told me tribal leaders are meeting with him and the priest later today. They'll have the church all to themselves."

"Bring 'em in alone and don't mix 'em with the elite, right?"

"Can't you stop working for awhile and just enjoy the art like everyone else? Many of them haven't seen this chapel since we finished it."

"I'll do anything for you. Anything you'd like from me right now? I have some ideas."

Rosa said nothing, but her wide grin and blushed face revealed her thoughts.

As so often happened inside the mission, necks craned and bent toward the ceilings. Mouths opened slightly in awe.

Nick and Rosa watched Carl patiently guide the new priest through the chapel, calling everyone by first name as he made introductions. The car dealer felt at ease and wore his San Xavier pride on his face.

Always the salesman, Nick thought, but he decided not to say anything to Rosa.

The new priest grinned constantly. In his brown habit and rope belt, he appeared as a humble friar who emerged from the Middle Ages. He seemed comfortable chatting with the politicos and business bigwigs who shook his hand. *He's good at small talk*, Nick thought. *Not me. I can talk at length with friends or sources, but not with strangers in a social setting like this. My writing does my talking for me. I'd much rather be alone with Rosa right now.* He looked over at her, and their eyes met. *I'd better get back to work and quit staring at her.*

Nick jotted down some notes about the priest. He guessed the friar was in his mid to late fifties. He had thinning gray hair with a bald spot on the top of his head. Veins ran like blue tributaries on his hands. His white skin meant he didn't spend much time outdoors. His girth required two yards of rope. He wore half-moon glasses, and his greenish eyes always extended upward, like a professor peering from his desk in a tiered lecture hall. Not a tall or short man, the priest in sandals stood perhaps five-foot-five. He laughed quickly and deeply.

Father McGraw fit cozily inside the church and among the sacred icons surrounding him. When he stood under the statue of Mary, Sorrowing Mother, it appeared that his robe flowed into hers.

The priest talked so much that tiny globs of white formed along the corners of his lips. Nick noted them as a distraction, at least to him, and he hoped the man would drink some of the free coffee or orange juice and wash them away.

"What do you think?" Nick asked Rosa. She wore a white lace dress and black sandals with straps, not her usual work garb. He'd seen her put the dress on earlier in the morning and commented that inside San Xavier she'd look angelic. He was right.

"He seems nice. He's gentle with people," Rosa said. "He and I are meeting privately tomorrow to discuss the project. Then we'll meet with the entire team. I'm sure after that I'll be a much better judge of his character. Carl has probably filled him in already and told him I'm an idiot and should never be invited back. The way Carl talks, he may have the priest convinced that he single-handedly raised the money for the church and did all the work himself. I hope the friar gets a good look at the walls we haven't done yet and sees what candle soot damage. Have you met him yet?"

"No, I was waiting for the crowds around him to thin a little."

They stood closely. He rubbed his hand on the small of her back and started sliding it down. She turned so that he had to quit, but her broad smile belied her protest.

"He sure has soft hands," she said.

"You talking about me?"

"Come on, Nick. I'm talking about the priest. He has never done hard labor. When he shook my hand, there was nothing there. I felt like I was grabbing the hand of a princess to kiss it."

"I've got a hand you can kiss."

"Nick! We're not in bed. We're at work."

"Complications, complications. There're always complications." Nick put his hands in his pockets. "I need to mingle. I think I'll go tell him to wipe the corner of his lips. The white stuff is driving me crazy."

Rosa beamed as her lover moved away from the table and into the crowd closer to Carl and San Xavier's new priest.

"Let me introduce you to Father William McGraw," Carl said before Nick stepped close enough to shake hands.

The priest offered his limp hand. "Father Bill, please. I'm delighted to meet you."

Carl interrupted before Nick could speak. "Nick is here doing a story on the conservation project for *Smithsonian* magazine. His story should help us greatly in our fund-raising effort for next year."

"Oh, how nice," Father Bill responded. "It's such a wonderful magazine. I read it often, and am thrilled that such a prestigious publication has chosen to do a story on our mission tucked away in the Southwest. You must be a talented writer to be doing an article for *Smithsonian*."

"Thank you. I understand you came here from Oakland."

"Yes, I've been there for the last five years. I'd been all over the world before returning to my native California. It's nice to be in the desert, though. Arthritis has bothered me in recent years, and I think this will be a good move for me. How about you, Nick?"

Impressive. He remembered my name. "I'm here from New York via St. Louis," Nick said. "I'm a former newspaper reporter who turned free-lancer several years ago. I'm afraid I'm not as well traveled as you."

"You still have plenty of time in your life to do that, my boy." Father Bill gently touched Nick's forearm. "Your name is Italian, isn't it? Are you Catholic?"

"My ancestors came from Italy, and yes, my family is Catholic. I'm afraid I haven't been good at maintaining their faith for myself, however."

"There's time for that, too, my boy. Perhaps you'd like to come see me for confession." The priest winked. He wasn't looking for a response. The white globs in the corner of his lips were growing. "Are you coming to the celebration of my first Mass on Sunday?" he asked. "It'll be a grand event."

"I think so. Two of the conservators and I are going to southeastern Arizona on Saturday to view the telescope being built by the Vatican and the UofA, but we'll be back for Sunday's Mass."

"Ahhhh, the telescope. Isn't there a problem with it destroying the habitat of the endangered red squirrels on the mountain? Mount Graham, right? I believe the Apache Indians also claim that the mountain is sacred and shouldn't be touched."

"I see you're well versed in the politics."

"I've read about it. The University of Arizona is in front of the project, but the Vatican's Arcetri Observatory is one of the original partners. In fact, you're writing for *Smithsonian*. Did you know that the Smithsonian Institution also was one of the original partners, but it withdrew from the Mount Graham project because it believed Hawaii's Mauna Kea site was a better location?"

"I didn't know that. I . . ."

Nick couldn't complete the sentence. Carl grabbed Father Bill by the arm and guided him to an elderly man and woman sipping coffee. Nick frowned at Carl, the man with the deal, the man with the power. He wondered how much Carl enjoyed breaking up his conversation with Father Bill.

"Hello," came a morning raspy voice from behind him. It smelled like coffee. He turned.

Elizabeth Smythe's bright eyes welcomed his glance. "Isn't he a jolly man?" she said, standing close enough to Nick so that the tip of her right breast rubbed against his arm.

"I suppose so," he responded, moving away from her. "I didn't have much of a chance to talk to him."

"Ali sure hung onto him awhile," Elizabeth said angrily, her brightness fading. "He talked to the new priest just like they were old friends. I barely had two seconds of time with him."

"Maybe they've met before. Ali has worked in a lot of churches during his career."

"I don't know how people can stand the Turk. He's never pleasant, and like my father, impossible to please. I have no idea what I've done to make him so sour toward me."

"Why worry about him? You're working for Rosa, not Ali."

"True enough, but I've tried to be his friend. There's no need for Ali to be so cruel. I guess once a commando, always a commando."

"Commando?" Even though the word left his mouth when he asked the question, he said it again to himself. *Commando?*

"Quite right," Elizabeth said. "Didn't you know? Ali was Mister Big Commando when he was in the Turkish military. Strange move from guerrilla warfare to the absolutely gentle world of art conservation, huh?"

Nick looked over to the corner where Ali stood talking to a bearded man in a business suit. The east chapel's grand recessed cross overlooked them. The conservators had brought its gilding and beauty back to life, and it towered colorfully above the people in the crowd.

Turning back to Elizabeth, he asked, "How long was Ali in the military?" He searched for the right question but knew he hadn't found it yet.

"Long enough to make it to the rank of captain. He was a leader of men. Can you believe it?"

"What about you, Elizabeth? You a commando?"

His abrupt question surprised Elizabeth but she didn't show it. "I can take care of myself, if that's what you mean," she said, still smiling. "No man is going to bully me."

"I know Ali doesn't like you."

"Thinks I'm a kid. If he only knew."

She turned to look at the crowd.

Nick didn't want the conversation to end. "Why did you want to come to San Xavier? I heard that you maneuvered to get here."

"Maneuvered? Where would you get that? Worldwide, people in the business know San Xavier as a wonderful opportunity for someone at my level. I was happy to get it."

"Did you have any help?"

"In what way?"

"Did you know anyone here who could help get you on board, like Father John?"

Nick could tell his question angered her. Her lips quivered a bit and her cheeks flushed, but the fake smile remained firmly set on her face. She could handle anything he threw at her, dammit.

"Come, come, Nicky. I like men, not priests." She moved closer to him and whispered, "Too bad you're not available. Why don't we get together before you leave Tucson and have some fun?"

He took a step backward. "You're right. I'm not available. You should have no trouble finding a companion."

"I manage to get out. I know how to handle men, believe me."

"I'm sure you do. I'll bet you like being treated like a goddess."

"What's wrong with that, love? I like it when a man thinks I'm his goddess."

"Where will you go when you leave here?"

"My experience at San Xavier should help me land jobs wherever I want, but I'm thinking of taking some time off for an extended holiday. Tucson has been tough on us."

"Where will you go? Europe?"

"I hope so."

"Being from England, you probably are most comfortable in Europe. I'll bet you've traveled over there."

"Indeed."

"Your family is there."

"Me mum is in England. There is no other family for me."

"Is your father dead?"

"I wish. I have no idea where he is, nor do I care. As I said, he's like Ali, a horrible man. I haven't seen him in years."

"Brothers? Sisters?"

The smile faded. Her eyes narrowed and turned steel cold. "Look, Nick, there is no such thing as family. People are friends or they are enemies. Blood relations mean nothing. A family member will break your heart faster than anyone else."

"You had a rough childhood?"

"My childhood is none of your business. I've told you too much already. I'm off to join the others."

She puckered her bright red lips, making the mole above them twitch. As she flitted away, she said, "Let me know if you'd like to get together."

Nick needed fresh air. He looked toward Rosa as he reached the door but two women he'd never seen before had her cornered and fired questions at her quicker than she could answer. Walking into the sweet morning brightness, he pushed on his sunglasses. He pulled out his notepad and flipped a few pages before jotting down some information. "I know I'm getting closer," he wrote.

Chapter 29

Nick wanted to interview Maria Gomez, the cleaning lady who discovered Father John's body. He'd tried before the new priest arrived at San Xavier, but Maria was better protected than a high ranking bureaucrat shielded by secretaries and public relations people. The women working in the church office wouldn't let Nick get near her.

At first, he went into the office and told the Tohono O'odham woman behind the front desk that he'd like to talk to Maria.

The clerk had a cheerful face and seemed eager to please. "I can see if Maria is available," she said. "Your name?"

"Nick Genoa."

The clerk mouthed the name and then disappeared into a back room for a couple of minutes. He heard whispering.

When she returned, the clerk, looking at the ground, said, "Maria doesn't want to talk to you."

Nick didn't know why his name had become poison around the mission, but he blamed Corona.

He needed another avenue. A reporter often did. He knew the first *no* never meant much.

The day after the reception for Father Bill, Nick sat in his rental car late in the afternoon and waited for Maria to finish working for the day. He felt confident that he could talk her into an interview if he could catch her alone, away from her protectors.

He also wanted to question Ben Johnson, the reservation police officer who witnessed the interrogation of Jimmy Longfellow. Johnson would be next.

Nick had read the police reports on the half dozen interviews that officers conducted with Maria after Father John's murder. He sought something more, a small thread that perhaps could aid his investigation. She had found the body. Maybe, just maybe, she forgot to tell the cops something. He believed he knew the right questions to ask.

As he sat, Nick thought about how the days had gotten longer during the time he'd been in Tucson. When he arrived in early February, he awoke and went home in chilly darkness. Now, in late March, the sun was still bright at five in the afternoon, bleaching San Xavier's white plaster exterior as though it were a cow's skull in the desert.

Nick hadn't previously met Maria, but Rosa described her as a short, slender woman with close-cropped black hair that had grayed. She wore large glasses on a thin, plain face. She didn't wear makeup to cover brown, unwrinkled skin. She walked quickly, but with a slight limp. Rosa also said that Maria didn't drive. A young man, probably her son, picked her up each day a little past five.

Nick occupied his time by reading a brochure handed out to visitors to San Xavier.

> *Masses:*
>> *Daily: 8:30 A.M.*
>> *Sundays: 8:30-10:30 A.M.*
> *Historical Lectures (20 min. ea.)*
>> *Every day (except Sunday) hourly from*
>> *9:30 A.M. to 4:30 P.M.*
> *No admission fee; free will donations accepted.*

The brochure also contained some information that he didn't know. Inside the church, the lion images on each side of the communion rail represented the Lions of Castille to honor the reigning family in Spain during the 1780s and '90s. The building to the west of the church had been named the mortuary chapel because under its floor were the remains of two pioneer missionaries of the area. A replica of the grotto in Lourdes, France, had been built on the hill east of San Xavier.

At 5:02 a battered yellow Chevrolet pickup pulled up in front of the church and parked down from the entrance, closer to the Indian school west of the mortuary chapel. A young man with shoulder-length black hair sat inside the truck. His eyes stared straight ahead, into the late afternoon sunlight. His only movement came from his fingers keeping beat on his steering wheel to a rap song on the radio. The windows were down, and his forearm hung out, swinging like a fishing pole.

Nick walked toward the truck at the same time that the woman with the limp walked from the courtyard of San Xavier.

"Maria Gomez?" he asked gently as he walked toward her. He was still about five yards away from her, but he wanted to get her attention before she reached the truck.

"Yes." She appeared worried that a strange man somehow knew her name.

"My name is Nick Genoa. I'm a writer working on a story on San Xavier Mission, and I was hoping that I could ask you a couple of questions."

"Me?"

"Yes, I know that you've worked here for years and you knew Father John."

The suspicious and painful look on her face drew the young man from the truck.

"What do you want?" he bristled as he stepped between Nick and Maria. He didn't bother to shut the truck's door. The radio blasted more rap music. The thin, tall Indian wore Wranglers, ropers, and a tight black tank top that revealed a strong chest and muscular arms. He wasn't a man to fool with.

Before Nick could answer, the woman said, "*Am owa s-ap'e, Tim. Heg o ge o'ohondam uvikwad.*" She turned back to him and said, "I told my son it's OK, you're a writer. What did you say your name was?"

"Nick Genoa."

She hadn't heard the name before. The woman in the church office had lied when she said Maria didn't want to talk to him.

"There's nothing I can tell you," Maria said. "I've already told the police everything I know. I've just come back to work, and it hasn't been easy."

"Yes, I know, Mrs. Gomez, but. . ."

He was unable to finish his sentence before her son grabbed her arm and led her to the back of the truck. He whispered something to her before she walked back to Nick.

"My son Tim is a carpenter who works construction throughout Tucson," she said. "He is a craftsman who has made his family and people proud. We all listen to what he says. He told me that perhaps if I talk to you it will relieve some of my pain and help take away my tears. It's been hard for me to get this thing out of my mind."

Tim looked at Nick and nodded. His round, thin unfriendly face signaled that he would grant an interview on behalf of his mother. Nick also could tell that Tim had no interest in meeting or getting to know a writer from New York.

"Do you have a car?" Tim asked.

"Yes, I'm parked right over there." Nick pointed to the parking lot south of San Xavier, which was dusty from the tourists' cars pulling out for the day. The yawning sky preparing to swallow the ball of sun to the west somehow told white folks that time had come to leave Indian land for another day.

"Why don't you follow us to my mother's home? It's not far from here."

As instructed, Nick followed the pickup into the desert foothills. The truck belched dust, never slowing for the growing number of barking dogs in the roadway. It merely swerved to avoid hitting them. Tim's arm continued to dangle from the open window of his truck.

Maria Gomez' small frame home on a dirt road was tidy and uncluttered. Throw rugs covered its concrete floors. Small golden-framed photos of children covered the top of a twenty-five-inch console television, certainly the most expensive thing in the small living room. *Maria's grandchildren*, Nick thought.

He felt comfortable as he sat on the three-cushion couch. Her son sat in the gray recliner next to the couch, watching Nick carefully but not speaking. Tim's eyes shifted from Nick to his mother.

"Would you like a cold so-ta?" she asked as she stood next to a small table near the front door. On the table and the wall above it were at least two dozen more framed pictures of family members from childhood to adulthood.

He declined. She walked into the kitchen, which branched from the living room, and returned with a glass of cream soda. She sat on the opposite end of the couch, looking refreshed instead of tired from her full day of work. Sitting on the edge of the cushion, her knees together and facing Nick, Maria in her white uniform could have been posing for a store catalog.

"How long have you worked at San Xavier?" Nick started. He wanted to establish as much rapport with her as possible before he started asking the questions that could bring back painful memories.

"More than ten years now. I worked for the priest before Father John and then him. Now I'm working for Father Bill. I am fifty-six years old and would like to work for the priests until I retire. Six or nine more years. I'm not sure if I'll quit at sixty-two or sixty-five. I'll get Social Security then. My children are grown and no longer live here, but my grandchildren visit often. When I retire, I will spend my time with them."

Nick could see the pride in her face. "Father John must've been a very special person," he said.

"A wonderful person. I never seen a priest more dedicated to the people than himself. He spent his life working for the church. Everyone loved him.

That's what made his passing so hard for all of us. We lost a man dear to our hearts." Maria crossed herself.

The interview went for about a half hour before Nick asked, "Would you like to talk some about how you felt when you found him?"

She grimaced. "I wondered when you would ask me."

"I have to."

"You're a nice man. You don't push hard like the police."

"I know you've talked to them many times."

"I told them over and over. There's no more to tell. I didn't even realize he was dead when I saw him on the floor."

She said it so quietly Nick wasn't sure he understood her. He slid over slowly on the couch, moving closer to her so he could hear her better.

Her head sank. "I walked into the kitchen and thought he was asleep on the floor. I don't remember much after that except that I started screaming in Spanish that he was dead. I don't speak much Spanish no more. I learned it from my father. He was Mexican. My mother was born on the reservation. My children speak Tohono O'odham but don't know much Spanish, so there's no reason for me to talk it. But for some reason I. . . . On that day, the words wouldn't come out in English."

"I know these questions are tough on you," Nick said reassuringly. *I'm surprised she isn't crying. I admire her stoicism.*

"Did Father John have a lot of guests?" he asked after a pause.

"During the day, Father John's quarters were always open. People came and went because they knew if they couldn't find him in the church or office, he would be at home. He never minded if people visited, even while he ate lunch. He was laid back and never raised his voice. He welcomed people with open arms. He'd invite his visitors to have lunch with him, even Indians. He loved everyone. He was like the friars who came here long ago. He wanted to be here."

"Did the conservators working inside the church visit him?"

"Sure," Maria said as though the question was silly.

"Any in particular?"

"All the Europeans visited. Father enjoyed talking to all of them, but he had trouble with the one that doesn't know English too good. Francesca something is her name. Even the three Indian boys working with them would visit Father, but the woman in charge, Rosa Zizzo, seemed to be there the most."

"Did he have a good relationship with Miss Zizzo?"

"They spent hours talking."

"What about Jimmy Longfellow?"

"Everyone liked Jimmy, including Father. They were friends. You ask anyone on this reservation, and they don't know how Jimmy could have done such a thing. He was a wino at times and had trouble with the law, but he was putting his life back together. If he was the one who did this, then he brought great shame to all of us."

"Do you have doubts Jimmy did it? The police think they got their man."

Maria said nothing, but Nick could tell by the movements of her face that she didn't like non-Indian police.

"Did Father John ever have guests in the evening?"

"I don't think so. There never was nothing messy in the mornings when I came in. He was a very neat man."

Maria scratched her head. "I just remembered something. If he did have a guest the night he was killed, the person smoked. That's it, it was the smell of cigarettes. When I first walked into Father John's quarters that day, I smelled it. It wasn't very strong, but it was definitely the smell of a smoker. I just realized it."

"The police don't know this?"

"I never thought of it until just now. I knew there was an odd smell when I walked in, but I was afraid to say anything about it because I couldn't remember what it was. You must think I'm strange, but now I know for sure. Father John didn't smoke and didn't let people smoke in his quarters. If he did that night, it must have been someone very special."

Nick glanced at Maria's son, who stood up and walked around to the back of the couch. He laid his hand gently on his mother's shoulder. "It's good that she talks now. She is remembering some things that she put far back in her mind. She gets them out, and they can no longer haunt her. The evil dreams will go away."

She held her son's hand and smiled. "Father John was loved by everyone on the reservation," she said. "It doesn't seem possible that he is gone or that an Indian killed him. Why would an Indian do that? For the gold? What would an Indian do with gold? Wherever he went, people would think he was a criminal if he had money in his pocket. Indians can't have a lot of money. White police don't want no Indian having money. That's a crime. And, unless Jimmy was crazy stoned, he wouldn't harm a priest. Maybe he didn't believe in God like we Catholics do, but he knew enough not to want to spend eternity paying for his sin."

Surprised, Nick asked, "Jimmy wasn't a Catholic?"

"He was raised one and still would go to church, especially after he started working there on the art project, but he liked the roadman, too," Maria answered.

"The roadman?"

Maria looked at her son. He shook his head and said, "*B g ñuikud i:da O'odham. Pi ic o sa'i ma:c hegai, a:cim.*"

Nick didn't understand why Tim suddenly quieted his mother. A minute ago, he wanted her to talk. "Please, Maria, I need to ask you a few more questions," he said. "I'm trying to help clear Jimmy."

Maria looked at her son and then the writer. "Tim's right. We don't know you and need to be careful. But I'll tell you about the roadman. He's the holy man of the Native American Church. Jimmy was spending more and more time with those people."

"Isn't that the church that a growing number of Navajos are joining?" Nick asked. "I heard about it last year when I was on the Navajo reservation.

Their sacrament is peyote."

"I don't know no more," Maria said, looking at her son again. His dark eyes were riveted on her.

"But you know he was a member of the Native American Church," Nick said. "Are Tohono O'odham becoming involved with it?"

"I don't know no more," Maria repeated.

"Why do you think he confessed?"

"It don't make a difference if Jimmy is guilty or not. Wherever he goes, people would stare at him and say he killed Father John. He was tired, lonely, and probably crazy from all those questions from the police. I know how the white police are. They asked me the same questions a hundred times. Over and over I had to tell them what I knew. Even though I told the truth my story probably changed. They probably thought I was lying. They don't like my people, especially young men like Jimmy who've been in trouble."

Tim walked to the door, ushering Nick out.

"Do you agree with your mother that Jimmy didn't have a chance?" he asked as he stood.

"*Pi it hebai wo sa'i hi: g Jimmy.*"

Nick looked back at Maria. "He's right," she said. "There was no way out for Jimmy."

Chapter 30

"Ben Johnson doesn't work tonight. He's at his other job at the new casino. You can find him there," the officer who greeted Nick at the reservation police headquarters said. Behind a protective sheet of glass, the Indian cop with dark, unkind eyes looked like a fish in an aquarium. He didn't smile.

The officer gave Nick instructions to Desert Diamond, one of the Indian reservation casinos that Arizona tribes won through lawsuits, mediation, and negotiations with the state. Desert Diamond was one of the largest. Its 500 slot machines drew people from throughout southern Arizona and splashed money on the Indian economy. Johnson worked there three nights a week as a security guard.

No matter how hard he tried, Nick couldn't collect his thoughts during his drive to the casino. He changed the dial on his car radio to a classical music station to try to calm himself and clear his head.

He kept coming back to Ali Bahadir, the conservator who smoked. Maria had smelled the acrid aftermath of a smoker just before she found Father John's body. The Turk had been to Spain before he came to Tucson and could've known about the possibility of stashed gold. He knew about churches and how they were supplied and used gold. Elizabeth Smythe said he was a commando in the Turkish military, which meant he had training in knife fighting. The unfriendly brute certainly would be capable of murder. Maybe he wanted to use the stolen gold to finance Turkish military activities.

Elizabeth smoked, too, at least when she drank. He remembered that she had asked for a cigarette the night they went to Sanchez's. Could Elizabeth be the goddess Father John wrote about in his fiction? Could she be capable of murder?

She hated men, but she knew how to manipulate them. She wrangled her way into the San Xavier project, perhaps knowing about the Díaz gold.

Of course the murderer didn't have to be a smoker. Nick needed more to go on than that. He also disliked Ali, which could be clouding his thought process and make the Turk so much easier to incriminate. He couldn't rule out Elizabeth. Francesca was a definite no. And Rosa? Forget it. He knew her too well. She couldn't kill anything.

Nick still didn't have enough hard evidence to take to the police. Theories weren't going to lead to an arrest. The condoms presented the biggest unsolved riddle. Who was the priest sleeping with? Could it have been Ali? The thought intrigued Nick.

The evening had cooled in the sixties. He drove with his windows down.

He found Desert Diamond easily. It wasn't far from San Xavier Mission. On the outside, the building that housed the casino looked like a large warehouse. Inside, it imitated a small, unadorned Las Vegas casino. Piped-in calliope tunes provided the music. Coins clinked into stainless steel trays. The place's smoke collided with Nick's eyes immediately.

Not that he wanted to see that much anyway, particularly the tired-looking people mechanically pulling levers on the slots. They were there to spend their hours and quarters, all of them probably thinking they could strike it rich through the luck of a pull button. One more pull. The next pull.

Cameras in the ceilings watched everyone. He walked toward the guard standing under a huge lighted sign ringed with blinking marquee lights that announced this place as Desert Diamond.

"Officer Ben Johnson?" he asked when he got close enough to the stone-faced man whose only movement came from his darting ebony eyes.

The man glanced at Nick for less than a second and nodded. He didn't speak, and he looked nothing like the movie actor or the Canadian world-class sprinter with his same name.

"My name is Nick Genoa. I'm writing a story on San Xavier Mission, and I was hoping I could ask you some questions about Father John Duvall and Jimmy Longfellow."

Johnson turned his head slowly to look at Nick. The officer had high cheekbones and skin the color and texture of parchment paper. He wasn't an old man, but the sun had made his face much older than his years.

"You from Tucson?" he asked as though that counted for something.

"No, I'm based in New York and am doing a piece for *Smithsonian* magazine. I met Jimmy while working with the European conservators inside the church, and I'm just poking around doing some work besides what the Pima County Sheriff's Department is doing."

"You're not a cop?"

" 'fraid not."

"The case belongs to the sheriff's department," Johnson said. "They have jurisdiction over the church and the land around it."

"I know that, but you were there when Jimmy was arrested and during his interrogation."

Johnson nodded again. He wasn't much of a talker. He barely moved. His right hand rested on the butt of his pistol. His eyes scoured the casino.

"Jimmy didn't kill nobody," Johnson said quietly.

"He confessed," Nick reminded the officer. "I read the transcripts of the interrogation."

"Scared," Johnson said louder, looking at Nick again. "There was no hope for Jimmy. The detectives threatened him with death by lethal injection. When they told him he had a right to a lawyer, they said it like a joke. Transcripts don't show none of that."

"They sure didn't show any wrongdoing by the officers," Nick agreed.

Johnson began a conversation as he surveyed the floor. He spoke slowly. "They had Jimmy cornered from the beginning. That's something the transcripts won't never show, neither. He was in a room with charts and photographs that showed everything about the murder. All Jimmy had to do was look at those pictures to start believing he was there when it happened. He just wanted to get it over with."

"If you believe that Jimmy was innocent and his confession coerced, why don't you do something about it?"

"The Tohono O'odham Nation is a sovereign nation. We govern ourselves and police ourselves. When something happens outside our jurisdiction, there is nothing any one of us can do except listen. The Pima County Sheriff's Department knows that. They only invited an observer because Jimmy lived on the reservation. We all knew I was not there to offer advice. My job was to be a stump, for the record, and to keep my mouth shut unless spoken to. I couldn't help Jimmy. He had to confess."

"Why didn't you go to someone and report the problems with the interrogation?"

Johnson smiled. "You still don't get it, do you? Do I look white?" He hissed the word white. "I'm an Indian. I may be a policeman, but I'm still an Indian. No one is going to believe the word of an Indian over the white cops. No one but another Indian. If you know anything about the Spanish missions, you know about the conquistadors. They took whatever they wanted, had no respect for the natives, not even the chiefs. That's how the white cops are today. No respect for the natives. I can tell my supervisors what I saw, but my department wouldn't get nowhere if we went to higher authorities. I don't want no trouble for me or my family."

Ten feet from them an elderly woman in shorts, short-sleeve sweatshirt, and sandals began screaming. Nick and Johnson looked at her machine as a stream of coins jingled into the tray. Lights flashed on the top of the machine and people began to gather around it. Johnson watched the action carefully but didn't move.

"If Jimmy didn't confess, they could've let him rot in a jail for a year while they checked out all the leads," he said. "They don't physically torture suspects, but they know all the psychology stuff. They screw with a suspect's head."

"Would you and other Indian police do the same with a white suspect?"

Johnson lifted his head and examined the writer. "Maybe. We have ways of getting even. Indians don't talk much to white folks, but we know how to take care of ourselves."

"I'll bet the Mexicans inside the jail know how to get even, too," Nick added. "You think they killed Jimmy because of long-standing hatred between Mexicans and Indians or because they thought he killed a priest?"

Johnson shrugged his shoulders and then said, "Who knows?"

Nick wished they were somewhere else. The noise and smoke of the casino, as well as the blinking lights above his head, gave him a headache. "I visited with another Tohono O'odham today who told me that Jimmy was a member of the Native American Church," he said. "Do you think he could have been hallucinating on peyote at the time and was capable of killing Father John?"

"I've known Jimmy all his life, and he was coming along OK. He was getting his life together. He and other young people on the reservation were getting into that church. But that was helping straighten him out. He was still drinking a little beer, but he wasn't no wino no more. He had problems with the law and was on probation when he was arrested this time, but his life was changing. He had a job. The Native American Church was teaching him to avoid negative thinking, not to speak bad of things."

Johnson scratched his chin, searching for what to say next. "The white man uses his church and the Bible and a preacher to be near God. Native American Church members have peyote. That's their preacher. Peyote gives Indians direct access to God. It's a healer and a guide and has great power, but it's only used in rituals."

"Did Jimmy smoke?"

Johnson didn't answer.

"Cigarettes," Nick added.

"Never."

"He did have some marijuana in his apartment. He told me that when I interviewed him after he was arrested."

Johnson nodded.

"He was in the Army and learned how to fight with a knife. His screwdriver killed Father John. You see any connection there?"

Johnson waved his head no. "That's another spot where whites and Indians differ. When white man goes into military, he's doing it for all kinds of reasons. Patriotism, maybe, or a job with meals. Maybe just to look good to the girls. When he gets out, he's nothing special. Just a guy out of work and looking for a job. For Indians, the armed forces offer steady work, something that is hard to find here. Being a soldier brings honor to an Indian, his people, and his land. He comes home a hero."

"What about the screwdriver?" Nick pressed.

"Indians aren't no good at lying or covering up something. No Indian is going to take a screwdriver and grind it down to a point. He'll use a knife or a gun. If an Indian killed Father John, he would admit it to other people in the tribe. Jimmy never did that. If you want to find the killer, look for someone who knows how to use a knife but wanted to blame an Indian. Look for a real good liar."

Chapter 31

Fog embraced the mountains surrounding Tucson. A surprise storm had drenched the desert and dumped snow on the peaks. Even though the forecast claimed sunshine by noon, Nick, Rosa, and Elizabeth departed for their seventy-mile drive to Mount Graham in near-freezing weather and grayness.

Nick drove the rental car. Rosa sat next to him. Elizabeth had the back seat to herself, reclining against one back door with her booted feet up against the other back door. She nodded in and out of sleep.

"I still think we should have postponed because of the weather," a worried Rosa said. "Or maybe left closer to the afternoon instead of mid-morning."

"We'll have no trouble," Elizabeth said, waking up from her nap and talking as if she knew.

"This is nothing compared to a New York winter," Nick said. "Quit worrying. Besides, it took too much effort to get the permits to visit the observatory site. The Forest Service closed the road to the peak because of the environmentalists who tried to block the telescope work. We're lucky we got clearance to visit when we wanted."

Each traveler wore hiking boots and a down-filled coat. Elizabeth also carried a backpack stocked with freeze-dried food and hiking gear. They'd been told to prepare for foul weather. Rain and cold on the desert floor meant snow and temperatures in the teens in the mountains.

"It seems strange that we're now in the desert, surrounded by cactus and bushes, and before long we'll be high in the mountains surrounded by aspen, spruce, and pine," Elizabeth said forty-five minutes out of Tucson. They climbed slowly as they headed east across the desert on Interstate 10.

"There aren't many places in this country where you can be swimming in the desert one hour and skiing in the mountains the next," Nick said. "In the northern half of the United States at this time of year you have to get on an airplane to get a change of weather."

Elizabeth cracked her window. "What's the peculiar smell in the desert today?" she asked.

"Greasewood," Rosa said. "It's something only the desert has. Whenever it rains, you can smell its bitterness."

Impressed, Nick asked, "How do you know about greasewood?"

"I read about it in a book. It's more accurately called creosote bush, but people in Tucson and the Tohono O'odham call it greasewood. Tohono O'odhams believe it's the first thing that grew, and from its lac, the resin it secretes, Earth Maker formed the mountains. When the lac dried, the mountains hardened. The lac is what gives the desert its distinctive smell after a rain."

Nick liked hearing her talk. He moved his right hand over and rested it on her thigh. She grabbed it and held onto it tightly, and he could tell the weather worried her.

By the time they reached the town of Willcox, the desert vegetation had changed to yucca, prickly pear, and tall grasses. Soon after, they were out of the cactus and into cedar and oak, creeping closer to the forest of tall pines. They were headed for 10,477-foot-tall Emerald Peak, one of the named landmarks on Mount Graham.

"I read that Mount Graham is in the southernmost well-developed spruce-fir forest in North America," Nick said, keeping his eyes on the road. As they aimed ever closer to the snowy mountains, he became concerned about ice. He hunched closer to the steering wheel and gripped it tightly with both hands.

Elizabeth started talking, and he glanced quickly at her through the rear-view mirror. Her young face had not started to show the signs of age. "I still haven't figured out why the Vatican wanted to get involved here," she said, now fully awake and sitting up. "Can't they do all the observing they want from satellites? Why does anyone need land-based telescopes anymore when there are so many satellites circling the globe?"

"I don't know much about astronomy, but I do know that there are some things that still can be done better from land," Nick replied.

Rosa hopped in. "Even so, this might not be the best place for a telescope. Of the original partners, some have pulled out and gone to better locations."

"I know," Nick said. "The Smithsonian and Ohio State left the project to the University of Arizona and the Vatican's Arcetri Observatory. The Max Planck Institute of West Germany was involved for awhile, too."

"Some two-hundred million dollars are going into this complex," Rosa added. "That's a lot of money when you have the red squirrels and Apaches to deal with."

Elizabeth unsnapped her seat belt and slid forward. She rested her elbows on the back of the driver's seat like a kid trying to get closer to her parents. She wore perfume, something flowery that would hang in the car for days. "The Vatican observatory director ridiculed the Apache claim that the mountain is sacred," she said. "The Apaches say Mount Graham is an area where their sacred dancers, the gan, emerged, but the observatory director said that's nonsense."

"Why would the Roman Catholics put down the beliefs of another religion when they rely on so many beliefs?" Nick said. "How in the hell would a Vatican guy be able to judge Apache religious beliefs or call them nonsense? Of course people are willing to go to war, kill, or do other crazy things over religion."

Neither woman added anything to his editorial. Each looked out the window, enthralled by the beautiful forest that was beginning to envelop them. The roads had been plowed clear. There were about six inches of fresh snow on the ground, a sea of white on both sides of the narrow highway.

Once Nick left the pavement and began working his way up the mountain on a dirt road, he had to follow precisely the instructions he'd been given for eight miles of skinny, unmarked paths. Because developers constantly feared sabotage, they left the roads to the observatory unmarked.

Several days earlier, someone had damaged two pieces of heavy equipment near the observatory. When the forest ranger told Nick about the damage, she also blamed environmental activists operating in the area.

The observatory site posed in front of them suddenly. There were no marquees, just two plain concrete towers that resembled giant gray eggs that had been laid on end in a meadow. The Vatican telescope structure was about 100 yards away from the University of Arizona's and on a higher grade. There were no footprints on the snow around either of the towers.

An unsmiling police officer in brown greeted the trio before they could drive into the fenced-in area surrounding the telescopes. He also blocked the entrance gate.

"May I help you?" he inquired as soon as Nick rolled down the window. The cold outside spilled into the car and brought the officer's frozen white breath with it.

"Yes, we're here for a tour of the Vatican telescope. I'm Nick Genoa from *Smithsonian* magazine."

The cop looked at the clipboard is his hand. "Yes sir, we have you down. Didn't know if you'd still come in this weather. It won't get into the thirties today. May I see some identification? Anything with a picture will do."

Nick pulled out his driver's license. His hands shivered. "Do you guard this area all the time?"

"Yes, reserve deputies from the Graham County Sheriff's Department provide security twenty-four hours a day, year-round."

"I understand you had some sabotage a few days ago," Nick said.

"It wasn't part of our area," the deputy said defensively. "There was damage to some state highway equipment a mile or so down the road. I guarantee you there won't be any problems inside the fences we patrol. We're not going to put up with any crap, especially from those seed and carrot eaters."

The deputy turned and pointed toward a small cleared parking area near the Vatican tower. "You can park right over there. John Peterson, one of their people, will meet you at the elevator entrance as soon as I call and notify him that you're here."

The Vatican tower was nothing special, just a round cement structure with two-foot-thick walls. A thirty-foot-wide satellite dish had been erected at the top of the other telescope tower.

"Not what I expected," Rosa said as Nick turned off the car's engine.

"Me neither," Elizabeth added. "I envisioned huge structures with a spectacular view of the valleys below. From here all I see is forest."

"They were built for looking up rather than down," Nick joked. Elizabeth looked crossly at him. He guessed she thought he was being condescending.

"John Peterson?" Nick asked as he walked up to the man waiting near the elevator door, the only entrance to the concrete structure. The man dressed in hiking boots, jeans, and a red-and-black plaid wool shirt stood at least six and a half feet. He was news-anchor handsome and Scandinavian, with thick blond hair and blue eyes. A neatly trimmed mustache and goatee added a few years to his face.

"Yes, hello, Mr. Genoa. Welcome to our complex."

"Please call me Nick. This is Rosa Zizzo and Elizabeth Smythe. They're the art conservators I told you about."

Peterson took his time looking at each woman. He enjoyed what he saw. Then he held out his hand and shook theirs enthusiastically. "Come on in," he added. "We're here twenty-four hours a day and don't get many guests. Three of us make up the working crew and three are on the sleeping crew. Work and sleep. That's it. It's nice to have some company, particularly lovely women. Sorry 'bout that, Nick. You're welcome here, too."

"Are the roads up to here always clear?" Nick asked in the elevator.

"Absolutely," Peterson said. "Even though there aren't many tourists coming and going, there is a steady flow of scientists and supplies. The road is maintained daily, even in the winter."

"Do you get much snow up here?" Rosa asked.

"It doesn't seem to be so bad yet," Peterson said. "This is my first winter here, but I've already heard stories of three-foot snowfalls and massive drifts. We're in one of the highest spots in Arizona. Most people think of southern Arizona as all desert, but this country is much more like the mountain country of northern Europe."

An hour later, Nick, Rosa, and Elizabeth sipped coffee in a window-less room with Peterson and one of the other six scientists working in the observatory. The tour had been informative, but because it was daylight and cloudy, there had been no opportunity for star gazing.

"I read that construction of the telescopes would ruin the habitat of the red squirrel, which eats nuts from certain pines up here," Nick said to Peterson between sips. "But it looks to me like the observatory was built in a meadow."

"Correct," Peterson said. "Most of the trees were taken out during construction of the roads. There is not a thick forest where the towers are. The thick tree area is on the slopes, and the red squirrel's prime habitat is the spruce-fir forest surrounding the top of Mount Graham. They live only on that mountain."

"So you don't think you're bothering them?"

"I know we're not bothering them, but that's not what the media think. The truth is that only about two-hundred and fifty trees were taken out for the site. There are thousands up here, so thick you can't see more than a few meters in front of you. The squirrels are tied to the rainfall and the number of pine nuts produced each year. These telescopes were allowed under a 1988 act of Congress, and all sorts of scientific studies were done that showed the squirrels would be fine. But then the environmentalists and the reporters jumped on the damn thing. Suddenly the mountains became sacred to the Apaches. We really don't concern ourselves so much with the environmentalists or the Indians. We're here to do a job, and this is a wonderful spot for astronomy."

Nick watched Rosa and Elizabeth as they stood and began to put on their coats. "We won't take any more of your time," he said. "We thought we'd hike while we're up here and perhaps spot a red squirrel or two. Can you tell us the best place for seeing them?"

Peterson smiled. "I've never seen one, but the deputies tell me that if you head beyond the meadow and into the forest, and go deeper into the mountain, there are plenty of them to see even in the winter. When you leave here, just walk out of the fenced-in area and head south. I've also heard there is a wonderful series of waterfalls on the mountain one mile due south of here. Do you have a compass?"

"Yes."

"Then you might want to check out those falls. I'd like to if I could ever break away from here. Be careful, though. This snowstorm will make hiking dangerous. And be careful of the cold and hypothermia. There's a lot of slippery ice out there."

Chapter 32

A melody of sounds drew the hikers deeper into the white mountains. The tops of the pine trees danced in the frosty wind, which rushed through the forest like ocean waves curling and crashing against a beach.

Birds surrounded them. The forest south of the observatory hid its creatures well, but the chirps were reminders that, even in winter, the mountain teemed with life. They also saw footprints of what they thought were deer, but hadn't sighted any red squirrels yet.

The trio walked along a narrow stream that they presumed would lead to the waterfalls. The snow crunched beneath them. "Try this water, ladies," Nick said like an excited schoolchild. Out of shape after nearly two months of not working out, he breathed heavily. Since meeting Rosa, he hadn't spent any time at the gym. He got his most strenuous exercise in the bedroom.

They were nearly at 10,000 feet elevation, and Nick could feel his lungs struggling to take in enough air. His knees were in the snow on the bank of the stream. He had taken off his gloves and was drinking the stream's icy water from his cupped hands. "I've never tasted fresh water from a stream before. It's ice cold."

"Are you sure it's OK to drink?" Elizabeth asked.

Nick laughed. "Why wouldn't it be? This has got to be water from melting snow, still untouched by humans. You should try it."

Elizabeth remained standing and mumbled something about animal shit polluting the water. Nick could see her white breath stabbing at the air.

Rosa kneeled for a taste of the water. "Ummm, this is wonderful," she said after sipping from her cupped hand. A second later, she added, "Do you hear that sound downstream?"

"Uh-huh. It must be the waterfalls. They can't be too far. We'll get to them if we follow the stream." He checked his compass to confirm that he knew what he was talking about. "We're headed south. I'm glad I learned this stuff in Boy Scouts."

The hikers pushed deeper into the mountain gorge cut over millenniums by the side-winding stream. They moved slowly along its banks because they were walking over icy rocks that had been rounded by the flowing water. It was afternoon, clear except for a few thin high clouds that couldn't stop the sun from reflecting off the snow cover. Even though the temperature hadn't climbed out of the twenties, Nick wiped sweat as it rolled over his cheek.

"This hike is for daring people," Rosa said, her arms out so that she would keep her balance on the path they cut through the snow. She was winded, and the sound of her heavy breathing mixed with that of the singing birds and ever-closer waterfalls.

Her companions waved their heads in agreement but said nothing. Each had a tough enough time just walking and breathing.

Within minutes, the stream at their feet ended into the openness of another canyon. They were at the edge of a cliff. The stream's flow toppled over the rocks and into the first of six small waterfalls. Each one was about fifteen feet long and emptied into a pond about the size of a backyard swimming pool, which in turn overflowed into the next waterfall. The icy water slid down the slick rock cliff until ending deep below, where once again the flattened, meandering stream headed through a gorge.

Oddly enough, a flexible black plastic hose tied to a huge boulder at the top of the cliff tethered down the side of the first waterfall. Someone, at sometime, had climbed down to the pool below them.

"Going down?" Nick joked as he grabbed the black one-inch hose and tested it for strength. It held him, and his confidence grew. "There's no other way to get down there unless you can fly," he added. "The cliff is too sheer."

"Maybe people slide down in the water," Elizabeth said. "The falls are about ass width."

Nick laughed. "I'll bet the moss in them would make the slide one hell of an experience."

Rosa frowned. "I don't think we should try that," she said quickly.

"We're only teasing," Nick said. "There's no way I'd try to slide down an ice-cold waterfall. Maybe in the summer, but not now. I'd freeze to the damn side. It'd be like licking a frozen pipe, which I actually did once when I was a kid."

"We should go back to the car," Rosa said. The skin between her fearful eyes wrinkled. She hugged herself in an attempt to stay warm.

"Come on, Rosa," Nick said. "Didn't anyone ever teach you that if you feel something, you should go for it? I think we can climb down this hose. It's plenty strong, and I'd love to get some pictures looking up into a waterfall."

"There's no way of knowing if that plastic will hold us."

"It's an inch thick, and I'm sure it's held lots of people before us. That's why it's here. I'll go down first just to make sure, and then you and Elizabeth can follow me if you want. I'll hold it steady from the bottom."

"I'll go," Elizabeth chimed. "It looks like fun."

"I won't," Rosa added. "If we all die as fools, who'll tell our story?"

Nick patted her arm and hugged her. "You don't have to if you don't want, but I've got to try it," he said, reassuring himself, and to a lesser extent, Rosa.

Nick had worked his way about halfway down the cliff when the hose broke. Lucky for him, he landed on the icy ledge next to the pool of water instead of tumbling to the bottom of the cliff. He didn't break any bones, but his badly twisted right ankle began throbbing with pain. He felt stupid for not listening to Rosa.

She screamed, "Oh, my God. Nick, are you OK?" She and Elizabeth dropped to their knees and looked down the cliff at him.

"Yes, I think so. What a tumble." He tried to stand. "I've really done it now. I'm going to need some help climbing out of here."

"I'll go back and get help." Rosa shouted. "Maybe we can get a helicopter in here."

"No, I don't want you to do that. This isn't an emergency. Let me think for a second. Besides, I'll probably be OK in a few minutes." The pain in his face betrayed him.

The three remained silent for an incredibly long time. The rushing falls drowned out the sounds of their heavy breathing. "I've got a rope in my backpack," Elizabeth said finally. "I borrowed it from Ali. I can lower it down and then we can pull you up."

"Good idea," Nick said. "The Turk comes through."

With a little help, he knew he could get back up the cliff and safely to the car. "Rosa, why don't you go back to the car and get my extra pair of gloves? These are wet and cold. I stashed another pair under the front seat. They'll help me climb the rope."

She jumped up to follow his instruction. "It won't take long. Don't try anything silly while I'm gone. Elizabeth and I will get you up here."

"Just remember, this isn't an emergency," Nick said. "When you get back to the car, don't bother the people at the observatory."

Before Rosa left, Elizabeth said, "I'll lower the rope to him while you're gone and when you get back, we'll bring him up."

"Just don't try to do anything silly while I'm gone," Rosa repeated. Her voice cracked in fear. "I'm never quite sure what Nick might do. I'll get back as quickly as I can."

Elizabeth took the heavy rope from her backpack after Rosa disappeared into the forest. She worked it with experience. She tied a bowline knot on the end for Nick. She wrapped the other end around a ponderosa pine two times before tying it off with two half-hitches.

"Put the rope around you," she shouted after she lowered it. He couldn't see what she was doing on the rocks above him.

"Will it hold me?"

"It'll hold you even if you slip while we're helping you up."

"I can probably just climb up right now," he said confidently. "My ankle hurts like hell, but I think I can make it."

"Just wait for Rosa and those warm gloves," Elizabeth warned. "She's right. It'll take both of us."

It took less than twenty minutes for Rosa to get back to the parking lot. The below-freezing coldness reddened her face, but she could feel beads of sweat rolling down her back. As soon as she reached the car, she thought about going to the observatory for help, but she remembered what Nick had told her. And she needed to return to him quickly.

Luckily, the car's doors were unlocked. She'd forgotten to ask Nick for a key. Rosa pulled the door open and stuck her hand underneath the driver's seat for the gloves.

The tissue she pulled out with the gloves puzzled her. It had dried blood on it.

No time to worry about it, she thought. She couldn't recall if Nick cut himself. Must have been something left over from the person who had the car before him.

She grabbed the pair of dark brown leather gloves and tossed the tissue into a trash barrel outside the elevator entrance to the Vatican telescope tower. Within seconds, she ran to her injured lover.

When Rosa got back to the waterfall, Nick stood awkwardly, ready to begin inching his way back up the cliff. She tossed him his gloves and grabbed the rope behind Elizabeth.

"This is going to hurt you worse than me," Nick groaned sarcastically as he started moving against the rocks. He hurt like hell, but he didn't want to tell Rosa. He had no choice but to pull himself out of this mess.

With Elizabeth and Rosa tugging from the top, he made steady progress back up to the top.

"I'm sure happy that's over," he grinned as he sat next to the stream and caught his breath. "I've got to get back into the gym. I'm ashamed at how out of shape I am."

"Thank God you made it," Rosa said tearfully. "We've still got to get you back to the car, but you can lean on us."

The two lovers embraced. Elizabeth said nothing as she took the rope from Nick and neatly wrapped it around her forearm before tying it to one of the straps of her backpack.

Nick hadn't seen the portion of the rope that had been nearly sliced through with a knife. He didn't realize how fortunate he was that it didn't snap and send him tumbling to his death.

With his right arm over Rosa's shoulders and his left over Elizabeth's, he hobbled back to the car.

Rosa drove back to Tucson, forgetting about the blood-stained tissue she pulled from under the seat. Elizabeth sat in the front, too, clutching her backpack. Nick, occupying the back seat, sat with his leg up.

"Maybe we should take you into an emergency room," Rosa said on the outskirts of Tucson.

"Oh, nonsense," he told her. "I'm already feeling a little better, and I don't think I'll need to do much walking the rest of the weekend. I'm going to Mass tomorrow for the new priest, and that's it."

"You should see a doctor, Nick," Rosa pleaded.

"If it's still bothering me Monday, I will, but for right now, what I need is a few aspirins, and a beer."

She smiled and said, "I need aspirin and a drink, too. This has been a crazy day. You could've been severely injured or even killed."

They got back to Tucson well after dark.

"Would you like to go have a beer with us?" Rosa asked Elizabeth when the trio pulled up to their apartment complex.

"Not tonight. I've got my exercise class." Elizabeth had said little during the return trip.

"We'll just drop you off, then."

Nick slid delicately into the front seat. His foot pounded in pain, the type he knew would linger for several days.

"Exercise class?" he said as Rosa pulled out of the apartment complex and headed for a tavern on East Speedway.

"Yes. She worries about physical fitness, but I didn't know she works out even on Saturday night."

Nick grimaced. "Now I really feel guilty. I promised myself before I came here that I was going to find a gym and work out. Look at me now. Maybe if I was in shape I could've taken that fall better."

Rosa reached over and gently rubbed his leg. "Try to relax. You've had enough pain today. You don't need to beat yourself up. Besides, I love you just the way you are."

"Where does Elizabeth go for her class?"

"I don't know. It's got to be someplace close, I guess, where she can walk. She has no car. She once told me that keeping her body in excellent physical shape is the most important thing to her. I believe it when she says she can take care of herself if she needs to."

Chapter 33

N ick sat impatiently on the couch in Rosa's living room, glancing at the television, waiting for her to finish doing her hair so they could leave for Father Bill McGraw's first Sunday Mass at San Xavier. The television chatter did little to hold his attention. Three panelists on a news show kept asking a U.S. senator about something happening in the Middle East. Nick watched the mouths moving but didn't listen.

He'd learned the routine with women early in his life. Man finishes getting ready first. Man waits for woman. Man learns patience or at least the pretense of it. If he fails to wait quietly, man angers woman. It's not acceptable behavior to sit in the car and wait. It's an unforgivable sin to honk the horn.

His ankle hurt, but he could hobble. Tired of sitting and fidgety, he called to Rosa: "I think I'll walk around the pool and exercise my foot. I'll wait for you at the car."

No answer came from the bathroom. He heard the snap of the end of a curling iron. There wasn't much privacy in her small apartment.

"Rosa, I think . . ."

"I heard you, *mio amore*. That's fine. I won't be long. Come back here after a few minutes and we'll walk to the car together. My hair is a mess."

Just before Nick walked out the door, Rosa opened the bathroom door and stuck out her head. He would have been satisfied with her thick, dark hair in its standard ponytail. She didn't need hair spray or a curling iron. "Are you sure your foot is strong enough?" she asked in her love song voice.

He smiled, telling himself he would wait for her forever if he had to, in or outside of the car. "I'm OK. It's still sore, but not nearly as bad as yesterday. The wrap you put on it helped. The walk will loosen it up a little."

"OK, I'll be out quickly."

Nick strolled slowly. He limped around the swimming pool and then aimed toward Elizabeth's apartment on the other end of the complex. He thought he'd ask her if she wanted a ride to the mission.

He knocked on the door. No answer. Maybe she'd gone to the health club, or called a cab to take her to San Xavier. A member of the Patronato may have come by to get her.

He knocked again. The door opened slowly.

"Nick? Sorry I didn't come to the door right away, but I was on the phone."

Nick looked into Elizabeth's gleaming eyes. She looked like a model even though she wasn't a beautiful woman. She had puffed up her bleached hair. It spread like wings on her shoulders. She wore a yellow springtime dress made of silk that clinged to her body and revealed her shape. White platform shoes added three inches to her height. She'd covered her face with a thick layer of foundation and painted her full lips bright red. Her fingernails matched her lips in color. She'd splashed herself with flowery perfume.

He was clean and neatly pressed, but suddenly he felt inadequate in his blue cotton slacks and white Polo shirt.

Nick stared at Elizabeth. She liked it. She expected masculine attention.

"Would you like to come in? How's your foot? Can I do something for you?" Her questions were gunfire fast. She didn't seem interested in answers.

"My foot's feeling fine, thanks. I'll come in for a second and call Rosa if you don't mind. She and I are about to leave for the church, and I thought you might need a ride."

Elizabeth moved just enough for Nick to walk into the apartment. He sat heavily on the living room sofa and dialed Rosa's number. As he did, he started fingering the rope tied to Elizabeth's backpack, which she'd tossed on the couch.

Quickly, Elizabeth grabbed the backpack and said, "Let me get this out of the way." She didn't realize that Nick had already seen the neatly sliced rope. Only a few strands were left where it had been cut.

He didn't tell her what he'd discovered. Instead, he concentrated on her every movement, hoping to get a signal from her that the rope worried her. Obviously, whoever sliced it assumed it would snap while someone—Nick Genoa—used it. But something had gone terribly wrong and he was still alive. He remembered that Elizabeth had said she borrowed the rope from Ali.

"Carl's picking me up," she said as she walked from her bedroom and stood in front of Nick.

He glared into her eyes and said, "Did you know the rope was cut?"

"What?"

His question surprised her, or at least she faked her outward appearance extremely well.

"The rope has been cut," he said again. "Did you know it?"

"Where?"

"Why don't you go get it and I'll show you."

He sat frozen until she returned. "Here. Look how close it was to breaking yesterday."

Elizabeth managed only, "Oh my God." She either told the truth or was one hell of an actress. She sat next to Nick and added, "Of course I didn't know. You don't think . . ."

"I don't think anything right now except that I'm a very lucky man. I'll see you in church."

As he hobbled out of the apartment, he turned quickly and looked back at Elizabeth. She stood in her doorway, unsmiling, watching him.

Thoughts played in his mind. *If the rope was Ali's, was it cut before the trip to Mount Graham? How would the Turk know it would be used, unless he was in cahoots with Elizabeth? Was the rope cut after I fell? Elizabeth knew how to handle the rope and tie knots, but if she's such an expert, why didn't she check it before using it? If I've become a target, what the hell will happen next?*

Like dominoes, his emotions flipped from anger to sadness to terror as he walked into Rosa's apartment and shut the door behind him. The phone rang. He flinched.

"Nick, is that you?" came the voice from the bathroom. "Will you get the phone? This damn hair of mine."

"I'll get it. Hello."

"Is Rosa there?"

"She's busy right now. Who's calling, please?"

"Carl Corona."

What an asshole, Nick thought. The guy knows it's me and he's treating me like a nameless receptionist.

"Can I help you?"

"Nick?"

"Yes. Carl?" He said it snidely.

"I just talked to Rosa and wanted to tell her something else. Father Bill invited a group of Franciscans from California and plans to give them a tour after lunch. I'm hoping Rosa and the other conservators can be there, to talk about their work."

"I'll ask her. We're about to leave."

"You're coming to the Mass?" The tone in his voice mirrored his antagonism toward the writer.

Nick had taken enough crap from the car dealer. "No, Carl, I'm going to Home Depot to buy a hammer and nails. What the hell's your problem with me?" His question cut like glass. He wished that they were face to face so he could see the bastard squirm.

Silence on the phone. Nick could almost hear Carl's wheels turning.

"What you write could help us here, or it could damage us greatly," Carl said slowly. "I think you've misunderstood me. I really have been supportive of your work from the day I met you. I just hope you and the others don't say anything today about the problems we've had."

"I'm sure the Franciscans know what happened, Carl. You can't go around stifling people."

"Why are you trying to solve a murder instead of doing a story on the art?"

Nick hated that question, even though it was valid. He'd been asked it too many times.

"The story has changed. I'll still do the piece for *Smithsonian*, but no one can stop me from looking into the killings and theft. That is as long as I'm alive."

Again, silence on the other end. More thinking. "Are you worried about your safety?" Carl asked.

"Should I be?"

"I think you should go to the police. Tell them what you've found. There's no reason for a writer from New York to be doing police work in Arizona."

"Tell them what? That there's an investigative reporter in town and he's looking into something? There's nothing illegal about that. I guess I could tell them Carl Corona's full of shit and has no idea what I'm doing. That won't make you look very smart, will it?"

"You don't need to be doing the work of the police," Carl said angrily, about to slam down the phone.

Nick clenched his fist. He would've liked to slug the guy to knock some sense into him, but it wouldn't do any good. He spoke to a deaf man.

He tried again. "Just for the hell of it, Carl, let's say Jimmy Longfellow didn't kill the priest. There's a killer out there someplace. And a treasure in gold. Don't you think there's still some investigating to be done?"

"I'm here to help you write the best story possible about our mission, not to help you empty out everyone's closet and look for skeletons. Father John is dead. Let him rest in peace."

"Jimmy is dead, too."

"Dammit, why do you keep comparing the death of an Indian to a priest?"

Nick enjoyed Carl's anger. Anger usually brought out honesty.

"Interesting comment," he said. "Particularly coming from a man who has spent his life doing great things for a desert church that was built to serve the Indians."

"The church helped lift the natives out of their ignorance. It has served them well for two centuries. You've been here two months, Nick. You have no understanding of what life is like here. We spent a lot of money and time bringing in the European conservators. It's also difficult getting a good priest. The conservators will be gone soon. Father John cannot be brought back. Everyone in Tucson has already forgotten about the death of a Tohono O'odham man who had a criminal record, was on probation, and admitted that he killed a priest. Enough damage has been done. If you create more, we'll be left cleaning it up long after you've gone. San Xavier is not a piece of hotel linen that you can come in and soil and then leave to be cleaned. It's a living thing that must be protected."

"Nice lecture. You forget one thing, though. What about the gold?"

"It never meant anything to us. After two centuries, it came out of hiding for one day. What do I care if it's found or not? It means nothing to anyone connected to this church, except more heartache and perhaps more death. The ownership of that gold would likely be tied up for years while various church groups wrestled over it. That it was found here could even be a signal to treasure hunters to sneak into the church and start breaking walls."

Nick abruptly changed the subject. "Was Elizabeth Smythe Father John's lover?"

"I told you before that Father John had his affair in Europe."

"You also told me that he traveled throughout Europe before he joined you in Spain. Did he go to London?"

"Yes, but he also went to Italy and other European countries."

"Isn't it possible that he met Elizabeth in London? He didn't wear his habit to Europe. He obviously had sexual desires. What if they met there, had an affair, and she followed him to Tucson?"

"Why are you asking these things? I've told you he wasn't having an affair here. I don't know who the woman was in Europe."

"Sure, he could have had an affair in Europe with someone you don't know. But isn't it also possible that Elizabeth had been to Spain and read the Díaz journal and then purposely sought Father John and the job at San Xavier? Or maybe they met, fell in love, and he told her about the gold. Maybe they plotted together to steal it."

"Why Elizabeth? Why not Rosa or Francesca? Why not Ali?"

"Are you trying to tell me something about the priest, Carl?"

"I'm not trying to tell you anything, except that I have no idea what went on in the priest's private quarters at night. I can't talk about this anymore."

"What about you, Carl?"

"Me? What?" Carl stammered.

"If you believe Ali could've been involved with Father John, then why not you?"

"I'm sick of talking to you. You're crude and slanderous. Who do you think you are? You reporters are all the same. You have no sense of privacy. You think you can ask anybody anything and get away with it."

"That's our job, Carl. And why are you sick of talking to me? You haven't told me a damn thing. You say he was not having an affair here, and then you say you have no idea what went on at night. You're so busy protecting the church that you've forgotten what's really important, like bringing a killer to justice. One of these people could be a killer. The key to solving the murder could be knowing who Father John slept with, man or woman."

The phone slammed loudly. Nick smiled. Carl had lasted longer than expected. Even if he told the truth and knew nothing about a local tryst between a priest and someone else, he helped Nick's effort to get the story. Carl had a big mouth. Within hours most of the conservators would know the details of his conversation.

Sitting on the couch in Rosa's front room, Nick silently wrote in his notepad until she emerged from the bathroom.

"Who was that on the phone?" she asked. He hesitated, once again mesmerized by her splendor. Her pale green serge dress made her olive skin radiate. She wore little makeup other than pale lipstick. And her hair looked great.

"Carl," he said finally. "He called to remind you to talk about your stunning beauty."

Rosa blushed. "I could discuss my beauty in about ten seconds. I'll be happy to talk much longer about the wonderful art in the church. I heard you raise your voice on the phone. Carl make you angry again?"

"He helped me with my story. He's quite the source and a real piece of work. He doesn't match Ali on the arrogant bastard scale, but he's close. Let's go. We don't want to keep all those people waiting. San Xavier's walls bowed to Christianity. Today, I believe everyone in the church will bow to your beauty."

Chapter 34

Nick and Rosa rushed in and took their seats only minutes before the procession started down the center aisle. The other conservators had saved them a place.

San Xavier overflowed for Father Bill's first Mass. Well-dressed people, all there to pay tribute to a new priest and an ancient church, squeezed into the simple wooden pews. People who couldn't fit in the pews stood in a row along the walls.

"*Ciao*, Nick," Francesca Vitucci said to Nick.

"Good morning to you. You look great."

She enjoyed the comment.

Nick and Rosa sat between Francesca and Ali. Elizabeth sat behind them with Carl. Francesca whispered something to Rosa in Italian. Ali and Nick nodded at each other but didn't speak.

Nick marveled at everything around and above him. "The people in the pews remind me of the angels in a wall painting in the tabernacle," he said to Rosa. "Plenty of colors."

"Shhh," she said.

"Come on, Rosa. Nothing says you have to enjoy all of this silently. Look at the bright faces. These people are in touch with their Lord, and their church."

She didn't respond. She watched an old Tohono O'odham man, dressed in new Wranglers and cowboy shirt, walk weakly down the aisle toward the sanctuary. His stumpy, gnarled right hand held tightly to the cane that kept his body upright. Despite his frailty, the strong-willed man refused help from anyone. Bound to make it to his destination on his own, he shuffled toward a pew near the front.

A young woman with two girls in tow, each wearing a blue and pink dress, caught Nick's attention. Like most of the Indian women, the mother wore lace on her head. A rosary dangled from her fingers. She was plain in dress and looks, but her face sagged with the weight of a troubled life. Her eyes never left the two girls.

A middle-aged Anglo woman with coiffured hair and drooping jewels sat close to Nick. She wore a mink coat, a full-length monster that would draw instant protest in New York.

What an assortment of people. Brown skin, tanned skin, white skin with rosy cheeks. High-heels, flats, sandals. High-tone people and those with no tones at all. It made no difference. They played only bit parts in the show that surrounded them.

During the service, Father Bill moved calmly. His soft voice was hard to hear. He spoke much more forcefully during his homily, and his words inspired Nick.

"I come to you with nothing, a simple man with no possessions other than the clothing that I wear," the priest told his followers near the end of his spiritual lesson. "There are no material things to distract me from my mission here, which is to bring to you the glory of our Lord. Our love of God must move us all past the recent tragic events at San Xavier. I can't replace Father John, and I pray for forgiveness for Jimmy Longfellow. Now we must move forward, and I promise you my love and patience during the time I'm with you. I pledge to you my energy. I pledge to our Lord my faith."

Nick hadn't been to church in years, and his mind kept recalling moments from his youth, when his father insisted that he go to Sunday Mass. On most Sundays Dad couldn't quite make it, but the two Genoa children had to. Church didn't make sense to him, and he grew to be like his father. He never considered himself a good Catholic.

He thought about his younger sister, Anne, wondering if she went to church regularly, when Rosa poked him gently in the ribs and brought him back. "Are you going to take communion?" she asked.

"No, I don't think I'm quite ready for that. You go ahead."

She put her hand on his shoulder and whispered, "I shouldn't either, but this service is so beautiful that I want to be a part of it."

"I thought we weren't supposed to be talking."

She poked him again with her elbow and then excused herself to join the growing line that snaked its way from the back of the church to the altar. Nearly every person in the crowded church lined up for communion. They stood silently, moving slowly toward their second before Father Bill.

He looked like he enjoyed each of them. "The body of Christ," he said over and over as he marched among his people. Most of the faithful held out their cupped hands, but many of the old Indians opened their mouths wide and stuck out their tongues in the traditional fashion they'd used their entire lives.

After the service, jolly Father Bill stood outside San Xavier's entrance, shaking hands. He seemed touched by the number of people who waited in line to greet him. After the last person walked past him, he went to one of the ramadas next to the church, where Indian women worked over open fires to make and sell fry bread. The smell of burning lard floated over the parking lot and into the church entrance.

An Indian woman handed him a piece of her fresh hot bread wrapped in foil. He opened it and took a bite, smiling broadly.

"This is delicious," he said.

The Indian women near him giggled.

He patted his stomach, which drew more giggles, and said, "I'd better save this for later." He rewrapped the bread and headed back into the church to join four Franciscan priests and Carl for lunch.

An hour later, Nick sat in the back of the church, listening to Carl dominate a tour that moved from the east chapel, to the west chapel, to the chancel in the middle. Rosa spoke occasionally, but Commander Corona took charge. None of the other conservators spoke.

From his vantage point, Nick surveyed each of the people in front of him. Like Father Bill, each of the priests looked gentle, calm, genuinely interested in everything being said. Carl the human jukebox never stopped. Just when someone else started to speak, it seemed another coin slipped into Carl's mouth and the record began again. Each of the conservators remained gracious, smiling, and, most of the time, silent. *They all look so innocent*, Nick thought.

Ali was the first to shake his head in frustration. He walked out of the church and into the sunny plaza for a cigarette.

Nick followed him. "Nice service, wasn't it?"

The Turk nodded and grunted. He had no desire to talk to Genoa. His eyes concentrated on his feet. He was a handsome man, intelligent, excellent at what he did. Nick could've liked him if he treated people a little more kindly.

"What's next for you, Ali?"

"Another job." He finally looked at Nick. "I notice you are limping. I understand you had an accident this weekend."

"I fell on my ass. Luckily, there's a lot of padding there and my ankle suffered the only damage." His attempt at humor drew nothing, not even the slightest smile.

"Your rope saved my life," Nick said after the two men had stood silently for a couple of minutes.

"My rope?"

"Yes, the rope Elizabeth borrowed from you. She had it in her backpack. She and Rosa used it to pull me back up the cliff."

Ali frowned. He took a deep drag on his Camel and exhaled slowly. "I don't own a rope."

Nick had no idea if he lied. "Elizabeth said . . ."

"She is an ignorant kid," Ali interrupted.

Leave it alone, Nick told himself. *Go back into the church and join the others. Quit being a reporter.*

He couldn't do it. "I thought maybe you learned how to tie knots when you were in the Turkish army, and you practiced on this rope."

Ali flicked his cigarette into the dirt. He buried it with his shoe. He looked at Nick as though the writer was wasting his time. "Army? Where the hell did you get that from?"

"I thought you were in the Turkish military, a commando or something."

"I was in our form of civil service, and I guarantee you I didn't carry a gun." He smiled finally. "The biggest gun I carried was a twelve-inch paintbrush to work on a painting from the thirteenth century before the Ottoman Empire. The second biggest gun I carry is my dick."

When Ali said the word, it sounded like *deek*. He said it seriously, arrogantly, not as a joke. Then he rounded his lips as though he had more to say, but instead he turned and walked back into the church, ending the conversation as abruptly as it began. He didn't want to be bothered by triviality.

Nick strolled back inside just as the tour ended. Rosa saw him and waved him to her side. Father Bill stood next to her.

"Your service was wonderful," she told the priest as Nick walked up. "Wasn't it just wonderful, Nick?"

"Yes, it was," he said, feeling guilty because he'd not been to church for so many years and hadn't taken communion. It had been more than a decade since his last confession.

"Your sermon was inspiring," he added.

The priest beamed. "Thank you so much."

"You really do go through your life without the material things we all seem attached to, don't you?" Nick asked.

"I have only my clothes and what the church supplies. Yesterday, I looked at the car that San Xavier provides, and I couldn't help but laugh. It shows just how much work there is to do at this very poor church."

"A VW Bug, or maybe a bus?" Nick joked.

"Not quite. It's a '76 Hornet."

They laughed. Rosa joined in, even though she'd never heard of that type of car.

"Hornet?" she said to Nick.

"It was made by Plymouth or Dodge, or maybe it was AMC. Luckily, there aren't many of them left on the road."

"This one is really a bucket of bolts, but it'll get me where I need to go," Father Bill added. "I don't do much driving. I'm just so happy it's blue instead of green."

Rosa didn't understand the Green Hornet joke. Nick did and smiled. "You say that the church provides the car?" he asked the priest more seriously.

"Yes. I think it's been here for some time."

"Father John would have used it?"

"And probably several before him." The priest laughed again.

"Father, do you mind if I take a look at it?"

"Not at all. It's parked behind my quarters. Do you know anything about mechanics?"

"Not really, although I had a '56 Ford pickup when I was in high school and was able to keep it on the road."

"Maybe you can tell me why it's dripping so much oil. I'm sure I need to have something replaced, but I have no idea what. I hope it doesn't need a lot." He paused and laughed again. "We might have to pass the collection plate an extra time."

Nick wanted to take a break, and the blue Hornet intrigued him.

"I'll go take a look."

He excused himself from the group. Rosa resisted. She wanted him to stay, but a gentle peck on her cheek assured her that he wouldn't be gone long.

The faded blue Hornet did indeed need a major restoration. Or a junk yard. The paint on the hood had been erased by years of sunlight, which left only patches of brown primer and surface rust. Dings and dents dominated the car, like it had been used more than once as a bumper car at a weekend carnival.

Nick leaned over, one hand on the hood, and looked underneath the car. As the priest had said: a leaky bucket of bolts. None of its engine gaskets seemed capable any longer of holding back oil.

The windows were rolled down. Or the glass was gone. The keys weren't in the ignition. Who would care? There wasn't even a slim possibility that the Hornet would be stolen. The car looked like hell.

He slipped carefully into the front seat, hoping not to put too much pressure on his sore ankle. He had no idea what he sought.

Wool Mexican blankets front and back covered the wounds in the upholstery. Nick opened the glove compartment. The registration and an insurance verification card, both in the name of the church, were inside a soiled envelope. A plastic scraper for the desert's few days of icy windshields, two small bolts, and a small package of Kleenex tissues were also in the glove compartment.

Why hadn't Carl provided something a little more current, or at least classier? I've never known of a priest—or anyone else running around in a Hornet that looks like this. As Father Bill said, comforts and possessions are not important to Franciscans.

He got out of the car and tried to open the trunk. No luck without the key, even on the old Hornet. He walked back to the front of the car, opened the driver's door, and pulled down the cracked plastic visor. The keys fell to the floor. So much for the priest's secret hiding place.

A bald spare tire and a well-used jack, nothing else, were in the trunk. Nick slammed the lid in frustration and walked back to return the keys to the visor. The cover of a notebook poking out from underneath the front passenger seat caught his eye. Another reporter's notebook, this one dustier than the one he had found earlier in the priest's quarters. He picked it up, blew on it, and then opened it.

The signature of John Duvall inside the well-worn front cover had faded like the car's paint job. Nick turned a few pages. Nothing unusual. The priest liked to doodle.

Nick flipped the pages until he spotted handwriting in the margin at the bottom of a page in the middle of the book. Father John's.

Old Pueblo Self-Storage. Unit 1958.

My lock.

Blackpool.

Once again, Blackpool. What did it mean? And why would a priest with no possessions rent a storeroom? Nick wanted the answers. He'd look up the address to Old Pueblo Self-Storage and check it out later in the day.

He returned to the church to pick up Rosa, thinking about what he'd say as soon as he saw Carl. Definitely something about the Hornet. The car dealer should provide a decent set of wheels for the priest. At least he could have the transmission and engine seals replaced. Or maybe bring donkeys back to the mission so Father Bill could travel in the same luxury as the priests who first came to San Xavier.

Driving home, Nick joked about the priest's car. Rosa looked at him strangely because she couldn't understand most of what he said. She looked at him crossly when he told her he needed to run an errand instead of joining her in her apartment. He said he would be back within an hour. He felt guilty and foolish for not telling her he planned to drive to Old Pueblo Self-Storage, but he knew he couldn't. It might be dangerous.

He stopped at a phone booth to look up the address. Not far from San Xavier. Nick drove there quickly.

A tall fence topped with barbed wire surrounded the mini-storage facility. A sign on the entrance gate instructed renters that they had to register at the office before going any farther.

The clean-cut attendant—tall, about eighteen or nineteen—looked like he belonged in a college classroom rather than in this place. But then today's Sunday, and Nick guessed the kid worked this job part time and attended the UofA during the week.

Nick signed his name as John Duvall, Unit 1958.

The boy looked at the signature and nodded his head yes. He didn't speak.

Nick got back into his car and followed the numbers to Unit 1958. That's when he hit the first snag. A heavy bold lock secured the door on the storeroom lock, and he didn't have the key. He got out of his car and walked up to the door, just close enough to step into a puddle of oil and grease. The Hornet definitely had been here, and not too long ago.

As Nick scraped the bottom of his shoe on the pavement in front of the storeroom, he spotted the butt of a filtered Winston next to the grease and oil stain. Red lipstick ringed the filter. He leaned over, picked up the cigarette, and put it in his pocket.

He went back to the office and told the attendant he'd forgotten his key.

The kid, who kept using his hand to push his straight blond hair off his forehead, looked at a peg board behind him. "Did you give us a spare key when you first locked your unit?" he asked in a deep disc jockey voice.

"I thought I did. Maybe I forgot to do that."

"There's no key here." He rolled his eyes and lectured, "We're open until eight tonight. You'll need to go get the key. Bring us a spare one, too, because as you know we don't supply the locks."

"Good idea," Nick said with a quick salute.

He was back at 7:30 P.M., well after dark, this time with a bolt cutter he purchased from a hardware store.

Once again, he told Rosa he needed to run an errand. Her facial expression said she doubted him, but he insisted he needed to check out one small thing for his story.

The storage facility's attendant had changed. Now a pimply-faced black-haired kid with brown skin stood guard. The morning clerk wore khaki trousers and a crew-neck sweater. This one wore faded jeans ripped in the right places. He wore an old, ragged Flowing Wells High School sweatshirt. Again, no smile, no attempt at customer relations. And, like the daytime clerk, he didn't ask Nick for identification to go along with the signature of John Duvall.

Once again, Nick signed in and headed for Unit 1958, which was in the back of the facility and out of the light and traffic. He parked close to the door so he would be partially hidden while he cut the lock.

A cool night had spread over Tucson. High clouds blocked the light from a half moon. The evening's light breeze brought with it the foul scent of sewage, a reminder of a nearby treatment plant.

As he walked to the storeroom, something moved on its roof and frightened him. Two doves fluttered into the night sky. His heart raced.

The cutter sliced through the metal cylinder like it was a hot dog. He flipped the switch on the wall next to the opened door. The bare light bulb's brightness caused him to squint for a second or two as he looked into the closet-sized room just large enough for stacks of boxes but too small for big furniture or equipment.

The two suitcases were placed side by side, flat on the floor, one large and covered in black leather, the other much smaller and brown.

Nick opened the small one first. It contained two propane tanks, one with the torch attached, a pair of metal tongs, and a paperback book titled, *Treasure of the Atocha.* He remembered seeing the book, or one just like it, in Robert Clarkson's gold shop in Phoenix.

The book described the fabulous treasure of religious items found aboard a salvaged Spanish ship that had sunk centuries ago. One of the items, a precious crucifix of emeralds and gold, was worth $500,000, according to the book.

Nick picked it up and skimmed through its pages. Clarkson's business card fell out of the book and onto the cold concrete floor of the storeroom. The book belonged to a dead man.

He picked up the card and put it in his shirt pocket. He took a deep breath, leaned over, and opened the black case.

The shiny yellow ingots had been piled neatly, all with their markings facing up. There were handfuls of silver-dollar-sized gold coins. The rich beauty of the foot-tall gold crucifix inlaid with emeralds and pearls impressed him the most, and he imagined it would be worth even more than the one pictured in the book.

He put one of the coins in his pocket and stood for a minute looking into the two open suitcases. *Should I call the police? Of course. But if I delay, perhaps I can solve the murder and clear Jimmy. How many people have died for this treasure? Just since I've been in Tucson three people have died. Why is this metal worth three people's lives? How many other people have been killed in the last two centuries because of some ingots, coins, and a crucifix?*

Nick closed the two suitcases and backed slowly out of the storeroom. He took the cut lock from the latch and replaced it with a similar-looking lock that he also bought from the hardware store. If the thief returned within the next couple of days, he'd have a problem. Nick didn't care about that possibility. He was about to ensnare a murderer.

Chapter 35

"I found the gold, Rosa." Nick's face had turned ashen even before he walked into her apartment.

"And I bought the Mona Lisa," she responded playfully before looking at him.

"No joke this time."

Rosa froze.

"I found the gold where Father John and someone else hid it," Nick said. "Thanks to Father Bill and San Xavier's damn Hornet, I stumbled across it. It's stashed not far from here in a mini-storage unit."

"Mini-storage?"

"It's a small storeroom that people can rent from month to month. Father John rented it. Whoever stole the gold knew about the storeroom. Either that or Father John put the gold there before he was killed."

"Sit. I thought you were joking."

Dinner had chilled. She'd planned a quiet Sunday evening with red wine, soft music, and a candlelight dinner of oven-cooked pasta with tomatoes, mushrooms, mozzarella, and a little bit of cream.

Nick sat with her on the couch. He pulled the stolen property from his pocket and handed it to her. Rosa put her hand to her mouth. "Father John a thief?"

"Probably. Or at least a lover who wasn't thinking straight. I found a notebook in his car. He'd written the name of the storage unit inside of it. I went there and found the entire treasure."

"What did you do with it?"

"Nothing yet. I grabbed this coin and left everything else where I found it. The treasure is safe, at least for awhile."

Rosa stood and ran her hand through her loose hair. "We need to go to the police."

"I can't yet, I . . ."

"Please, Nick, please. You can't do this on your own."

"I'm too close to figuring it out. I think I can solve this thing."

He asked her to sit down again. He put his arm around her shoulder and held her tight enough so that she practically moved onto his lap. He tilted his head back and let the air from a table fan cool him.

She hugged him. "Why do you care so much about it?" she asked. "I'm worried now. This could get dangerous. We're done here. We're leaving in a few days, and we'll have the rest of our lives together. Let the police deal with Tucson, Arizona. Just tell them what you have found."

Nick thought about her comment and said nothing. He examined her lips, covered, as usual, with pale red, almost-pink lipstick. She never wore dark red lipstick.

"You're right," he said. "Who the hell decided to make me Dick Tracy? I have a good life, made even better by the first woman I've ever truly loved. We've got good careers and we could go through life without struggling. An anonymous call to the sheriff's department could end my involvement. Problem is, this damn story is like a magnet, and it's pulling me stronger than any story ever has. It's like your art project at San Xavier. You couldn't give it up before the job's done."

He took his arm from her shoulder and put it to his side before sitting more stiffly. He pushed the button on the fan to let it oscillate. "You know, Rosa, in all the years that I've been a reporter and writer, I've covered all types of stories.

Check passings. Babies in their mothers' arms. Speeches. Traffic accidents. Trials. Murder. Mayhem. Features about famous people. Travel stories. You name it, I've done it, always meeting my deadline and pleasing my damn editor. Nick's always come through with any assignment he's been handed. But in all of those years, I've never written a story that really cut any ground, that meant anything to a large number of people. Here's my chance, and I can't quit. I'm too close."

"Do you care more about your story than about us?"

A silly question, they both knew, but she had a right to ask it. He reacted politely.

"Of course not. But Jimmy was killed because people thought he murdered a priest. This time, the Indian didn't do it. His family and his people deserve to know who did. The guy drank, had trouble with the law, lived in a cage we call a reservation. He was easy to blame."

Rosa nodded. "Maybe the police were wrong about Jimmy. But if they were, that would mean a killer is out there, possibly free to kill again. Your life could be in great danger. Mine, too."

"I worry about you all the time, and of course I'm scared. But I can't walk away from this story yet. You came to San Xavier and made it beautiful again. You helped these poor people feel good about their most glorious landmark. I think I can help them, too."

Nick stood and walked to the television set. These apartments didn't furnish remote control. He switched stations and shook his head in dissatisfaction. Finally, he turned it off and walked back to the couch. He stepped slowly and a little awkwardly, but his ankle was improving rapidly. The four Tylenol he took a couple of hours earlier helped.

"Did you know that the rope you and Elizabeth used to pull me up the cliff yesterday had been cut with a knife? All that was left were a few strands, and the damn thing could've broken at any time."

His comments startled Rosa. "Oh, my God. I didn't see any cuts in the rope."

"Neither did I. I'm not even sure where it was sliced. It could've been wrapped around the tree at the top and not been a problem. On the other hand, it could've sent me tumbling to my death at just the right time."

"You don't think I . . ."

"No, I don't," he interrupted. He grinned and said it again, "No, I don't." Then he added, "Do you remember Elizabeth saying that it was Ali's rope? I asked him about it today, and he said he doesn't own a rope. One of them is lying, or they're working together."

"I've known Ali for a long time, and even though he's not a nice man, I don't think he's a murderer. He's not known to be a liar, either. Pompous bullshitter, yes. Liar, no."

Nick began smoothing his mustache with his fingers. "I'm not sure about Ali. His arrogance hides a lot, and I believe he could kill, especially for gold. If it's his rope, though, why would he cut it before our trip? He didn't know we'd need it. No, if it's his, he's got to be in it with Elizabeth and they planned something for both of us on the mountain."

"Please, Nick, I'm scared. Go to the police."

"With what? If I go to them with what I have now, there's not enough evidence to charge or convict either one of them. I need to set up some sort of trap."

Rosa shook her head no. "You might get killed."

He didn't want to think about that, even though he believed her. "It could be dangerous," he said. "You should stay out of it."

"Stop it, Nick. I'm already in it. If you're unwilling to go to the police, I won't either. I want to help you."

"I have no idea how to set a trap, but what do you think of this? You spread the word among the conservators tomorrow that I'm close to solving the case. Don't say anything about the gold. Then I want you to tell Ali that you and I are going to have a moonlight dinner at the park down the road on Monday. Tell Elizabeth the same thing, but say Tuesday. Tell Carl, too, but make it Wednesday. It's important that each of them hears a different day. Then leave the rest to me."

Rosa cocked her head. "The park down the road? Too weak. No one will fall for that."

"You're right. Tell them anything you want. We just need to be someplace where the killer thinks we're alone."

"Why don't we tell them that we know about the storeroom and the gold? Then whoever knows about it will go there and try to move it."

"Or be scared away. No, I've thought about the storeroom thing. The killer thinks the storeroom is a safe place. Could be for years as long as the rent is paid. And I checked on that. Father John is prepaid for a year. They don't keep a record of who brought in the money. It was probably paid in cash. There's only one thing that can screw up our trap. If the killer goes back to the storeroom in the next couple of days, he won't be able to get in. I changed the lock."

"Then we need to make sure we don't act suspicious."

"Precisely. Act normally. Just let people know that we'll be alone someplace private and dark. We've got to get the killer out alone, thinking we're two lovers not paying any attention to what's going on around us. I'm sure the killer believes I've got to die."

Rosa lifted her hand to her open mouth. "I'm terrified."

"So am I, but I won't let anything happen to us."

She doubted him. "You're a tough man to be with," she said.

A sinking feeling gripped Nick. He'd heard that line before. His wife used it on him and it cut like a razor. "I just need a little more time, Rosa. Please stick with me."

"How much time?"

"Until I catch the murderer." He turned and walked into the kitchen, giving her a minute to think. He returned to the couch to tell her, "I've got a little insurance here."

He was holding two Sony microcassette recorders in his hand. "I picked up another one of these today so that you'll have one, too. They're small and powerful enough to put anywhere and still pick up everything. I'm going to leave one with you and take the other one to my apartment. Keep it running when you talk to the others. I'll do the same. You can hide it in a pocket. It's got a built-in microphone."

"Why do we need to do that?"

"You've got to trust me on this one. It could provide the evidence we need. We'll stay together as much as possible, so you shouldn't need yours much. As long as you're working inside the mission, nothing is going to happen to you."

She still looked worried. Before Nick could say anything, she recalled the blood-stained tissue she'd found underneath the seat of his car a day earlier.

"Did you cut yourself recently?" she asked.

"What kind of bloody question is that?" he joked.

"No, really, I'm wondering if maybe you cut yourself. When I came back to get your gloves yesterday, I found a tissue underneath your seat. It was stained with dried blood."

"Where is it now?"

"I threw it away at the observatory. I didn't think it was anything, except that I couldn't remember you cutting yourself. Maybe it was left there by the person who rented the car before you."

Nick paused. Things were beginning to come together for him. "Rosa, is there any chance that maybe one of the conservators drove my car and I didn't know about it?"

His question embarrassed her. "I knew you wouldn't care."

"Of course I don't care, but who took it, and when?"

"Remember that Friday night that I wasn't feeling well and told you not to come over so that I could go to bed early?"

"That was also the night that Robert Clarkson was killed in Phoenix."

"Oh, my God." With her comment, Rosa began to cry. "Elizabeth asked if she could borrow the car. She said she couldn't get a rental car because it was too difficult for foreigners without a major American credit card."

"Why did she want it?"

"She said that she, Ali, and Francesca wanted to go out to dinner, and then she was going to spend the evening with a man she'd met at the health club. I didn't ask questions. If Elizabeth was having an affair, I was sure she didn't want me to tell anyone about it. She told me as much, and that's why I didn't say anything to you. When they were done, they put the keys under my doormat."

"Do you think Elizabeth kept the car the entire night?"

"She told me that Ali and Francesca were going to drop her off at the club after dinner and then return the car. She said her friend would bring her back in the morning. I went to bed, so I don't know when Ali and Francesca brought the car back."

Chapter 36

Monday morning. The *Daily Star* was on the kitchen table, unfolded and read, next to a slice of half-eaten toast. Nick worked alone in his apartment. He'd moved to the couch, with his computer on his lap and the phone nestled on his shoulder. He'd drained a pot of coffee and had another one brewing.

Phoenix information had the home phone number of the late Robert Clarkson. A woman answered after three rings.

"Mrs. Clarkson?"

"Yes."

"My name is Nick Genoa. I'm sorry to bother you at home. I'm writing a story about an art conservation project at San Xavier Mission in Tucson and interviewed your husband for the story."

"I know who you are. Lucy told me about you. You talked to her not long ago. I'm sorry you had to learn about my husband over the phone. You're not going to use my name in any story, are you?"

The widow sounded gruff, impatient. He pictured her as well-heeled, strong-willed, middle-aged, wearing plenty of jewelry, and living in a fancy home. She didn't seem devastated by the death of her husband.

"No, I'm not going to use your name," he said. "I'm just trying to sort out a few things, and I was hoping I could ask you a couple of questions."

"I don't mind talking to you. I'll help in any way that I can."

"Mrs. Clarkson, I . . ."

"You can call me Emily."

"Thank you, Emily. When I talked to Lucy last, she said she told the police everything she knew. I'm sure you have been interviewed over and over by the police, too."

"They still haven't arrested anyone. I told Bob a hundred times over the years not to work alone late at night. It's unfortunate, perhaps I should say deadly, but that's the only way some people will buy or sell gold. They're afraid to be seen during daylight hours."

After a pause, she continued. "If he would have listened to me, maybe he would be alive now."

Nick let her ramble, like he would any survivor. No law said she had to talk to a reporter. If she controlled the conversation, or thought she did, she'd say whatever she wanted and likely keep talking. If she got scared or angry, or faced tough questions, she could easily slam down the phone.

"When I talked to Lucy, she said she was doing inventory and that nothing had been stolen," Nick said.

"Nothing was stolen. Bob had more than a million dollars in inventory in the showroom and more in the back storage area. As far as we could tell none of it was taken. The killer wasn't interested in jewelry. He just wanted Bob dead and wanted to leave as quickly as possible." After several seconds of silence, she added, "If only the robber would have known that nothing was worth death to Bob. He always said he'd help a robber carry out everything in the store if it would save his life."

"What about something besides jewelry? For example, when I visited the store, I noticed that there were also books on the counters. Were any of those taken?"

"I have no idea about that." The tone of her voice showed that she thought the question was silly, out of left field. "Bob constantly bought reference materials. They were not even entered on the inventory lists."

"Did your husband buy any gems that night? Or sell any?"

"Not as far as we could tell. At least there was no cash register record. Bob's register was computerized. It recorded the date and time of sales or purchases, and his last sale that day was shortly before he closed at six. Bob would never buy or sell any jewelry or metal without recording it."

His line of questioning headed nowhere. Emily Clarkson spoke openly and candidly, but she wasn't helping him. Nick changed direction. "Did the police tell you that a car was heard screeching away from the store sometime after midnight? Lucy told me about it."

"Yes. That's been all over the news. What hasn't been in the newspaper or on TV is that the police wanted to know what kind of cars Bob and I drove. We have Cadillacs. He had an Eldorado. I drive a Coupe DeVille. The car that left the scene was a small car."

"Did anyone see it?"

"A couple of people in the area said they saw a small car, probably one of those small tin boxes from Japan."

"Did they see the color?"

"Black, which happens to be the color of Bob's. But his Cadillac was still parked in the alley where he always parked it. My car is white."

Nick's rental car was maroon. He knew that at midnight in an unlit alley, maroon could have looked black. He feared that the killer's car and his were the same.

"Do you plan to reopen the store?" he asked.

"Oh, no. I never knew much about jewelry. Not like Bob. He was the expert, one of only a few certified coin appraisers in the world. Did you know that?" Her voice had softened.

"Yes, I'd been told he was one of seven."

"You know quite a lot about Bob."

"Not really. I only interviewed him once. I'm so sorry about what happened."

"Thank you."

Nick fingered Clarkson's business card, which he held loosely in his right hand. Raised gold lettering on off-white background, much nicer than the ones he had at the *Times*. "And you won't reopen the store?"

"No. I've already been approached by several jewelers about buying the inventory. Bob owed a lot of money, but I'll be fine after we sell everything and pay the bills."

"Thank you for your time, Emily. If I have additional questions, may I call you back?"

"Yes."

Before he could say goodbye, she interjected, "I didn't tell you about the thrupny-bit."

"The what?"

"Thrupny-bit."

"Sorry, but I don't know . . ."

"It's an English three-pence piece, a small silver coin. This one was all silver, which means it was minted before the nineteen-fifties when they quit using the all-silver coins and went to nickel-brass plated coins. Lucy found it on the floor when she was taking inventory."

Nick didn't understand. "Someone took it from a display case?"

"No, Bob never sold British coins. And this one had a small broken hole in it. I think it was a charm that must have broken off a bracelet."

"Do the police have it?"

"Yes, we gave it to them. They hadn't found it when they went through the store. Makes you wonder how thorough they were, doesn't it? Anyway, I don't think it's much of a clue for them. If it was the killer's, why would a man be wearing a charm bracelet?"

"Indeed," Nick said. "Thank you for your time, Emily."

Next, Nick called Edward Newton at the Guggenheim in New York. He got through quickly. The secretary recognized his name.

"Mr. Newton, we haven't spoken before. My name is Nick Genoa. I'm doing a story on the conservation project at San Xavier Mission for *Smithsonian* magazine."

"I've heard so much about you I feel like I know you, Mr. Genoa." He talked softly, effeminately, his congenial, professional voice free of a New York accent. "I'm so happy we finally have a chance to talk." Nick pictured a refined gentleman who, like him, had moved to New York for his career. A dark wool suit, white shirt, and silk bow tie. Penny loafers over argyle socks.

"I wanted to call you before I finished up the story," the writer said.

"You're nearly done? How nice. I plan to be in Tucson within the next few weeks to look in on what the conservators did this year. My reports tell me they have done some stunning work. They're special people, aren't they? Isn't the news about Saint Ignatius just wonderful?"

Nick couldn't answer the questions as rapidly as Newton asked them. He did a quick search through his mind for Saint Ignatius. He remembered. "Yes, the conservators found a fully carved wooden statue underneath what they thought was a plaster statue."

"Truly remarkable." Newton took a deep breath before he continued. His answers were slower, more thoughtful, than his rapid-fire questions. "The X-ray examination of St. Ignatius at the University of Arizona's Medical Center confirmed it. That finding can help us in restoration efforts at San Xavier and throughout the world."

"I've learned a lot about the art world while I've been here," Nick admitted. "It's too bad there's been so much tragedy to go along with the beauty."

"I hope you didn't call to talk about that. I feel such sadness over what happened, but I pray that it doesn't mar the wonderful work that has been done."

Nick got the message. He decided to hold the challenging questions for awhile.

"Have you been to San Xavier?"

"Isn't it beautiful?" He stretched the word into *beauuuuuuuu-ti-ful.* "I was there before we first hired the Europeans last year. The church was everything Carlos Corona of the Patronato San Xavier told me it would be. It's the finest example of an art-filled Spanish colonial church in this country. The only one."

"The conservators have made it even better."

"They're the best in the world," Newton said confidently. "The colors in that church deserve to be displayed in their full glory. Can you imagine the impact that church must have had on people two centuries ago? Today we have color photography, films, computers, television, and emerging technology to bring us the visual wonders of the world. The only visual experience in the lives of the Indians at Bac was San Xavier. How spectacular those paintings and sculptures must have been when the people first saw them. They were great teaching tools."

"Could I ask you a few questions about the conservators?"

"Of course you can. When will your story run?" *At least the guy's cooperative, but he sure is disjointed or perhaps nervous,* Nick thought before he answered the question.

"It'll run sometime in the fall, I believe. It depends on whether a rewrite is needed and how good the photography is."

"*Smithsonian*, right? Yes, you already told me that. Fine magazine. Fine magazine. The quicker your story runs, the more it could help us in fund-raising. But then, you wanted to ask about the conservators. I didn't mean to change the subject."

"No problem. I know you've worked with Ali Bahadir and Rosa Zizzo before."

"I hope you're not going to try to corner me like that other reporter did. A friend of yours, wasn't he? Mitchell somebody, I think I remember. I'll tell you the same thing I told him. The conservators were hired because they're the best. My reputation is on the line whenever a museum or other institution calls for a reference. I'd never give them anything less than the best."

Newton didn't need to get defensive. Nick just wanted him to answer a couple of questions. "Didn't you hire Rosa Zizzo, and then she hired the others?" he asked.

"Quite right."

"I guess Francesca Vitucci and Elizabeth Smythe came highly recommended."

"Francesca was well known, at least in Italy. Rosa vouched for her. Elizabeth is a newcomer. I hadn't met her before, but she called me several times asking about the project. She really wanted the job."

"How would she have known about it?"

"Our profession is quite incestuous, actually."

Nick liked the way Newton said the word. *Act-shoo-a-lee*. Like he was English, or trying to be.

"Everyone seems to know what is going on, where, and to whom," Newton continued. "It's very possible Elizabeth learned about it at school. She was near graduation from the University of London, or had just completed her studies. It has a terrific program in art conservation."

"Maybe someone told her. Is it possible that someone wanted her here? Wanted her to be part of the project?"

"Anything's possible, Mr. Genoa. Like the others, she had an impressive resume, although quite thin. She just didn't have the same quality of field experience as the others. A few years of field work under her belt and she'll be widely known around the world. The Tucson experience will become a good feather in her hat. It's something all interns would like to have. She's fortunate."

"You said her resume was impressive. Do you have copies of all of their resumes?"

"Yes, they're on file here."

"Could you possibly fax those to me? Their background information will help while I'm writing the story. You know how some people are about talking about themselves."

"Yes, I can have them faxed to you."

"There's a fax machine in the office of my apartment building. Let me go get the number and I'll call you right back."

"Before you do that, could I ask you one question, Mr. Genoa?"

"Sure."

"Carl Corona has kept me updated on what's going on down there, I mean beyond the conservation project. I know that you're looking into the killings of Father John and the young Indian man and the theft of the gold, beyond what the police are doing. Do you really think it could have been one of the conservators and not the Indian?"

"I think there are some big holes in the police case against Jimmy Longfellow." As he spoke, Nick thought about Carl. He would love to know what the car dealer had told Newton about him and Rosa. He wouldn't ask.

"Yes, Jimmy Longfellow," Newton said. "Poor fellow. I was so sorry to hear about his death, too. But the police didn't close their case, did they?"

"Police are busy people. They have plenty of bad guys out here to deal with. As soon as they think they've got one of them, they focus on the next. There's still a treasure of gold that needs to be returned to the church, and they're certainly still pursuing that because they have no clues."

"Any idea where the gold could be?"

"Not yet, but I'm sure it will turn up." Nick lied.

"I hope that someday I can get a look at the gold. The religious items rightfully belong to San Xavier. I suppose the gold does, too."

"I suppose."

"It would be awful if one of the conservators was involved," Newton added. "Do you really believe that?"

"Like you said, anything's possible."

"I'll be happy to help you however I can. I hope the resumes are useful."

Nick liked the man. He wondered how quickly Newton would tell Carl about their conversation. Should he ask him not to say anything to anyone?

He decided not to. At this point, the more Carl and the other conservators knew about his digging, the better.

"Thanks for your help," Nick said. "Let me go get that fax number, and I'll call you right back."

The faxes from New York arrived in the middle of the afternoon. As soon as he read them, Nick knew he had enough. He didn't want to move too quickly, however. The murderer needed to come to him.

He called the mission and asked to speak to Rosa. It took several minutes before she got to the phone.

"Rosa, can I see you alone? We need to talk."

"About what? We're very busy."

"I can't tell you on the phone."

"You're serious, aren't you?"

"I'll pick you up in twenty minutes."

Chapter 37

"It's Elizabeth."

Nick hadn't spoken until they parked at the top of "A" Mountain, a peak on the west side of Tucson that's been a sentinel over the city since its beginnings. A few other cars had made the trip to the top and parked alongside Nick's. Not far away, two teenagers sat on a large boulder, holding hands and looking toward the tall buildings downtown.

"How do you know?" Rosa asked.

"There's no doubt in my mind. She's killed two men and was indirectly responsible for Jimmy's murder. She was also Father John's lover. Met him in Europe and wrangled herself into the San Xavier project in the hopes of finding the gold. She was the one he called his goddess in his writing."

"I don't know what to say. I hired her."

"Sure you did, but she had the credentials for it, and you hired her based on what Edward Newton told you. Had you seen her complete resume, which is on file at the Guggenheim, you would've seen that she's from Blackpool, England."

"The nickname!"

"Uh-huh. And she has a black belt in karate. Another reason to give her a nickname with *black* in it."

"She's an expert in the martial arts?"

"Yep. That means she would've had opportunities to train in knife fighting or using ropes."

"My God."

Nick shook his head. "Everything was in front of my eyes, and I didn't see it. Remember the night we went to Sanchez's? Elizabeth asked for a cigarette when we were all walking out. She admitted then that she smokes when she drinks. Maria Gomez smelled cigarettes in Father John's quarters the day after he was killed."

"She had everyone fooled."

"Elizabeth is an expert at lying. She's crafted some incredible lies since she met Father John and joined all of you in Tucson."

"How do you know she killed Robert Clarkson?"

"First, she told you a lie to borrow my car. And Clarkson was killed with a knife by someone who knew how to do it quickly. It's not easy to do. You don't just stick someone and he dies. His widow also told me that a three-pence charm was found inside the jewelry shop after his murder. Certainly that would be something that an Englishwoman would wear."

Rosa put her hand to her mouth. "I told Elizabeth about Robert Clarkson."

"Of course you did. I told you in innocence what I'd discovered about Spanish gold when I visited him in Phoenix. You told the others unwittingly. There was no malice in that."

"Except it got a man killed."

He reached out and held her hand. "Stop blaming yourself, Rosa. The only thing you're guilty of is hiring the world's best conservators and being extremely loyal to your team."

"But I . . ."

"Come on. Let's get out of the car and take a walk."

The spring day comforted the couple as they walked. The sky's single cloud floated slowly beneath the brilliant sun. A slight breeze cooled Nick and Rosa. The huge "A" painted for generations by students at the University of Arizona towered behind them on the mountain. Tucson glistened in front of and below them. The centuries-old tall saguaros on the side of the mountain, like street signs with arms, beckoned people to the fragile desert.

"Do you think Ali was involved?" Rosa asked as they looked south on Mission Road, so named because that was the route to San Xavier before freeways.

"I'm not sure yet, but I don't think so. Elizabeth lied when she told me he had been a Turkish commando. Arrogant? Yes. Sexist? Yes. But not a killer. I don't think Carl was connected to it, either. It must've been a sinister plot between Father John and Elizabeth to find the gold and run away together. Things just got complicated and out of hand once you and the others found the gold. Elizabeth also never figured on my investigation."

"Jimmy wasn't involved?"

"Not at all. Elizabeth used him to her advantage just like she used Father John and perhaps all of you. Jimmy made an incredibly easy mark."

"Are we an easy mark? Do you think Elizabeth wanted to kill both of us on Mount Graham?" Nick could see the terror in her face as she asked the question.

"That's what I'm afraid of. When I fell, she must've seen it as an opportunity. She cut the rope and hoped it would break and I'd plunge to my death. And then you'd panic and try to rescue me. She could easily push you over the side, too. Then bury the rope. Then go get help and scream hysterically that two lovers had plunged to their deaths and she could do nothing to prevent it. God, it all seems so simple now. She was so close to doing it."

"Elizabeth a murderer. She's so young and has such a bright future in front of her. I still don't want to believe it."

"You'd better. Gold can make people do crazy things, and she doesn't have it yet. A hell of a lot more could still happen."

"Why do you think Father John would get involved with her?"

"I think he went to Europe on vacation, not intending to tell people he was a priest and not intending to meet a woman. He wanted to travel and do some research on San Xavier. That's how he and Carl learned about the Díaz journal. Elizabeth probably wasn't looking for a lover, either. He visited the University of London where she went to school, met her, and probably told her about the mission. She wanted to get herself in a position to do post-graduate work at a great site such as San Xavier. She's smart enough to quickly manipulate the vulnerable priest. He told her about the possibility of the gold. Then all she needed to do was perform with plenty of sex and make pledges of love and an escape to a far-away paradise."

"But why did she need to kill such a gentle man?"

"And a tormented man. He fell in love, but then felt guilty as hell about it. He had a treasure in gold delivered to him and thought his lover could help him. He believed Elizabeth. Problem is, even if they'd escaped he probably would've ultimately turned himself in. He couldn't have hidden his dark secret forever."

Rosa shook her head in agreement. "Poor Father John."

"He never saw it coming," Nick added. "He must have invited her over on the night you found the gold and helped her move it. She probably came to him after having a few drinks and smokes. She smoked more in his quarters, maybe drank, too. She knew exactly what she needed to do. She needed the courage to kill him."

"Do you think she cared for him?"

"Absolutely. You and the others who knew him always said he was a good man, easy to talk to, very compassionate. She needed to be in the right frame of mind to kill him."

"She kept two of the coins and hid the rest. Then she put those two in Jimmy's house."

"Losing two coins meant little to her because she still had ninety-eight of them left. I'm sure Jimmy told her he never locked his back door. He made it simple for her."

"They must be talking about me in the mission right now. I ran out and waited for you right after you called. Maybe that wasn't such a good idea."

"Don't worry, Rosa. There's little left to hide from the others. I'm also sure Elizabeth has suspected something for a long time. I think she's just hoping now that the project will end and she'll fly back to Europe without getting caught. She's like a rattlesnake, though. She *will* strike if she needs to."

They stopped walking for a minute and embraced. Quail called each other in the distance but remained invisible in the heavy brush. Nick felt Rosa trembling and wondered if she could feel his shaking.

"Are you going to the police now? Tell me you are, Nick."

"Not quite yet. They might screw things up again. I want Elizabeth to catch herself. I also want to make sure that no one else is involved."

"You can't . . ."

"I've got to. We can wait another day or two. Elizabeth might fall for our trap if you let it slip we're going to some quiet place for dinner tomorrow night."

"I don't like this. It's too dangerous."

"Let me take you back to work. You've got to act normally in front of Elizabeth and the others."

"Is there such a thing as normal? Aren't we all becoming monsters? I can't live if something happens to you."

"Just a little longer, Rosa."

Chapter 38

Another storm had moved inland from California, and unusual cold had embraced Tucson. The cloud cover cast a pall over the desert and at midday the city looked as dull as it did at dusk. The radio weather reports predicted rain in the valley and snow in the mountains.

Nick had dropped Rosa at the mission and returned to his kitchen table and laptop computer. He could hear the mumbling of an afternoon disc jockey from his clock radio in the bedroom. He worked better with some background noise and even had his recorder running next to the radio to pick up a few songs.

His story had been budgeted for 5,000 words. With photography, it would be a large spread in the middle of the magazine. His editor had told him it could be the cover story if the pictures were good enough. Although he'd been given a lengthy word count—more than most magazines allowed—Nick knew that by the time he synthesized his months of notes and tapes, it would be a challenge to keep the story at the length *Smithsonian* ordered.

Who to keep in, who to leave out? How to start, how to finish? He struggled over his latest draft, too lost in thought to realize that someone else was in his apartment.

The swift, powerful kick to his side sent him tumbling. The wallop damaged his ribs, and his head slamming to the floor knocked him out cold.

He awoke on his bed, neatly bound with duct tape and rope so that he could move only his head, which pounded like the bass drum in a rock band.

"You should've died when we were pulling you to safety, but the damn rope didn't break," Nick heard as he focused on the figure at the foot of the bed.

"Blackpool."

"Interesting, love. You know my nickname. I hate it, but it came with my black belt in karate."

"And Blackpool, England, on the Irish Sea. Your hometown, Elizabeth."

"You've been a good reporter." Her odor revealed that she'd been drinking and smoking. She wore thick makeup, with bright red lipstick, neither of which went with her stained sweatshirt, jeans, and hiking boots. "Quite the appropriate nickname. Father John knew it, too. A slip, I'm afraid, perhaps made while we were in bed. He liked using it because it made him smile. No problem. The pitiful, lonely, stupid man thought he'd fallen in love."

Nick tried moving. No luck. He wanted to rub his throbbing head. It felt hot and huge. Every movement made his side feel like he'd been booted again.

He couldn't let her know the terror he felt. He screamed inwardly: *No! No! No! You're not going to kill me! I'm not going to die right here! God, please help me!*

"I was wondering when I'd finally catch you," he managed. "I thought it would be when Rosa and I were out alone. You're supposed to be with the other conservators at San Xavier."

Elizabeth smiled crookedly. "You catch me, love? Other way around, don't you think? I suspected that you knew it was me and that I would need to surprise you on my schedule rather than yours." She said schedule the English way: *shed-jewel.* "You're the only thing now keeping me from getting away with the perfect crime. Of course if you told Rosa, I'd have to kill her, too. I planned that for Mount Graham, but things didn't quite work out."

Nick squirmed again. No good. Too much pain. The rope and tape were bound too tightly. "You left a hell of a trail," he said. "You're a liar, easily caught. You also borrowed my car on the same night Robert Clarkson was killed, you're a karate expert, you're a smoker, and Father John used your nickname in his writing. I have to admit, the Blackpool thing had me going awhile."

"My, my, how intelligent you are."

"I didn't know for absolutely certain it was you until I read your resume. Another stupid move by you. Your resume is on file at the Guggenheim. You shouldn't have mentioned your black belt in karate. That gave you the expertise with knives. Once I read that, and saw where you were born in England, the evidence against you was rock-solid."

Elizabeth lifted her chest proudly. "I'm quite accomplished with knives. As we move up in the ranks, we're taught to defend ourselves against anything, including attackers with knives. That training has helped me learn quite nicely how to kill someone with a knife. It's a wonderful weapon. Silent and efficient. It has given me power over other people. As for my birth town, there is nothing I can do about that. The one mistake I made was letting the nickname slip to John."

Elizabeth walked closer to Nick. He wondered if this was the end of his life, the second she would make a deadly slice with a knife or kill him with her powerful hands. In his thoughts he told Rosa he loved her with all his heart. He kept repeating it to her, hoping that somehow she could hear him. At this moment he was powerless. Elizabeth had complete authority over him. This second he was alive. The next second, any second, he could be dead.

She pulled a knife from her pocket. "Any last requests before I cut you just enough so you bleed to death slowly? I promise to make yours much slower than Robert Clarkson's. That short and fat gross man deserved to die just for being a slob."

"You didn't need to kill him."

"Oh, but I did. He'd become a witness who could identify me."

Nick wanted her to keep talking. "You left your calling card when you killed Clarkson."

She looked confused.

"Your three-pence charm."

"I wondered about that," she admitted. "The fat slob thrashed around just enough to get his nails into my bracelet. It was dark. I didn't know he'd torn off the charm until a day later. And even then I didn't know if it was in his shop or outside. I was a little worried that it was in your car, but I didn't see it when we went to the mountains."

"That charm was clearly English. The cops will figure it out before long."

"A gift from me mum. I'm truly sorry I lost it. And please don't try to bullshit me, Nick. You're not nearly as good at it as I am. We both know the police in Phoenix can't trace a fifty-year-old coin to someone in Tucson, someone who will be out of the country in the next couple of days."

"Too bad I came to San Xavier."

"Yes, if you hadn't, things would be much smoother now. Of course, if you would've come and just done your story on the project, you'd be with your sweetheart Rosa on the way to a wonderful life in Europe. The cops thought they got their man. All I needed to do was complete my work here and then go back to Europe. The gold would be safe where I hid it for months, years. It made no difference."

"Old Pueblo Self-Storage?"

She said nothing, but the creases in her forehead revealed her growing fury. She had the eyes of a cougar ready to strike. "You've been a hell of a story," he added. "The more you tried to implicate the others, the deeper I looked at everything. I wanted it to be Ali because I don't like him, but I also had to dig to make sure it wasn't Rosa."

"You shouldn't have kept at it. Along the way you dug a grave for Robert Clarkson and now you."

"But why Father John? He wouldn't hurt you."

"Right. But he would have confessed at some point. In Europe he wanted to hide from people, not let them know he was a priest. But he couldn't hide forever. Once I humored him, let him empty his passion in me, he told me there might be gold at San Xavier. He wanted to find it and escape with it. The gold and sex became his sins, a nightmare he'd ultimately reveal."

"He loved you."

"So much he didn't see the screwdriver coming. When he realized he'd been stabbed, he smiled in disbelief, as though it was his fault that he accidentally walked into something. He was stupid like other people. He thought sex meant something as emotional or ridiculous as love."

Too busy talking, Elizabeth didn't see the shadow moving behind her. Nick saw it, and he knew he had to keep Elizabeth busy. She moved closer to him, and opened the pocket knife. Its five-inch blade looked deadly. He didn't know if the shadow would make it to his bedside in time to save him.

"How do you plan to do this?" Nick asked.

"Quite professionally. A few cuts in the right places and you'll die on a nice *shed-jewel*. If you need a little more pain as you expire, I'll be happy to poke you in the ribs."

Just as she moved the knife toward Nick, his laptop computer smashed her in the head, hurling her onto the bed. Quickly, Rosa lifted the computer again and slammed it into Elizabeth's back, knocking the wind out of her. The knife fell to the floor.

Elizabeth tried to stand. Rosa smashed her again, and she dropped like a marionette with its strings cut.

Rosa started crying uncontrollably and lifted the computer once more to strike Elizabeth when Nick shouted, "That's enough. She's not going anywhere. Untie me and then dial nine-one-one."

She dropped the computer and moved to her lover, touching his face before she began trying frantically to untie the rope. Tears dripped from her face onto his.

"Get the knife," Nick ordered. "Just cut the rope. Forget trying to untie it."

"Oh, *mio amore*, are you OK?" she sobbed.

"Not right now. But I'm alive, thanks to you. Can't say the same for my computer, though. You shattered it on this lump of shit on the floor. Good thing I've got everything on a disk. I had the cassette recorder running, too, and got everything she said."

Nick struggled painfully to his feet. He used a portion of the rope to bind Elizabeth's hands behind her back. She offered no resistance. Her only sound was a painful groan.

Rosa went into the other room to call the police.

"How did you know to come in here?" he asked when she returned to the bedroom. "You got here just in time to save my life."

"You're a lucky man," she said, catching her breath. They embraced. She ran her fingers through his hair as she spoke, as though she still needed to make sure he was alive. "Elizabeth wasn't at San Xavier when you dropped me off. I thought it was odd and got a little suspicious. I called a cab. She didn't answer her door. Then I looked toward your apartment and saw the door ajar. I heard the talking in the bedroom when I came in. Thank goodness your computer was on the table. I couldn't think of what else to hit her with."

Chapter 39

Nick browsed through a copy of the *Daily Star* while he waited for the flight to New York. Tucson had changed since he'd been here. So had he.

The city's winter chill had given way to springtime warmth, which in turn would entice the torrid days of summer.

Nick had done a hell of a job in Tucson. He caught a vicious killer, cleared the name of an innocent man, and recovered a treasure. Because of him, an Indian community would regain some of its honor.

Tucson had brought him Rosa. For the first time in years, he felt secure, once again with a strong heart and restored confidence and self-esteem. In about five hours he'd be home, or at least at Kennedy Airport. Then after a few more days, he'd be off to Rome and finally able to relax.

Carl had brought Nick and Rosa to the airport. The car dealer would be worried until he actually saw the published story in *Smithsonian,* even though Nick assured him the magazine wasn't interested in a tale of sex, murder, and an insane conservator. Elizabeth's trial and punishment would be well covered by the daily media. He would write stories about his investigation for other magazines.

They shook hands as enthusiastically as the first time they met. Carl told Rosa he'd like her to manage the project again next year.

Nick leaned back slightly in the uncomfortable plastic airport chair and reread the story spread across the bottom of Page One of the *Star.*

The family of a Tohono O'odham man falsely accused of killing a Catholic priest and stealing a fortune in gold from San Xavier Mission filed suit against the Pima County Sheriff's Department Monday, claiming he was coerced into confessing.

The suit on behalf of Jimmy Longfellow seeks a minimum of $3 million in compensatory damages and an unspecified amount in punitive damages. It also claims that Longfellow, who had lived on the Tohono O'odham Reservation, suffered "excruciating mental torture" the days before he was killed inside his cell at Pima County Jail. Officials have blamed Longfellow's slaying on Mexican gang members operating inside the jail.

The suit was filed in U.S. District Court in Tucson. The sheriff's department, Pima County and the two detectives who interrogated Longfellow, Ashton Anderson and Thomas Leigh, were named as defendants.

It charged that the "coercive, cruel and relentless" grilling by Anderson and Leigh caused Longfellow to confess.

Pima County Sheriff's Department officials refused to comment on the suit Monday, but spokesperson Cynthia Crowley said the suit was baseless. Pima County Attorney Thomas Clausen also refused comment because he said he had not yet read the suit.

Anderson and Leigh could not be reached for comment.

Longfellow was 23 years old at the time
of his death. He had been working as an aide to
a group of European conservators hired to restore
the interior art at San Xavier Mission south of Tucson.

The sheriff's department now has charged
English art conservator Elizabeth Smythe with the
stabbing death of Father John Duvall in February
inside his living quarters at the mission. Smythe
also is charged with stealing a treasure in gold
coins, ingots and religious items.

Smythe is currently under police guard
at Tucson Medical Center, where she is recovering
from injuries she suffered during a scuffle at
her apartment building shortly before her arrest.

Police said she will be transferred to Pima
County Jail in the next day or so, where she will
be held without bail.

The missing gold was recovered from a
mini-storage unit in south Tucson. Investigators said
Smythe admitted that she put the gold in the storage
unit the night of the priest's murder.

"She said she planned to keep it there
until things cooled down and she could figure
out how to get it out of the country," Crowley said.

Along with the Tucson charges, Smythe was
accused of first-degree murder in the slaying
earlier this month of Phoenix gold dealer Robert
Clarkson. Smythe is charged with slitting Clarkson's
throat after she discovered that he possibly could
link her to the stolen gold.

Joseph Milner, one of the attorneys filing the suit on behalf of six members of the Longfellow family, said family members are now trying to pick up the pieces of their lives. "This senseless act of police brutality caused their son's death and brought great suffering to them," he said outside the courthouse after the suit was filed.

The suit claims that although sheriff's detectives did have probable cause to arrest Longfellow, who was on probation after spending 18 months in prison for assault, the officers pressured him until he confessed.

The suit follows two other cases in recent months in which murder confessions obtained by sheriff's departments in Tucson and Phoenix proved false.

Walter "Trapper" Gable, who had a history of mental problems, was arrested last year in the 1990 slaying of a woman at a picnic ground after he confessed to deputies in Tucson. He was released two months later when another man confessed that he and a girlfriend committed the crime.

Gable sued the county for his wrongful jailing and ultimately settled out of court for nearly $2 million.

Also last year, four Tucson men were arrested in the 1991 Buddhist temple massacre west of Phoenix in which six monks, a nun and two helpers were killed. After extensive questioning by deputies in Phoenix, each of the four men gave separate confessions.

The four men were freed when investigators failed to produce any physical evidence against them and after homicide weapons linked other people to the killings.

Each of the four Tucson men has filed multimillion dollar lawsuits against the Maricopa County Sheriff's Department claiming they were coerced into confessing.

"Hey, mister, you saving that seat next to you for anyone?"

Nick looked up from his newspaper. Rosa looked splendid in a dark, flowery dress, black stockings, and black high-heels. Her full, pale lips smiled. She had let her thick hair fall freely, and it drifted with the air-conditioned breeze in the airport terminal. She wore her Mickey Mouse watch with a new black leather band. In each hand she carried a plastic bag from a gift shop at the airport. The arms of a pair of green glass saguaros were hanging out of one bag.

"I needed a few more souvenirs," she smiled.

"Can't have enough saguaros," Nick said. "Your family will love them."

Their plan was to fly together to New York, where he would stay a few days, send in his completed story, and make arrangements for someone to care for his home on Long Island for at least the next year. Then he'd join her in Italy.

He grinned. "You sure look terrific in a dress. Have I told you that yet today?"

"Twice," she murmured. "You're just used to seeing me in my work clothes. Don't get too used to these. I'll be back to work soon and into my grubby clothes."

"Or out of them."

"Nick!" She tapped him on the arm slightly, imitating a slap. They both knew it wouldn't take a hard smack to send pain surging through his body. His ankle had mended, but his ribs were still sore from Elizabeth's kick. It had been only a week since she nearly killed him.

"I'll miss you. Are you sure you don't want to stay with me in New York?"

"You know I'd love to, but I have some commitments to take care of in Rome."

He ran his hand through his wavy hair. "We'll be apart awhile, and I want you to keep thinking about what I'm going to do with you when I get to Italy."

"I can guess."

They both laughed. They held hands as they sat, soaking up what else they could of their experience in Tucson. Nick folded the newspaper and placed it on the empty seat next to him without showing it to Rosa. He would fill her in on the lawsuit another time.

"Did you see Francesca before she left?" he asked.

"Yes, this morning. She was anxious to get home."

"She OK?"

"Of course, although I don't think she'd be interested in coming here again. She's happier at home, where there's plenty of work and she's with her partner."

"What about Ali?"

"He leaves for Spain tomorrow."

"Yeah. I got a chance to talk to him yesterday and apologize for any pain I caused him. At least we respect each other, I think. He told me he appreciated my good work here."

"Ali is a proud man, and I'm sure he welcomed your apology. I know he's been affected by what happened here, but he'll never admit it."

"He's headed for another job. San Xavier won't mean much to him after a few days."

"Probably not. Perhaps you'll see him again. I'm sure he'll turn up on one of my projects in the future."

"I suppose I could learn to appreciate the guy. Too bad he won't allow people past his tough exterior. He's not nearly as bad as he seems."

As they waited for the announcement to begin boarding, Nick thought about Jimmy Longfellow. Too bad he hadn't lived to see the beauty brought back to the White Dove of the Desert. Jimmy and the other Tohono O'odhams were a great help to the conservators. There would be another project next year, but the Indians would be the permanent stewards of San Xavier's art.

He turned to Rosa. "So what happens once we're together again?"

She smiled. "I've got another church job in Austria. Some spectacular murals from what I hear. We'll spend about a month there, and then we can go wherever you'd like. Now that there is no more Soviet Union, there'll be great jobs coming up throughout eastern Europe. There are many untouched churches there, and we could have great experiences in some famous old ones."

"And in hotel rooms all over the world."

"Nick," she said again, much softer. "We'll always make time for that."

He put his hand high on her thigh just as a good-looking, square-chinned man in a uniform announced that their flight was boarding.

"I'm not going to like people interrupting us in the future."

She leaned over and quickly kissed him on the lips. "Neither am I."

ACKNOWLEDGEMENTS

While the characters in this book are fictional, there certainly are some real characters in my life who helped greatly in the evolution of this book and its production. Carol Gurney, Elizabeth Baldacchino, Salima Keegan, Dawn DeVries Sokol, and T.J. Sokol are responsible for helping make the manuscript publishable. Dr. Bernard "Bunny" Fontana, a wonderful man and historian, and the consummate expert on San Xavier Mission, always supplied me with useful information.

Cecil Schwalbe, a "frogman" (herpetologist) at the University of Arizona in Tucson, read the book in its final stages and pointed out what could have been some embarrassing errors in fact. Carol Schwalbe, a former editor at *National Geographic* magazine and now a journalism professor at Arizona State University, also was a great help in directing me to some people who could help me in the process of writing fiction.

Thanks to *Arizona Highways* magazine, too, for assigning me a story on the actual art conservation project at San Xavier.

—Bruce Itule

The Gold of San Xavier is available at bookstores or through the Thunder Mountain Publishing Co. Website (www.thundermp.com or www.thundermountainpress.com). You also can e-mail the author at bruce.itule@thundermp.com.